Gordon Lang
For Führer, Folk and Fatherland

Gordon Lang
For Führer, Folk and Fatherland
©2008 Conflict Books, London E3
All rights reserved.
Printed in Germany 2008 by buchwerft.de, Kiel
ISBN 978-0-9558240-0-5

Gordon Lang

For Führer, Folk and Fatherland

A tragedy of self-deception

Conflict Books

By the same author:

The Carnoustie Effect/Warfare in the 21st Century

(In German:)
'...die Polen verprügeln...', vols. I and II
Das perestrojanische Pferd

This is a novel written around recorded fact. Actions and words of Soviet leaders are reproduced accurately. All that has been invented is the notion that the same officer was involved in Germany's dealings with the Russians from 1917 right up to 1944. In reality, no one man treated with the Kremlin all the way through. Relations depended upon a succession of military men, diplomats and politicians.

The Erlenbachs, the Albrechts, Erika and her mother, Marion and her family are fictitious. So too are Dr Armbrecht, Colonel Lüdershausen, Major Otto, Alexei Fyodorov, Preiss, Steinegger and the British and American occupation personnel. All other named persons, from Baron Romberg to Seaman Kurockin, are real. The military, diplomatic and political conspiracy happened exactly as described. Agreements, minutes and records made at the time survived the war, and can be read in government archives.

And yes, Communists who fled to Russia really were…
But no. Better not spoil it for you.

Best wishes,

Gordon Lang

To Alison [illegible], a good

Tommy	9
Claus	17
Conspiracy	35
Cupid	49
Avus	63
Erika	75
Bliss	89
Nürburgring	107
Expectations	125
Julia	141
Fulfilment	157
Solidarity	175
A model Communist	185
All change	201
Insult to injury	213
Wolfsschanze	227
Shuttlecock	241
Flight	255
Charlottenburg	267

Tommy

They took him down from Heidelberg in a truck. The driver, an overweight sergeant with a bull neck, was one of those who had mastered the art of talking incessantly while never pausing in his chewing of gum. As soon as he was finished with one stick, the sergeant spat it out, flicked it from the window of the truck and unwrapped another with the fingers of one hand, keeping his grip on the wheel with the other. Once, it looked as though he were going to complete the fingertip unwrapping while simultaneously using the same hand to change gear, but in the end he moved the gear lever first and slid the fresh gum from its wrapping afterwards.

'What's your handle, buddy?'

'Tommy'.

'Whereya from?'

'New York'.

The sergeant slapped the wheel with his gum hand. 'Well, welcome to the club, buddy! We got half a dozen New Yorkers at Neckarsulm. You'll be right at home. So what part you from yourself? I'm from the Bronx'.

That was no surprise.

'Long Island'.

The sergeant looked at Tommy sideways. 'You putting me on?'

'No'.

'So why ain't you an officer? You got money, kid?'

'No'.

'Hm. Only Long Island guys I ever met since I been in the service, they was all officers, and all with money, you could tell'.

'Well, I don't have any'.

'Maybe not, but your folks'.

'I bet we're one of the poorest families on Long Island'. It wasn't true, but he needed to get the sergeant off the subject.

'Well, you're not an officer, so I suppose it figures'.

No, Tommy was not an officer. His number had come up in the draft, and he had been content to go into the army as a private, do his time, and go back home. He was pleased that his first posting after basic training had been Germany. It happened as he had hoped.

'Been at Heidelberg long?' the sergeant wanted to know.

'Five and a half weeks'.

'Fly in, or Bremerhaven?'

'Flew. To Frankfurt'.

'Yeah, that's the only way to travel. These ships to Bremerhaven, you never know what weather you're going to hit. Or what weather's going to hit you'. The sergeant laughed. He thought he was a wit. 'Great part of the country, this. You'll like it. Full of old castles and things, and lots of wine. You drink wine?'

'Sometimes'.

'It won't be sometimes here, buddy. It'll be all the time here, you'll see. Kinda gets a holda you. Me, I been a beer drinker all my life. Then I come over here and they have all this wine. In Belgium it was, my first time. They didn't have no beer where we was, and then we liberated this cellar full of wine. Before you know it, you're tipping it down like water'. The sergeant sighed. 'When I get back to the Bronx it'll be back to beer for me. Won't be the same, but I can't drink wine in the Bronx, not with my buddies. Course, most of the guys here sticks to beer, but not me, buddy. Chance to try something different, don't waste it, that's what I say. In fact, there's another thing. Have you seen the broads here? They're just fantastic'.

'I noticed that in Heidelberg'.

'You know what's so good about them? The great variety. All them blue-eyed blondes, Teutonic superwomen, and then them others with real black hair. I tell you, kid, you're spoiled for choice'.

10

The commentary went on all the way upstream along the river valley, right into Neckarsulm. In the middle of the town, the sergeant turned onto a road whose surface was concrete, not tarmacadam. 'Know what they call this road?'

Tommy didn't.

'Why d'ya think it's made of concrete?'

'No idea'.

'They call it the Panzerstrasse. Built by the Nazis to carry the weight of tanks going between the barracks and the railroad depot. They moved their stuff by train, guess that's why we had to knock out their tracks. This road's indestructible'.

Ahead, at the crest of a low hill, the Stars and Stripes waved over a gate with barriers and a checkpoint. Tanks with white five-pointed stars painted on their sides could be seen parked between long barracks buildings.

'You're here now, buddy. Better get your papers out'.

It took nearly two months before Tommy could organize a jeep for a private journey. Heading east out of Neckarsulm, he found himself passing what had once been flourishing vineyards. After only a few miles he slowed the jeep to enter the small mediaeval town of Weinsberg, with its extraordinary castle on top of a conical hill. Too symmetrical to be real, Tommy told himself.

At Weinsberg he turned the jeep south. On the passenger seat beside him lay a map, folded so that the section he needed was uppermost. The precaution was unnecessary. Tommy had studied the whereabouts of his destination and impressed the route into his mind. A half hour later and there, unmistakably, was the house, not quite hidden by trees. Tommy braked for the turn, changing down as he slowed.

Part way along the drive, three poorly dressed children shot out yelling from among the trees, darted across the way in front of him and disappeared into the copse opposite.

Tommy braked, drove the final yards to the house in bottom gear. Well, the place was still standing, but who was living in it?

11

DPs, buddy, is how the bull-necked sergeant would have put it. The house had been commandeered by the authorities to accommodate displaced persons.

There were something approaching seven million displaced persons in the Western occupation zones of Germany. Most were from Eastern Europe. They included concentration camp survivors, people who had been deported to the Reich to work as forced labour and some released prisoners of war who could not return to their home countries because the Russians were in occupation there.

A team from the United Nations Relief and Rehabilitation Administration was running this requisitioned house. It was not a camp, the UNRRA men assured Tommy. It was an assembly centre.

Why had Tommy come? Had the army sent him?

No, the army hadn't sent him. He had just wanted to see the house.

Why, if it wasn't an official visit?

'My parents knew the man who owned it. Do you know where he is?'

'It was an old lady who was the owner. She died just after the end of the war'.

'Her son, that was my parents' friend. What about him?'

'Disappeared. That's all we know'.

It was to be expected. 'No further information?'

'About the son? Can't find anything at all. There was a daughter, though, lived in Stuttgart. But she was killed in the bombing'.

No, they couldn't let him look round. He wasn't family of the late owner, was he? The place was full of East European refugees, most of them Romanian. Some were gypsies. Private visits could not be accommodated.

It was all right with Tommy. There was nothing for him to look at. He had never been to the house before, and it would mean nothing to him.

12

Perhaps he could find out more in Berlin. He would go there on his first leave.

Charlottenburg had certainly been one of the upper class areas of Berlin – after all, hadn't Frederick the Great resided here, and even Napoleon for a couple of years? Now aerial and artillery bombardment had created an equality in devastation. War the great leveller, no pun intended, Tommy said to himself.

The roadways had been cleared, and that was something, but there was little otherwise that was back to normal. Where expensive houses had been, bricks were now heaped in sometimes towering piles. Chimneys pointed like fingers to the sun, the dwellings to which they belonged collapsed alongside them. The odd house was still standing, suggestive of an object dropped at random into a desert. The occasional wall was there in strange isolation, and here and there half a house, rich wallpaper and elegant fireplace bizarrely exposed.

People were living in these ruins. In the main, cellars had survived and were accommodating several families. Street names had come through, or at least been restored. Otherwise, nothing was recognizable. This was an entirely new landscape.

Names were posted up everywhere. If not chalked on what remained of a doorway, they were written on either a sheet of paper or a piece of cardboard.

Hanna Schmidt. Where is she? Information please to Red Cross, Wilmersdorf.

Neumanns now at Steglitz, Unter den Eichen 17.

Tommy had no expectation of finding the house he sought. He was performing a duty, going through the motions.

It was there. Still standing.

Or was it? It looked like the house, but how could anyone tell, when there were no features in the surroundings from which to take a bearing?

The name, though, carved into the stone, had survived.

13

Yes, it was the right house. And it looked reasonably intact. Walls pockmarked from bullets. Heavy duty, too, the sort fired from aircraft. But no walls breeched, and the roof still weatherproof, by the look of it.

Someone was living there, that was obvious.

Could it be? Was it possible? He might not have been killed, despite what the UNRRA official had said. Maybe since the man had two homes, and homes were at a premium, the authorities had thought that it was all right to take the bigger one from him.

Tommy ignored the bell push, thinking that it too might have become a casualty of war. He lifted the cast-iron knocker and let it fall.

A chubby man of middle years opened the door. His dark hair was thinning, and he was wearing the uniform of a corporal in the British Army, without his forage cap.

No, the owner's dead. Killed. Sorry, mate, can't tell you any more. Wait a sec, though. Maybe the colonel knows something. You'd better come in while I ask him.

The corporal turned out to be batman-cum-clerk to a lieutenant-colonel in the military administration of the British sector of the capital. To Tommy's astonishment, the colonel received him, a GI private, with the same courtesy which he would have accorded to a fellow officer.

'May I ask what is your interest? This isn't an official inquiry from the Americans?' The colonel knew perfectly well that it wouldn't be. They would have sent an officer, not a private, if the man were on a war criminals list or anything like that.

'My parents knew him. When they knew I was posted to Germany they asked me to see if I could find out whether he had survived the war'.

'I see. Well, I'm sorry to tell you that it appears he didn't. Missing, presumed killed, officially. And that's all we know, I'm afraid. There are no details on record'.

'Missing. So there might be a chance he could turn up?'

'I think you can take it that it means killed. Very, very few turn up alive. A lot of those unaccounted for are in Russia, of course'.

'Could he be a prisoner in Russia, do you think, sir?'

'I wouldn't say that, but it is a possibility. They must have a lot over there, though whether they'll ever come home is a different matter. Then again, we don't even know if he ever came anywhere near the Russians. The Army seems to have lost all record of him after he was sent off from his headquarters on some mission or other. No one knows what it was. That was at the beginning of 1945. What happened to him after that is anybody's guess'. The colonel shrugged. 'In any case, the Russians don't cooperate with the Red Cross'. A light smile. 'Nor with us, as your own people know. We checked with German Army records, of course, when we requisitioned this house. Address of next of kin was East Prussia, but his family has disappeared, too. And with the Russians there...'

'I see. Well, thank you, sir'.

'There is one other place you might enquire. He had a country home besides this house. Down in the south somewhere. We know he didn't turn up there. I could find you the address'.

'Thank you, sir. I've been there. It's a DP camp now'.

Dead, presumably, but no known grave. There were a few million of them. Well, he had promised his parents that he would check it out, and he had checked it out. It had been a simple matter of honour to fulfil the obligation.

As Tommy left the house, he saw that the British corporal had swung open the twin wooden doors of the garage. This was a building which had evidently suffered some bomb damage, but since been repaired and tidied up. Before it stood a Humber car with British Military Government number plates. Tommy stood and peered into the gloom inside the garage. The corporal was bending over a low white shape, manipulating a spanner. He saw Tommy and straightened up.

'Don't seem possible it's survived, does it?', he called. 'Not when everything else round about's been flattened. It's a good 'un, too.

Needs tyres, though, if I can find some this size. Tyres like gold at the moment'.

Tommy stepped closer. The car was propped up on bricks.

'Had the motor running', confided the corporal. 'Once I got a battery on it, started straight away. Will be of use to somebody some day'.

The same car! There had been a love story, too, hadn't there? Tommy had gathered a certain amount, but the grown-ups had never told him any details.

It wasn't just his parents who had known the man. Tommy remembered him, too.

He had been to this house before. And been taken for a drive in that car. Hitler had been riding high then.

Claus

When the bullet smashed through Claus's lung, he felt not pain but the sensation of having run straight into the buffer of a railway locomotive.

A half stumble more, and Claus pitched forward on to his face. Why, he wondered, is my nose touching the earth? And what are all those feet doing, running past me? There was noise, too, a crack-crack-cracking and some duller, heavier sounds. What was it that the din reminded him of?

There was a sudden light-headedness, and Claus wondered if he were going to faint. Perhaps he had fainted already, and it was only the shouts of 'Sani! Sani!' which had roused him.

At any rate, they were lifting him now. He was lying on a hard, flat board and they were carrying him over rough ground, bouncing him up and down, jiggling him this way and that as they ducked and zigzagged.

It was the movement that brought the pain. It was a pain which, of course, would have set in some time, anyway, and it set in now. Claus's back began to burn and he felt as though a red hot nail were inside him.

A jolt. Movement ceased, but not the pain. The two bearers tossed the word 'lung' at the dressing station orderly, picked up an empty stretcher, and at once headed out again to bring in the next poor devil.

Pain had brought sharp consciousness, and with it remembrance. All morning the Tommies had been giving it to them. Those Highlanders had come on at them like madmen. The only way to stop them had been practically to wipe them out.

Then it had been their turn to give it to the Tommies. Claus's company stayed heads down for nearly an hour while mortar shells tore the British numbers into fragments. His men were silent but some, he could tell, were praying.

Then the signal.

Claus, in the lead, made perhaps sixty yards before that single Lee-Enfield round cleaved its way through his ribs.

Claus had visited comrades in dressing stations – twice he had arrived too late – and knew how overworked the personnel always was. It surprised him now that a sanitäter appeared at his side after only about ten minutes. In that time only two of the men close to him had died.

Claus was trying not to pay too much attention to his fellow patients, nearly all of whom were clearly much worse off than he. Instead, Claus lay there with closed eyes, seeking to ignore the pain in his chest and listening to the battlefield symphony. Interesting how individual rifle shots were never quite swamped by the overlapping machine gun rattle. Mortar fire, of course, had no chance of being heard when the big stuff came over and made the ground shake. Surprisingly, though, it was possible occasionally to distinguish a hand grenade – or was that an illusion?

The sani, as a medical orderly was always called, rolled Claus onto his side and held him there while a doctor took a quick look at the wound in his back. The doctor nodded and moved away to another casualty.

The MO had looked, seen the larger opening in Claus's back and known that the bullet was not still inside. That was a blessing. There was more than enough to do round the clock in this damned war, without yet another fiddly operation to remove a bullet. A clean shot straight through the lung could heal itself. If the young lieutenant didn't start coughing up blood, he would be all right and fit to go back into action in no time. They would know by the morning. If the man was still alive then, he could be away to a field hospital and probably shipped more or less at once back home for a short convalescence. Lucky beggar.

Claus was indeed lucky. This was 1916, and they could do wonderful things nowadays.

Whatever it was that the sani applied to Claus's back, it stung like hell. Claus was thankful that he just managed to hold in a yell. Even through the pain, he could feel that the hands which applied the

18

dressing were practised and skilful. The sani turned Claus over and began to clean his chest wound. This was a much simpler job, and the dressing here was applied in no time. Entry wounds were always neat, and usually bled little. It was the exit hole, made by the bullet as it went out through a man's back, where the biggest damage was done. Claus knew this well enough. He had seen plenty of exit wounds in both friend and foe, the dead and the still living.

The orderly had removed Claus's tunic, with its mud, blood and lacerations. Now he fished his patient's pay book out of a pocket and copied down the details. Leutnant Claus-Dieter von Erlenbach. His family would be relieved, no doubt, on being notified that the lieutenant was only wounded. It could always be worse. And next time probably would be.

Claus's wound was clean, they injected him with something to dull the pain and moved him behind the lines next day. Only a week later, Claus was on a train for Germany. Recovery from a shot through the lung was not really such a quick business, but the front hospitals were overfilled and overworked. If a man could recover at home with some attention from a civilian doctor, there was no good reason to maintain the overload at the front.

All the carriages of the hospital train were filled to bursting with wounded. Among those in the compartment with Claus were two amputees. Poor beggars! They had no chance of rejoining the fight.

He himself was lucky. A few weeks' rest, and he would be fit as a fiddle, able to play his part again in Germany's struggle.

It took several hours to load aboard the mass of wounded and crippled. The casualties had, after all, to be brought from a whole string of different field hospitals, and could not be expected to arrive all at the same time.

Claus was tired, and before the train began to move was close to falling asleep in his seat. He dozed off as soon as they were rolling eastwards, and when he woke realized almost with shock that the sound of the big guns was growing quieter. Why did Claus feel shame to be leaving the field of action, guilt because he had not died when others had and so many were still dying? He should be happy, he knew, and was of course pleased at the expectation of seeing his family. Yet still some shadow interposed itself. He was leaving his comrades to bear all of the burden. Silly to feel ashamed, he knew, because he couldn't help the situation, but all the same...

One could barely hear the big artillery now. On either hand, fields at peace, crops ready for harvest. Livestock. Flocks of birds.

Birds! They never saw any at the front. Claus had always enjoyed listening to birdsong, and had heard none for months.

Tantalisingly still just inside France, the train turned into a siding and halted. It waited for an hour, until a long transport drawn by two locomotives began to rumble past from the opposite direction. Packed with troops from Germany on their way to the front, most of them for the first time, this train clearly had priority. It was more urgent to throw fresh men into the battles than to bring casualties home.

Home! It was more than he had been expecting, and more than so many of his poor comrades would ever enjoy.

It had begun to rain before Claus's train jerked and clattered forward, to roll at last across the border into the Fatherland. The downpour was unrelenting as far as Koblenz, where the few walking wounded, Claus among them, were able to leave the train and continue their journeys alone. Claus wished his fellow travellers good luck and stepped onto the platform.

A railway station in persistent rain is a dreary place, but he was back in Germany, and that was all that mattered. The wound in his back was giving trouble, and the dressing needed to be changed, but Claus gave that no further thought once he discovered that a train leaving in just over half an hour's time would take him all the way home without any further changes.

Impatient now, Claus began that final stage of his journey with mounting elation. Then suddenly he was tired, very tired. He all but fell asleep as he sat, until the landscape metamorphosed into those Württemberg hills and forests whose every line he could have drawn from memory. The sight roused him into full alertness. This, the south western corner of the Reich, was the countryside which housed his earliest memories. There was the River Neckar, and there, there on its eminence, solid and welcoming through the curtain of rain, was Falkenstein, the Erlenbachs' estate. Behind it the woods where Claus had learned to shoot, below them the ranks of vines, orderly and dark in the rain, on either side the fields which he had roamed until dusk. Was there a tree anywhere which he had not tried to climb at some time or another?

The train was slowing. Claus was pale, he knew, had lost a lot of weight and felt weak, but he held himself properly erect and when the train halted did his utmost to alight with something approaching his customary briskness. There on the platform was his mother, not fooled for an instant, on the edge of tears but not letting them appear. Erlenbachs did not show their feelings in public.

And there was his sister Inge, two years younger than Claus, and at eighteen suddenly a beauty to turn all heads. It had been just over a year since Claus had last seen his red haired sister, and in that short time she had blossomed. Well, well.

Claus's father, a departmental head at the Foreign Office, was not present. His duties kept him for most of the year in Berlin, where the Erlenbachs had a villa.

The family tried to spend as much of the year as possible at Falkenstein, and there was no question that the country was more suitable than town for Claus's recuperation. It was hoped that his father would be able to travel down from Berlin to join them soon, at a weekend, perhaps.

Things had been pretty tough at the front, goodness knew, but Claus was surprised by the changes which had taken place at home, where he had näively imagined everyone to be carrying on as normal.

Economy seemed to be the new watchword. There was no car to take them the three miles or so home. Waiting instead with a closed carriage was his father's factor, Schaub, who these days was running practically everything at Falkenstein.

Claus had learned to drive the family car while he was growing up. In the months before joining the army he had spent hours driving as fast as he could through the corners on the roads round the family estate. During quiet moments at the front Claus had remembered these thrills with relish; on the train journey home he had begun to look forward to speeding round Württemberg's country byways. Now, though, the British blockade was cutting so deeply into Germany's supplies of oil that it was impossible to justify unnecessary civilian motoring.

Still, it was like old times for the three of them to be sitting behind a horse, listening to the plodding click of hooves and watching the raindrops flicking from Schaub's whip.

To be carrying four people uphill, they would normally have used a two-horse carriage. They were lucky, Claus's mother confided, still to have even one horse, and this one now did everything on the estate from ploughing to carting produce to town. The Army's demand for horses was insatiable. Not only had practically every available animal been requisitioned; oats to feed them were collected by the authorities as soon as they were harvested.

It was a characteristic of Falkenstein that as one approached via a series of bends, different parts of the house were revealed in a succession of glimpses between trees. The whole picture was not exposed until one rounded the final turn. To Claus, the ancient masonry with its turrets and leaded windows seemed as resilient and indestructible as the Fatherland itself. This was what they were fighting to preserve.

Half of the Erlenbachs' pre-war personnel had gone, leaving the tireless Schaub to take on many of the duties which once would have been the responsibility of others. This mattered less than it might have, since many of the rooms were now closed for the duration, and social activities had been abandoned as the war lengthened and food rationing made itself felt.

Claus found that he was breathless, and stiff from the journey. Back in his own bed, he slept without dreaming until the afternoon of the next day. He had had no sleep like that since going to war, two years ago.

Over the next few days, they all came to see him, the neighbours and the old friends, some with little presents. Two girl cousins called, wanting to know all about his wound, and with the gramophone wound up Claus did a little gentle dancing with each.

Visits were very tiring, and Claus was relieved each night to withdraw to his old room and fall at once into deep slumber. He had frequent dreams about the front, both reliving the deaths of close friends and imagining those of others.

The family physician, Doctor Armbrecht, called regularly to inspect and tend the lieutenant's wounds. 'You're just about the quickest healer I've ever seen', he told Claus. The outer wounds, both front and back, were clearing up fast, and Claus's increasing strength suggested that his lung was recovering just as well.

Claus's father came for one night only, talked with his son from dinner until bedtime, and was off back to Berlin immediately after breakfast.

The grape harvest began two days later, among sunshine which smothered the hillsides with layers of gold leaf. As a boy, Claus had delighted not just in snipping off the fruit but in carrying a packed wooden butt on his back down the hillside to the press. Of course, the estate hands saw to it that he never had too much to carry, but Claus had enjoyed playing the role of worker for those few days each year. He remembered now how much he had missed this activity in the immediate pre-war years, when the family had joined his father on an embassy posting to St Petersburg.

Falkenstein had always had its own vintner and bottled its own vintages. Falkensteiner Trollinger had made a great deal of money for Claus's forebears, and anyone who could lay his hands on a bottle of Falkensteiner Spätlese was considered fortunate indeed.

Now the vintner had gone to the war – had fallen on the Marne in 1914 – and Falkenstein grapes were taken to a collective winery for pressing along with the harvests from all the local vineyards. This year's wine would be bottled and labelled under the name of the village. It was disappointing, but not as frustrating as being forbidden by Dr Armbrecht to attempt carrying the heavy wooden butts on the slopes.

23

Yet Claus knew that must not do anything to delay his return to fitness. It was his duty to see that he went back to the front as soon as possible. It would be sheer irresponsibility to do anything which might hinder his recovery.

All the same, the estate was desperately short of hands. All the villagers were joining in on the local slopes, making a collective effort to bring in the vintage in the minimum time. Claus pottered about among the harvesters, doing whatever he could to help, without over-exertion. The sunshine, he was sure, was speeding his recuperation, and his breathing was nearly back to normal.

His mother did not break the news until the 1916 vintage was in. All the district grapes had been pressed and fermentation begun before she told him: 'That will be the last, Claus. We're going to have to pull out the vines and grow some root crops'.

It was beyond contention. They were lucky to have been able to keep their vineyard for so long, when all the staples such as meat, bread, flour, fats and even potatoes were severely rationed. There had already that spring been noisy protests by hungry crowds on the streets, and the new Food Office was finding it almost impossible to see that the theoretical ration allowances did in practice reach everyone. To sacrifice the Falkenstein vineyard in the interests of the Reich; that was little enough. Others were making higher sacrifices. The main thing was to bring the German people safely through the war to victory. Afterwards they would plant new vines. It would take some years before these produced any yield, but what did that matter? Wine was just another casualty of the struggle, and far from being the most significant one.

The telegram arrived while Schaub was outlining arrangements for uprooting the acres of vineyard. Leutnant von Erlenbach, Claus, was ordered to report at once to the infantry barracks at Pforzheim, for medical examination.

As soon as he put on his uniform, Claus could both feel and see how much of his lost weight he had regained. Somehow, just the sight of the grey cloth around his chest seemed to make him stronger. The figure that Claus saw in the mirror, as he made sure that his belt buckle

24

was placed perfectly dead centre and his cap sat exactly square, was that of an athletic young man of medium build, not quite six feet tall, with a more or less round face, bright blue eyes, a nose that managed to be straight without appearing pointed, a solid chin and the sort of complexion usually described as fresh. The cap was hiding light brown, reddish hair.

Claus set off for Pforzheim in some excitement. It surely wouldn't be long now, and they would let him go back to France. As soon as he returned from this examination he would take one of his guns into the woods and see about shooting some game. It wasn't as much fun as fast driving, but it would put him back into some sort of form.

If it had not been an institution of the German Army, one might have thought that the scene inside the Pforzheim barracks was one of chaos. It was of course nothing of the sort. The German Army did not permit chaos, and the intense, almost frenzied multiple activities going on simultaneously were the product of system and logical planning.

Infantry training was a continuous process. In came an assorted swarm of young civilians every few weeks, and at the same interval ranks of fit and smartly turned out soldiers marched out with packs and shouldered rifles to the railway station, where they boarded trains for one or other of the fronts.

Germany was fighting in Belgium and France, against the Russians and Romanians in the East and against Italians in the Alps. The need for soldiers was enormous, and during their hurried training the recruits learned to march, to obey orders without question, to handle, dismantle, load, fire and maintain rifles, to crawl through mud, to pitch tents and bivouac, to dig latrines and to fight with bayonets. They learned how to read maps and use compasses, how to recognize officers of different ranks by their insignia, and how to address them correctly. They learned the correct military way of making a report, and how to find their way across country at night.

All this they learned, and a great deal more. When they had learned it all, they went on simulated battle courses. Then, it was deemed, they were ready for whatever the front could throw at them.

25

At any one time, separate groups of recruits could be found drilling or being trained in different elements of this curriculum.

When Claus entered the barracks, he was saluted by the guards at the gate and at once encompassed by familiar sounds. Drill sergeants were putting three separate squads through their paces on the square. Physical training instructors had men running, vaulting and climbing ropes. Bayonets were being fixed and suspended sacks of straw run through in noisy charges. Through it all sounded an intermittent crackling from the firing ranges.

The elderly Medical Officer gave the impression of being harassed. He pursed his lips when he saw from Claus's papers the date of the wound. 'Already?' he muttered.

Claus went up and down steps for the MO, blew into a tube to raise a column of mercury, breathed deeply in and out while a stethoscope was applied, and showed just how long he could hold his breath. He was measured and weighed.

Both satisfaction and resignation were discernible in the MO's manner when he turned to the paperwork to record his findings. 'You've recovered remarkably quickly', he told Claus. 'Now I suppose they'll be sending you back to the front pretty soon'.

'I hope so'.

The MO was an expert at keeping pity out of his look. He had seen too much.

Passed fit for front line service. That was all that mattered to Claus. Now it was simply a case of waiting for orders.

There was no doubt that his mother was worried, that in some perverse way she wished for her son to have had a more severe wound which would keep him at home longer – preferably until the war was over. Of course, she did not show her worry, either by word or gesture.

Inge had not yet attained such maturity. She told her brother frankly that she wished he were not going back to France. Claus laughed and told her that little girls didn't understand. Yet even as he said it he was

26

looking at Inge's face and figure and knew that she was no longer a little girl.

Over the next few days, Claus's bag with his small bore shotgun was impressive. He brought down partridge and woodcock and added a dozen hares to the kitchen stores. Exertion no longer tired him, and he roamed the fields and woods all day with his gun and a couple of dogs.

Claus was impatient now, and when his orders arrived he tore open the official envelope without bothering to pick up a paper knife. Then he froze, and re-read the lines. No, he had not been mistaken. Leutnant von Erlenbach, Claus, was ordered to report to the War Ministry in Berlin in two days' time.

A desk job? Surely that wasn't what they had in mind for him? It had to be a mistake. And if not, why was he ordered to the ministry? Claus was a fighting man, with two years' front line experience. They needed experienced men at the front. Hundreds of thousands of untried recruits were being fed straight into the lines fresh from a hasty training. The way to get the best out of these youngsters, the way to preserve as many of them as possible, to make the most effective use of their capabilities, was to have them led by junior officers and NCOs who had been through it all, who knew what they were doing. Tying someone like him to a desk was simply a waste. Heaven knew, there weren't enough junior officers surviving.

In any case, Claus was a Württemberger, and Württemberg had its own War Ministry. So too had Saxony and Bavaria. Even though it was true that since the start of the war the Prussian institution had in effect become the Imperial War Ministry for the whole of the Reich, why summon Claus to Berlin rather to the Württemberg ministry in Stuttgart?

Claus fretted all that day. Next morning he took a train for the capital. He would spend the night at Haus Schwaben, the family's Berlin home, in order to be at the Wilhelmstrasse first thing on the following morning.

The Erlenbachs' villa, in the superior quarter of Charlottenburg, had been such a jolly place while Claus and Inge were small. That night, with only his father and himself dining, what had always seemed such a cosy atmosphere was unexpectedly barren.

Was he going to be stuck here for the rest of the war, going off to the War Ministry each morning, while his father headed for the Foreign Office? He would feel like a rat every time he thought of his comrades at the front.

His father, tall and lean with a dark, full moustache, had never discussed his work with his family, and he did not do so now. Nor did he ask his son any questions about the front. Claus had of course told him why he had come to Berlin, that he was puzzled and sure that his summons was a mistake. His father made no comment.

The two of them discussed the war only in general terms. Before they went to bed, they had emptied a bottle of Courvoisier cognac between them.

The Kaiser's and Prussia's War Ministry had always seemed to Claus to radiate solidity and power. A hundred times he had walked or driven past the daunting building, which stretched for quite a length along the Wilhelmstrasse. Now he entered the great grey edifice for the first time.

An orderly gave Claus the number of an office on an upper floor which took fully five minutes to reach via broad staircases, some thickly carpeted corridors and others whose floors were tiled. Many of the doors which Claus passed bore no numbers. His destination turned out to be only an anteroom, a reception area, where a corporal invited visitors to sit, pending an audience.

Claus was wearing a new uniform which he had ordered as soon as he arrived home from the front. He sat bolt upright on a chair with a wooden back and told himself that he could never spend the rest of the war cooped up in an office building like this, impressive though it was. The whole thing had to be a mistake. When he was older, perhaps, long after the war had been won, and he was a general, or a colonel at least, then he might have a part to play in the planning and organization of his country's defence. But for now...

His ruminations were ended when a buzzer sounded on the corporal's desk.

'Please, Herr Leutnant. You should go in now'. The corporal rose and opened the door into an adjoining, well furnished room.

As Claus advanced towards him, a tall, dark-haired captain with a neat moustache came from behind his desk. Claus was relieved to see someone close to his own age, an officer who, like himself, wore the Iron Cross, First Class. This man too had seen action, and would understand Claus's need to return to the front. If this was the officer who arranged the postings, rather than some old man set in his ways, Claus could surely talk his way out of a desk job.

The captain, whose name was Albrecht, extended his hand and introduced himself. 'I congratulate you on your recovery, Erlenbach'.

'Yes, I'm absolutely fighting fit, Herr Hauptmann', Claus told him. 'I'm strong enough to start for the front today'.

Albrecht smiled. 'Your appointment is with Oberst Lüdershausen. We must go straight in'.

Only as the captain turned did he reveal his disability. He walked faultlessly, but in turning needed to spin on his heel, rotating legs and trunk together. Whatever his wound had been, it restricted the turn of his upper body.

But I'm not like that, thought Claus. I don't need to be stuck here at the ministry like him. I'm still perfectly fit.

Albrecht ushered Claus into a third room, spacious, with high windows and a superb mahogany desk. Behind the desk a solidly built man – it would not have been fair to call him fat – sat making some notations in the margin of a report. Closely cropped grey hair, age perhaps mid-fifties; it was difficult to tell. At any rate the colonel's whole appearance suggested that he was someone who stood no nonsense.

Claus came to attention at regulation distance before the desk, eyes fixed two feet above the colonel's head.

'There are nothing but first class reports about you, Leutnant'. The colonel had stopped writing. 'Iron Cross, First Class, for crawling out under heavy British fire despite wounds, to rescue your company commander. You have since been wounded a second time, and are now fit to return to service. You have proved yourself at the front, Erlenbach, and the Reich has need of you elsewhere. You are a French speaker'. It was not a question. 'French, English and Russian too, I see. The Russian is unusual, but I see that you spent six years in Russia while your father was at our embassy in St Petersburg. You went to school there'.

The colonel glanced up from the file open in front of him. 'Erlenbach, you will go to Bern as assistant military attaché. Your regiment has been informed, and you will report at our embassy in Bern one week from today. With immediate effect you are promoted to Oberleutnant. Good luck, Erlenbach. I am certain that your services will be invaluable to the Reich. Albrecht will issue you with your papers'.

That was that. Claus was back in Albrecht's office within a minute of having left it.

'Cognac, Oberleutnant?' The captain was already opening a bottle. 'We must drink to your promotion as well as to your new posting'.

Bern? Assistant military attaché? It was all a little unreal. Claus took the glass offered him and tried to organize his thoughts.

Albrecht raised his glass and clicked his heels. 'Congratulations, Oberleutnant'.

'Thank you, Herr Hauptmann'.

They emptied their glasses together.

'This isn't at all what I expected', said Claus. 'I wanted to go back to my regiment'.

Albrecht clapped him on the shoulder. 'Don't worry. You've already done your bit at the front, and you'll still be serving the Fatherland. It's a distinction, you know. Not everyone can do these things. You've been carefully selected'.

Selected? But he had never applied for any such posting.

'It isn't the way these things are usually done', Albrecht admitted, 'but there's a war on and we have to cut corners. Don't forget, you're only going to be an assistant. That means a sort of general dogsbody. It's a wartime temporary posting'.

Claus thought he knew the obvious explanation for what had happened, but when he confronted his father that evening he met with indignant repudiation.

Yes, his father was in an ideal position to know whenever an embassy applied to the War Ministry for a junior officer to be attached, but no, he had not used the old pals' network to secure Claus's posting away from the front line.

The denial was only too believable. Claus knew his father. Such things happened, no doubt, but never in a thousand years would his own father dream of placing family before duty to the Reich. Not even to reassure Claus's mother. In any case, his father had never lied to him, had from Claus's boyhood answered every question frankly. It was unthinkable that he should lie to his son now.

'I'm as surprised as you are', protested his father. 'No one has spoken to me about you, and no one has asked any questions. The War Ministry has selected you for this post purely on merit'.

'Merit! You talk as if this is some sort of reward. Shipping me off to a neutral country in the middle of a war is a punishment. I want to go back to the front, where I belong'.

'Want? You want? Since when does a German officer concern himself with what he wants?'

It was unanswerable, and Claus knew it. One could not refuse a posting in wartime. That would be tantamount to desertion.

'Has it occurred to you', his father asked, 'that this is a prime posting that you have been given? Switzerland is important. We need the Swiss as a channel to our enemies – and yes, diplomacy goes on during a war just as it does in peace. Give it a little thought and you might realize that diplomacy is even more important in war. I don't doubt that you will be doing the Reich a far greater service in Switzerland than at the front. I imagine you'll be surprised to find how much useful work there is for you to do. In any case, we do our duty where we are sent'.

They did indeed. It was the essence of Prussian martial discipline. Württembergers were not Prussians, but all the Reich, not just Prussia, needed to obey that code now that Germany was fighting for her very survival, surrounded as she was by enemies on all sides.

But useful work in Switzerland? It didn't seem possible. Yet there was one thing: it was better than staying in Berlin. Any sort of social life in the capital would be just an insult while his friends were at the front.

Claus had his orders and his accreditation for the Swiss. He still had five day's convalescent leave, and would spend these with his mother and Inge. At Falkenstein he would, after all, be already three quarters of the way to Switzerland.

'Your mother's better off staying put for the time being', his father told him. 'No sense her hurrying back to Berlin as things are. The whole place is becoming far too hectic. Not a lot of fun being here, with all this wartime traffic. No one has any time for anything. It will do your mother far more good to enjoy a rest and some decent weather in the country for as long as she can. And Inge, too'.

His father was unquestionably right. Claus wasn't sure that Berlin was a place to enjoy at the moment. Nothing but grim bustle in the overcrowded streets, and tired looking civilians.

Claus left the capital early next morning. As he expected, train timetables were being disrupted by the needs of military traffic. By the time he alighted at the small station by the Neckar it was already late evening.

Despite his mother's skill at hiding her feelings, she could not conceal her relief that Claus would not after all be returning to the front. Claus had to let her believe that he was looking forward to his new post. Inwardly he found it difficult to suppress his guilt. The trouble was, he really had made a complete recovery to full strength. He felt as fit as he ever had. Only activity could help assuage his self-reproach. On each of those last few days he tramped out across the countryside with gun and dogs. It wasn't what he shot that was important; just the fact of doing some shooting.

It was more like a holiday farewell than a wartime parting when his mother and sister saw Claus off at the station on the first stage of his journey to Switzerland. Claus had been witness to many tearful scenes on railway platforms; all natural enough when the people involved did not know whether the leave-taking would be their last. Claus's posting, on the other hand, was a guarantee of surviving the war.

It might make my mother and Inge happy, Claus reflected as the train heaved itself into motion, but it's a burden I shall carry for the rest of my life. Most of Europe in arms, and here I am heading for an island of peace and normality.

It did not help that Claus was travelling in civilian clothes. Being out of uniform made him feel even more like a man dodging the call of duty. Civvies, though, were regulation. Switzerland would not let combatants through her borders, and if Claus did not now have diplomatic status he would not be allowed in.

Both the Swiss and the Germans were sensitive about who went in and out of their countries during hostilities. Controls at the small German frontier station of Gottmadingen were understandably stringent, and no less so at Thayngen, the first station on the Swiss side. Luggage was subjected to particularly close scrutiny.

Now Claus experienced some of the advantages of his unwished for diplomatic status. Despite his being the soldier of a warring nation, passing through to the Swiss side was for Claus without annoyance. His accreditation freed him from the more irksome formalities. Irritation came with a long wait for the Swiss train to depart. Some 230 passengers had to be checked through before steam could be fed to the cylinders and the journey into the Swiss heartland begun.

Bern was bright, but sober compared with Berlin. It offered its residents little of the entertainment and commercial gaiety which characterized the German capital in peacetime. Bern reflected instead the character of its people: industrious, prudent and perhaps even a touch introspective.

33

Yet the overall atmosphere of dedication, both inside the embassy and outside in the city, suited Claus. His father had been right. There was plenty of work for him to do. The embassies of all the belligerent nations, and the American one too, were probably busier at Bern than anywhere else. The city was alive with rumours and speculation.

Within a week Claus was so immersed in reports – analyzing, summarizing and forwarding them – that he was beginning to enjoy the challenge. What he was doing might after all prove useful service. It wasn't just a matter of collecting reports and passing them along; what counted was the analysis, deciding what was genuine and what so much smokescreen, error or sheer fantasy. By the third week, Claus's feelings of guilt about not returning to the front were beginning to subside. The Ambassador, Baron Gisbert von Romberg, was not merely courteous and considerate, but kind to all the embassy staff. Claus liked him and by the end of the year had settled in completely to his posting, remorse striking him now only when he read casualty notices from the front.

Conspiracy

'You speak Russian, don't you, Erlenbach?'

The Ambassador's question came out of the blue.

'Certainly, Excellency'.

'There are a number of Russians here that we should take a look at. Revolutionaries. Enemies of the Tsar. One of them is going to address Swiss workers at Zürich on the…' Romberg lifted a paper from his desk and consulted it. '…the 22nd of this month. You're our only Russian speaker, and we need you to go along. It's a public meeting, pushing to start some sort of revolution here, no doubt. We need a full report on these fellows, what calibre they are, how many of them, what resources they appear to have, who's behind them, any indication of what damage they might be able to do in Switzerland, and so on'.

It wasn't a military matter. They were sending him because they needed a Russian speaker, but the meeting wouldn't be in Russian, would it?

'Of course not', Romberg confirmed. 'No use talking to Swiss workers in Russian. The main man, a fellow called Ulyanov, will be speaking German. He won't be alone, though. You might just pick up something between him and his associates. Long shot, I know, but it's worth a try'.

Well, it was contact of a sort with the enemy.

Dull, though. A cold January night, a shabby hall, a few dozen militant artisans, phrases which seemed to Claus to be just talk, to have no practical meaning at all. Claus had not before seen an agitator at work, or been close to militant proletarians. He felt that he could live contentedly without repeating the experience.

Pushing to start a revolution, the ambassador had said.

Hm. At the end of a wordy evening Claus saw no reason to fear that Swiss workers were on the point of rising up to overthrow their government. Even the Russian speaker, the balding and bearded man

Ulyanov, acknowledged that revolutionary aspirations were premature. 'We older men', he conceded, 'may not live to see the decisive battles of the coming revolution'.

Noting in his report that Ulyanov had been introduced to his audience under the cover name of 'Lenin', Claus summarized the revolutionaries' promptings as 'nothing dangerous'.

Just seven weeks later, the Russian government lost its grip on power. Tsar Nicholas II abdicated.

Claus and the entire embassy personnel followed these events with almost feverish interest. It looked as though war-weary Russia, some of whose troops were deserting and whose navy was in revolt, would soon ask for peace. This would free valuable German and Austrian forces from the Eastern Front for a decisive push in the West. It promised to be the turning point that Germany needed.

The new Russian government, led by Alexander Kerensky, failed to oblige. Kerensky announced his determination to continue the war, and Russian forces continued to fight along the entire length of the Eastern Front, from the Baltic to the Black Sea.

Staff at the British and French embassies were jubilant. By chance, Claus saw two French attachés, in back-slapping mood and clearly already well into their cups, entering a city centre restaurant. The establishment was one which German diplomatic personnel avoided. British, French and Russians had their own particular haunts, Germans and Austrians theirs.

Then America entered the war. It could be a matter of only a few months before the first American troops would reach the Western battlefields. Clearly a massive increase in effort would be necessary if Germany were to achieve victory before then.

The Kaiser's General Staff responded to this threat with what must have looked like a stroke of genius. Top secret orders arrived at the Bern embassy, and the Ambassador sent for Claus.

'Erlenbach, you are to accompany me on the most delicate of missions. We have to contact your Russian revolutionary friend, the one who uses the cover name Lenin'.

Claus would not have called the revolutionary a friend. He was, after all, an enemy alien. And one who had been on the run from the authorities for ten years. Though in January Claus has heard Lenin admit that he did not expect to live to see the overthrow of his country's order, the would-be revolutionary had now been thrown into a fever by the Tsar's abdication. He was desperate to return to Russia, but his way was barred by enemy territory.

'He hasn't slept since news of the revolution arrived', Lenin's wife confided. 'He's been making all sorts of incredible plans. First he thought we could travel by aeroplane, then he realized that was impossible, and now he's thinking of disguising himself with a wig and trying to return to Russia by way of France, Britain and the North Sea. But he's afraid of being arrested en route, or of his ship being torpedoed by a German U-boat'.

'No need to worry about any of that now', the Ambassador told the balding revolutionary. 'We shall find a way to get you home. And soon'.

The German offer was simple: Germany would help Lenin reach home to assume power, if in return he would take Russia out of the war.

The next few days were as hectic as any that Claus had experienced at the front. Claus would not have believed it, but it really was possible to fight for one's country using only paper, just as with firearms.

Only a week after America's declaration of war, Claus boarded a train at Zürich along with Lenin and a group of his fellow-exiles. Claus thought them the oddest bunch he had ever seen. Wild looking, half of them scruffy, not a gentleman between them. A few women, and even some children.

One character in particular attracted Claus's notice – a round-faced fellow, with thick curling hair and thicker pebble-lensed glasses, who seemed to have a lot to say for himself. His name was Sobelsohn. Once the train was under way, Sobelsohn lit up a curved pipe of the style seen in Sherlock Holmes illustrations. Smoking, reflected Claus thankfully, at least shut the man up for a while.

When the train halted just inside Germany, the arrivals were greeted in cool but correct fashion by two officers whom Claus had not met but had been told to expect. The travellers alighted onto Gottmadingen's single platform and were directed into the third-class waiting room, where the officers checked their paperwork as quickly as possible.

Waiting for the group was a special train consisting of only one passenger carriage and a baggage car. A third class compartment with wooden seats at one end of the carriage was to be occupied by the escorting officers. A line drawn with chalk on the floor of the corridor separated the escort's end of the coach from the main part of the carriage and its travellers. None of Lenin's party was allowed to cross this line.

Three of the four doors to the carriage were locked and sealed. Only the fourth, opposite the officers' compartment and so on the German side of the white line, was left unlocked.

As long as Germany and Russia remained at war with one another, the travellers were enemy aliens normally liable to internment on reaching German territory. The General Staff's ingenious solution to this difficulty was to escort the Russian exiles through the Reich in a sealed train and for that train to be accorded the status of a travelling embassy. This meant that for the purpose of this one journey the carriage was recognized by the Germans as inviolable Russian territory.

Locked inside their carriage, the travellers were to have no contact with German nationals during the trip.

Such was the importance accorded by the General Staff to Lenin and his accomplices that the personal train of none other than the heir to the German throne, Imperial Crown Prince Wilhelm, was held up for two hours at Halle in Saxony, to allow the mobile embassy through.

At Berlin, Lenin's special train was halted for nearly twenty-four hours, and there the theoretical ban on contact with Germans was disregarded. A General Staff officer wearing civilian clothes – Claus never discovered his name – visited the train at the Potsdamer Station to make arrangements for the remainder of the operation. By the time that Lenin steamed on his way, the returning revolutionary knew that he was to receive massive German financing once he reached Russia. More than forty million gold marks had been earmarked for his efforts.

The General Staff was prepared if necessary to smuggle Lenin and his companions into Russia through the front lines of the Eastern Front. For obvious reasons of safety and simplicity, another route was to be tried first. The sealed train went on from Berlin to Sassnitz on the Baltic coast, where the returning exiles boarded the ferry Königin Viktoria, bound for the Swedish port of Trelleborg.

All being well, the German officer escort's job was done. The question now was whether the Swedes would let the Russians enter their country. Lenin's party was to attempt the rail journey through Sweden and Finland direct to the Russian capital of Petrograd, as St Petersburg had now been renamed. Only if the neutral Swedish authorities refused them transit were the travellers to return to Germany for the clandestine and perilous trip through two embattled armies.

The Swedes made no difficulties, and the hazardous attempt to pass the Russians through two opposing front lines became unnecessary.

Seven days after leaving Zürich, Claus was back at his desk in Bern, while Lenin arrived at Petrograd with his followers, welcomed on the station platform by a noisy gathering of revolutionary-minded sailors.

While so much was going on, Claus found it infuriating to be cooped up in an office, far away from both the action at the front and the scene of any further conspiracy.

The trouble was, Claus had meanwhile developed a taste for this kind of backroom activity. He had never been interested in the diplomacy in which his father engaged; that had always seemed to him far too tame. Like any red blooded young man, Claus wanted action. If the chance came now to go back to his regiment at the front, he would leap at it. And yet...

Fortune had given him an opportunity to see a great conspiracy at work – a conspiracy which, if it were successful, would make history. The experience had woken in him a new kind of appetite, and its longings were making him restless.

He would walk through the streets of Bern, looking into the bright cafés and the stores, lingering sometimes at the displays of food which he knew people at home simply could not obtain any longer, saunter sometimes through parks or sit for a while beneath huge trees, and all the while he wondered what Lenin and his ragtag disreputable crowd were doing now that they were back on home soil.

Lenin had been given large sums of German money, and it was these funds which kept him and his party going. Practically Lenin's first action on arrival back in Russia was to buy a new press for his party newspaper. Ten new titles were founded, and some 1,500,000 copies of revolutionary journals were soon being produced every week with German funding. The common theme repeated over and over to the soldiery was: Bayonet your officers. Go home. End the war.

In October, gangs of Lenin's Red Guards seized the Winter Palace at Petrograd while Russia's elected government was in session. The Red Guards were reinforced by military and naval mutineers, so that the palace was stormed by something approaching 7,000 armed men in all. The palace was guarded only by a women's battalion and some young cadets.

The Red troops overcame this fragile guard and placed the assembled legal government of Russia under arrest. Only Kerensky himself, who was not present, escaped and fled into exile.

Such was the armed coup d'état which the Communists passed on into history under the misleading title of October Revolution. The news brought general rejoicing throughout German diplomatic and military circles, but as Ambassador Romberg was quick to point out, it had not been a popular revolution of the sort with which one might perhaps sympathize. It had involved the violent overthrow of a democratic and legal government, with the illegal arrest and abduction of the elected representatives of the people. The actual Russian Revolution had taken place seven months earlier, when the Tsar was compelled to abdicate and a democratic government established. Lenin's Communists had played no part in those events, and the happy period of a young democracy had lasted for the Russian people little more than a half-year before being wrested from them by violence.

Still, it was the situation which Germany wanted, and no one was complaining. Lenin had so far spent 11,566,122 German marks, and the German Treasury released a further 15,000,000 marks to him one day after his coup.

It remained only for Lenin to earn his pay by taking Russia out of the war, so freeing the forty-four German divisions on the Eastern Front for a last offensive effort in the West.

Fighting stopped on December 6. Germany was now free to move a million men across Europe for an offensive against Britain, France and the USA. She was also able to empty the Ukraine of grain to feed fifty million Germans who were suffering the effects of Britain's maritime blockade.

Satisfaction at the successful outcome to the General Staff's brainwave did not last long. A renewed German offensive on the Western Front came to a standstill after fifteen days. Reinforcements transferred from the East were more than counterbalanced by the added weight on the Allied side of 1,473,190 fresh American troops with first class equipment.

Germany had played her last card, and the High Command made an urgent recommendation for armistice negotiations 'to avoid a catastrophe'.

Claus could not believe it.

Had it all been for nothing? Häberle, his head and right leg blown up into the branches of a tree, where from a certain angle they suggested a cancan dancer executing a high kick. The rest of Häberle was never found, and three days later, when there was a lull in fighting, they brought down the two parts and wrapped them together for burial. The inseparable friends Ingelfinger and Haberkern, still side by side when they were both practically sawn in half by the same machine gun burst. The brains and blood sprayed over Claus's face when a sharpshooter took the top off Lehmann's skull while the two of them were talking. Ever-cheerful Müller, who would do anything for anybody, disappeared completely when a shell landed where he stood. They had found not even as much as Müller's belt buckle. Dr Grau, the earnest young academic, head taken clean off by a mortar round as he

41

advanced, inexplicably remaining upright for an instant before collapsing like a marionette whose strings had been cut. Erxner, screaming for an hour before dying out there in a shell hole with a French bayonet in him, while they were all pinned down by sniper fire, unable to reach their comrade.

The thousands Claus had seen, the sacrifices of millions he had not seen, the privations suffered by people at home, the exhaustion of the nation's wealth and resources, the imaginative institution of the sealed train. It was impossible that it had all been for nothing.

Claus did not even think of the British bullet through his lung. That was of no account. He would give his life instantly now – wouldn't they all? – if this would reverse the outcome.

Just twelve months after Lenin's assumption of power, Germany and the Austro-Hungarian Empire had followed Russia's path to revolution and military catastrophe. Their monarchies were abolished. The General Staff had taken a brilliant and expensive gamble with Ulyanov alias Lenin, and the gamble had not after all saved Germany. What had seemed like a good idea at the time had produced the inverse effect. It was the General Staff which had saved Lenin, a wanted fugitive already resigned never to seeing the realization of his designs.

Claus had not cared for Lenin, either at Zürich or on the train. To Claus, Lenin seemed to possess an almost inhuman coldness. Now the reports from Russia which passed across Claus's desk confirmed that impression. Lenin's Soviet Russia was to become more despotic than the old régime, his Cheka secret police more ruthless and omnipresent than its Tsarist precursor, the Okhrana.

A manual for members of the Cheka which reached Claus instructed Lenin's thugs that they had to murder people not for anything that they had done, but for what they were: 'We are not waging war on individuals, but are annihilating the bourgeoisie as a class. Do not look for documents and evidence about what the accused has done or said. The first question to be put to him must be what class he belongs to, what are his origins, his upbringing, his training, his occupation'.

Claus was appalled when an official announcement by Grigory Zinoviev landed on his desk. Claus had clear memories of Zinoviev, who had been with Lenin on the sealed train. Now Zinoviev named a figure for annihilation by the Cheka: ten millions. 'Of the hundred million people in Russia under the Soviets we must win ninety million for our cause. Where the rest are concerned, we have nothing to say to them. They are to be exterminated'.

Claus had not forgotten the impression made on him as a boy when he read a novel by an English lady. It was the story of a German count who created a living human being, only for his creation to turn into a monster and kill the man who made it. Just like the fictional Count Frankenstein, Germany too now seemed unwittingly to have created a monster in Soviet Russia.

The news reaching Bern from Germany was scarcely more encouraging. Severe food shortage had been a major cause of the German revolution, and now, despite the armistice, the Allies were continuing their blockade. Hundreds of thousands of troops were returning from the front to find conditions for their families worse than they could have imagined. Germany's new provisional government had its hands full, trying to keep order and struggling to organize food supplies.

The transition to a republic and the end of hostilities had not led to any changes of personnel at the embassy, and Claus was beginning to fret about what direction his peacetime duties might take.

'I expect', the Ambassador suggested to him one January morning, 'that your father will be going to negotiate with the Allies soon'.

Claus had not thought of that, but yes, it was probably true. The armistice had only put a stop to the fighting, not settled the terms of the peace. These were still to be negotiated. As one of the absolute top men at the Foreign Office, Claus's father was certain to attend the talks as a right hand to Germany's chief representative.

'The Allies are set to gather at Versailles', said the Ambassador, 'so it looks certain that's where the talks will be held'.

Any day now, Claus told himself, I'll receive one of those neatly written notes of my father's, telling me that he's off to France.

43

No word had come when the leaders of the Western Allies sat down together at Versailles. Claus's father had not gone to France because no German delegation was invited.

It soon became apparent that the purpose of the Versailles Conference was not peace negotiations between the belligerent parties on both sides, but a meeting between the Allies to work out the conditions which they would impose on Germany.

It was May before a German delegation was summoned to attend. Its members, Claus's father among them, expected to be invited to sit down together with British, French, US and Italian representatives. They would hear the Allies' demands, put their counter suggestions, and negotiations would begin.

'Nothing of the kind', Claus's father told him later. 'There were no talks at all. Never once did we meet the Allies. It was outrageous. They treated us as if we had signed not a ceasefire, but unconditional surrender'.

The Allies had decided on the peace terms which they would exact, and simply summoned German representatives to receive them. The completed treaty – 248 pages – was presented to the Germans as an ultimatum. The French Premier, Georges Clemenceau, announced that war would be resumed if the terms were not accepted in full.

Count Ulrich von Brockdorff-Rantzau, heading the German delegation, was not intimidated. He refused to sign.

On June 20, Marshal Ferdinand Foch, the Supreme Commander of Allied Forces, received orders to advance into Germany on the evening of June 23, if the peace terms were not signed by then. On Sunday, June 22, the Paris newspaper Excelsior published under the ominous headline 'If Germany does not sign...' a threatening map showing the line-up of Allied forces along Germany's borders, with arrows indicating invasion into the Reich. An airship was pictured heading towards Berlin.

'Should the Weimar government not sign our peace terms' explained Excelsior, 'the armies of the Entente will open an offensive across the Rhine, starting on Tuesday morning. A cavalry screen will cover the advancing infantry, who will be protected by tank battalions and massive artillery. Airships and above all huge squadrons of aircraft will attack the enemy's cities'.

Clemenceau had made the Germans an offer which they could not refuse.

Fresh delegates were despatched from Berlin with orders to sign. Claus's father, having supported Brockdorff's stand, was not among them.

More than three quarters of a million Germans had died through malnutrition during the war itself, and deaths were still mounting due to continuation of the Allied blockade. Now Germany, whose sick, elderly and infants were dying in large numbers every day through lack of food, was ordered to hand over much-needed livestock to the Allies: 140,000 dairy cows, 40,000 heifers, 4,000 bulls, 30,000 ewes, 1,200 rams, 10,000 goats and 15,000 sows. The dying could only intensify.

The young German republic was ordered to reimburse the Allies for the entire cost of all war losses and damage sustained: an unspecified sum whose size would be determined at some time in the future. The Allies reserved the right to demand goods and materials from Germany as and when their wish for them might arise.

To five of her neighbours, Germany was forced to cede provinces amounting to an area the size of Scotland. 7,325,000 Germans were placed under foreign rule – equivalent to the combined populations of Scotland and Wales.

The greatest difficulties were caused by giving Poland what became known as the Polish Corridor, a stretch of German territory reaching north to the Baltic. This action detached East Prussia from the remainder of the Reich – akin to having Cheshire, Shropshire, Herefordshire and Gloucestershire occupied by a foreign power, so that travel to and from Wales would mean first passing through hostile territory.

The military conditions imposed were intended to render Germany defenceless against any attack by her neighbours. Germany was forbidden to build or possess submarines, aircraft (including airships), anti-aircraft weapons, tanks, armoured cars, anti-tank weapons, poison gases and heavy artillery. The Army was to be limited to 100,000 and the Navy to 15,000 men.

The Army could become an internal police force, and nothing more. Germany was not permitted to import or export weapons, military equipment or ammunition. The equipment of the new rump forces was specified in detail. Its manufacture was to be permitted only in certain licensed factories and workshops, under the supervision of an Allied Control Commission.

All of this was justified by the claim of Germany's sole guilt for the outbreak of war. 'What they have done at Versailles', said Claus's father, 'we could have done to France after Napoleon – and with complete justification, after all the wars and suffering that French ambitions have spread across this continent for more than a thousand years. We could have given French territory to her neighbours, we could have tried to bleed France dry, we could have stripped her army down to a laughable size in a perfectly justified attempt to stop her waging war on anybody again. We didn't do this to France, because we are not stupid. If we had done it, what would have happened? In twenty-five years France would have been back on her feet again, and not just back on her feet but with forces ready to go all out for revenge'.

Never had Claus heard his father raise his voice, not even to the most obtuse servant, but he raised it now. 'Well, they shouldn't be surprised if other people react in the same way. It's a matter of honour now, for every man to work to overturn this'.

The Erlenbachs could not know it, but even on the Allied side the severe terms met with opposition. While the conference was still in session, Britain's Prime Minister David Lloyd George declared that he could scarcely imagine 'a more powerful cause for a new war' than detaching German territories and people and placing them under the rule of other nations. 'In my view', Lloyd George warned, 'the proposal by the Polish Commission, to place 2,100,000 Germans under the rule of a people who have never in their history shown their ability to rule themselves, must sooner or later lead to a new war in Eastern Europe'.

No attention was paid to Lloyd George's earnest plea to act like impartial umpires who had forgotten all the passions of the war.

Claus did learn that the American President Woodrow Wilson had left the conference in disgust, and that the economist John Maynard Keynes had resigned as a member of the British delegation in protest at the harsh punishment proposed for Germany.

He did not hear how the Allied Supreme Commander, Marshal Ferdinand Foch, reacted when he learned in June 1919 of the penal nature of the dictated terms.

'That is no peace', Foch warned. 'That is an armistice for twenty years'.

Cupid

The girl was blonde, blue eyed and very nearly as tall as himself. Claus found himself following her without having made a conscious decision to do so. It was almost as though he were an automaton, drawn along in the girl's wake.

The hospital staff were very apologetic. Severe staff shortage and an overload of patients had thrown the day's timetable right out. Doctors were still examining patients, nurses were attending to dressings and there were ward cleaning duties yet to be performed. Everyone was very sorry, but there could be no possibility of admitting visitors for the next hour at least. If people preferred to wait rather than call again later, they would find chairs and benches in some of the alcoves off the corridors.

In one corner there was even a small table with four wooden chairs, and it was here that the girl was heading. A middle-aged couple took two of the seats, and Claus pulled out a third chair for the girl. The smile which she gave him when she turned her head in thanks was, Claus thought, the loveliest he had ever seen. His head began to swim.

Claus took the final seat and the middle-aged couple at once began a conversation with him and the girl. They hoped that they would not be kept hanging about waiting too long, but of course they sympathized with the overworked hospital staff. There seemed to be more people ill these days than there had been during the war.

The girl blamed the Allied blockade, which ought to have been lifted as soon as fighting stopped. She herself was visiting her aunt, an elderly lady seriously ill as a result of the food shortage.

The contrast between conditions in the Reich and those in the Swiss land of plenty was certainly dramatic. It had been a hot midsummer day when Claus's orders arrived. He had been at Bern for more than two years, and hoped to be posted back to his regiment. Instead, he was assigned to the War Ministry in Berlin for unspecified duties. Except that it wasn't called the War Ministry any more; it was now the Reichswehr Ministry. The Reichswehr was the Army.

Another desk job.

Some consolation came in his simultaneous promotion to captain. Like all soldiers, Claus would have preferred to have earned his advancement on the battlefield. The Bern posting had perhaps robbed him of that opportunity, but he must not think of himself. There was a job to be done in rebuilding the Reich after the damage inflicted on her at Versailles, and unlike so many of his comrades Claus was still alive to do his bit.

Not on the Wilhelmstrasse, though. As well as being renamed, the ministry had been moved some streets away from the heart of government to the Bendlerstrasse.

'For myself', Baron Romberg told Claus as they shook hands in farewell, 'I'm sorry to see you go. You've done an excellent job here. But the Army knows where it can use you best. There's an uphill struggle ahead for the Reich, and I know that you will perform valuable service. Good luck and goodbye'.

It surprised Claus that leaving the embassy should prove a wrench, after he had for so long ached to return to his regiment. He had become attached to Romberg, who had been kind to him from the day of his arrival.

'Yes', said his father, when Claus arrived back at their Berlin villa. 'Romberg is one of the really old-fashioned sort. As courteous as the day is long'.

Claus was in Magdeburg now to visit an old front-line comrade who lay in the hospital there after losing both legs.

'You know they confiscated all German assets abroad?' asked the girl. 'Do you know what that means? The patent rights alone are worth billions of marks. It's an additional penalty, a hidden one in addition to the so-called reparations which are being demanded. No one knows how much German assets worldwide are worth, but the Allies are sharing them out between them. They're just bloodsuckers'.

The question of patent rights had not occurred to Claus, and it was obvious that the other two at the table had not thought about them. Did it take a girl to open people's eyes?

50

The destructive peace terms imposed on Austria roused the girl to similar indignation. Claus was astonished. What girls talked like this? While the conversation was on political matters, he himself remained noncommittal. Politics was to him a distasteful subject and he regarded it as unfortunate that his duties and his family connections had sometimes forced him to mix with politicians. He did not like any whom he had so far met, and avoided opportunities to meet any more of them.

Rather than speak himself, Claus preferred to listen to the girl, who spoke good sense, and to gaze at her while she spoke. It was apparent that the girl was extraordinarily intelligent, and better informed than most of the public. It was, though, her astonishing beauty which dazzled him, the lyrical sound of her voice which held him spellbound. As he looked and listened, Claus forgot the hospital, noticed nothing of his surroundings, did not even see the middle-aged couple.

'You may go in now'. A powerfully built sister with the hint of a moustache was striding along the corridor. People were rising, some making comments, hurrying towards the diverse wards.

It all happened so quickly that Claus had no time to react. In battle his thoughts and movements were lightning itself, but faced with this girl all he could do was behave like a tongue-tied, clumsy marionette, springing up to draw away her chair and setting off with her back down the corridor. Before he could think of a word to say, they reached the entrance to the ward where the girl's aunt lay. The girl smiled, said goodbye, and was gone through the swing doors.

Numbed, Claus took two wrong turnings in his search for the amputees' section.

As soon as visiting hours were over, Claus shook his comrade's hand, wished him good luck, promised to come again and hurried towards the main hospital doors. People were leaving the building alone, in pairs and in small family groups. Had the girl beaten him to the exit?

She was reasonably tall, and ought to be easy to spot. Claus peered along the street in both directions. The girl was not in sight.

Claus had bought one of the first cars to be produced by Daimler after the war, a convertible Mercedes Sport. It was parked in the street near the double doors. Claus climbed into the leather driving seat and watched as the departing stream of visitors dwindled and came to an end. It was apparent that the girl had been too quick for him.

It was a long shot, but Claus had nothing to lose. He started the motor and drove off. Down the street he went, then round to the back of the hospital. The girl must already be farther away. Having circled the building once, Claus widened his circuit to begin a systematic search of all the streets in the area. The farther he drove, the more desperate he became. The girl was not to be seen.

Claus had covered every major road, every side street and every back lane within a mile of the hospital before he stopped the car and sat there motionless, to reflect. The girl had escaped him. He would never see her again.

On the drive back to Berlin, Claus felt as miserable as he could remember. It was worse, far worse, than taking a bullet through the lung. The body at least healed itself; all one had to do was wait. But waiting was not going to bring this girl back to him, the girl of whom he did not realize that she was important to him until she left.

Like a fool, he had not thought, while he was gazing at the girl and listening to her voice, that the experience would come to an end. Now she was gone.

That Claus was intolerably unhappy was apparent in his driving. Normally he exulted in rapid motion, flinging the open Mercedes through bend after bend with panache. Now he simply sat there holding the wheel, no longer actively in charge of the machine, but simply letting himself be carried along. This was not driving as Claus understood driving. The journey to Berlin took an hour longer than it should have.

It was silly, really. Not only had he not expected to see the girl; this morning he could not even have imagined her existence. They had sat next to one another for less than an hour, and they had talked a little. Yet now that she was gone it was as though an essential part of himself had been ripped away.

Claus spent the entire drive kicking himself. How could he have been so stupid as to have said nothing, to have made no effort at introducing himself so that they could meet again? It had been a once in a lifetime opportunity, and he had wasted it.

His sister Inge had married, and at the wedding Claus's cousins had ragged him. When are you going to marry, then, Claus?

The only answer he had was to laugh. Marriage had not entered his mind because he had been too busy, too earnest in his service for the Fatherland. The thought had simply not arisen.

Now there was nothing for him but to immerse himself in his work. Heaven knows, he told himself, there's enough of that.

What concerned Claus immediately was the question whether, with the Army soon to be cut down to 100,000 men, there would still be a place for him in the service. He could, he knew, devote his life to running Falkenstein. Goodness knew the place was going to take years to put back on its feet. New vines needed to be planted, and these would spend the first four or five years of their life putting down a root system. There would not even be any flowers, let alone grapes, before the middle of the 1920s.

Rebuilding the estate would be a fascinating challenge, but it was not what Claus knew that he must do.

Not only no tanks or aircraft but no anti-tank or anti-aircraft guns – the intention at Versailles had clearly been to render Germany defenceless and at the mercy of her rapacious neighbours any time they chose to attack. Well, they would see about that. As his father had said, it was a matter of honour now for every man to make a nonsense of the Allies' aim. The French and the Poles could go hang.

What Claus could do personally about Versailles, he could not yet imagine. The first thing was to follow his orders to report at Bendlerstrasse to a Major Otto.

The major turned out to be a shortish, jolly man with exceptionally bright eyes, a dark upturned moustache in the Kaiser style and an irreverent sense of humour.

'You know some of these Russians', were practically Otto's first words, and Claus was not sure whether it was a statement or a question. 'We're a kind of filter here, sorting out what goes to Intelligence and what to Major Schleicher's Political Department. Reports from all over the world, of course, and we need you to deal with what comes in from Russia. A lot piled up already, I'm afraid. Tomorrow, though, there's a treat for you. You'll be meeting one of your old friends'.

Otto's often flippant manner was deceptive. His was a mind of the severest practicality. 'I don't need to warn you, Erlenbach, that your duties, and everything in this department, are top secret. We are living in strange times, and the things we do here are likely to be unorthodox. But you wouldn't have been posted to me if you hadn't already proved that you could do the most delicate jobs with the utmost discretion'.

At nine o'clock next morning, the two men left the Reichswehr Ministry together. A grey Benz tourer was waiting, and they climbed into the rear seats.

It took three quarters of an hour to reach the villa at Grunewald. This was the most expensive residential quarter in the country, where strict regulations ensured that houses occupied only a small part of each land parcel, so that the whole area remained a mass of forest. Max Reinhardt had lived here, and the physicist Max Planck was a resident. So too was the head of the electrical giant AEG, Walther Rathenau, who had been in charge of Germany's raw material supplies during the war and made superhuman efforts to avert his country's collapse.

While the army driver held open the door of the Benz for his passengers to alight, Claus glimpsed the water of a lake. Which of the Grunewald lakes it was, he had no idea. Nor did he ever learn whose house it was they were visiting.

A large man with every appearance of a plain clothes policeman admitted the two officers to the building and led them along a broad, wooden-floored hallway. At a heavy oak door he stopped, knocked on the dark wood, opened the door and stood aside for the visitors to enter. The plain clothes man, if that's what he was, closed the door behind them and himself stayed outside.

It was a large and comfortable room with robust-looking rugs, heavy oak furniture and abundant leather seating. A picture window revealed a terrace and immaculate gardens, backed by the dark green forests which gave Grunewald its name.

Only one person was in the room, and Claus recognized him from the pebble-lensed spectacles and the Sherlock Holmes pipe which he was sucking.

Otto beamed at Claus like one springing a surprise party. 'You know Karl Radek, of course'.

Claus knew Karl Sobelsohn. He had never heard the name Radek. Another cover name, presumably, like Lenin.

Sobelsohn had been the life and soul of the party on the train journey from Zürich. That was two years ago, and in memory Claus could still hear the over-loud laughter that had bellowed out from the compartment where Sobelsohn was holding court.

Claus had to play the game now, and call the man Radek. The Russian, who remembered him, had come to Germany as the official Soviet delegate to the founding congress of the German Communist Party. He was now, it appeared, enjoying the protection of the state and receiving a series of important visitors.

'Enver Pasha's been here, hasn't he, Karl?' asked Otto in his jovial way.

Radek was happy to confirm it. 'He was one of the first'.

The Turkish General and former War Minister Enver Pasha had been an architect of the Ottoman constitution and the driving force behind his country's alliance with Germany. What could he have in common with a Bolshevik?

Radek clearly felt at home in this grand villa, where just as clearly he did not fit. Host-like, he was smiling at the two soldiers as they settled themselves in armchairs facing him.

A few preliminary remarks and queries on both sides, and Radek came to the point. 'Your enemies are our enemies. You know that. They've taken German land and millions of Germans and given them to the Poles. They've sent troops into Azerbaijan and Siberia to try to give Russia back to the Romanovs. The same people. They've been ruling the world for long enough, and it's time to stop them'.

'We'll not disagree', put in Otto.

'Where our two countries went wrong' – Radek was winding himself up – 'was in fighting against each other. Well, we can correct that. Must correct that. The new Germany and the new Russia, united, will put these butchers of Versailles in their place'.

'Exactly how?'

'The first thing is to realize that we have the same interests. You can't tolerate the new Polish state, and we certainly don't approve of it. You've suffered at the hands of the Allies, and we're suffering through them. We both need to rebuild. We need both to be economically strong'.

'Soldiers know nothing of economy'.

'But there are plenty of people who do. Rathenau's been here, you know'.

'No. I didn't know'.

'Rathenau's not going to bow to the Versailles terms without resistance. He knows what's to be done. He's already organizing an industrial mission to Russia'.

Good lord, thought Claus. A man like Rathenau working together with that gang of cut-throats.

'They'll be off any day now. Rathenau's firm of course, and Professor Junkers. A whole bunch of them'.

'With what object?'

'Trade. You need it. We need it. Our industry needs to get back on its feet. Your industry needs to get back on its feet. They've banned Junkers from building aircraft. He's going to see if he can build them in Russia'.

An hour longer the two officers listened to Radek's urgings against 'our joint enemies, the victors of Versailles'. His arguments made sense.

Germany, saddled with sole responsibility for the war, had become an outlaw, a convicted criminal among nations. In this, she was no longer alone.

With the brutality of the Bolshevik régime becoming apparent, the young Soviet Russia was also finding itself ostracized. Russia's cause had not been helped when Lenin announced that the Bolshevik seizure of power was no more than the first step towards world revolution. Look at what he'd said as early as March last year, telling the Russian Communist Party congress to prepare workers for 'the new war' and to see to it that they spent at least an hour each day learning how to fight.

Talking about 'the new war' while the old one was still in full swing! No wonder Britain, France, the United States and Japan had sent in troops to aid 'White' Russian forces who were fighting to overthrow the Bolshevik régime.

'Do you know where he got the name Radek?' Otto asked Claus while they were being driven back to the ministry.

'No idea'.

'He was thrown out of the Social Democratic Party in the Ukraine for embezzling funds. Apparently there's a word Kradek, meaning thief, in some Ukrainian dialect or other. He seems to have been proud of the name and started writing for Communist newspapers under the pseudonym K. Radek. His name is Karl, anyway. He just became K. Radek instead of K. Sobelssohn'.

Claus was amused. The name fitted. The whole crowd of them in Lenin's party had looked like criminals, and the way they were behaving now that they were in power simply bore that out. Claus had to admit, though, that this Radek was looking a bit more respectable now than he had on the train.

It was soiling to have to deal with such people, but if the interests of the Reich demanded it… A soldier had frequently to lie down in the dirt, and duty was duty.

Claus's work at the ministry brought onto his desk newspapers and official documents of all sorts from Russia, along with an endless stream of typed and handwritten reports on developments there. This intelligence originated from a diversity of sources whose integrity was frequently an open question. Deciding what was real and what was fantasy, sorting out the accurate from the exaggerated, the mistaken or the plainly misleading, this Claus found fascinating.

'Ah! The Russian expert'. The words greeted Claus as he passed another officer in a ministry corridor one morning. Claus stopped. He had seen the other man somewhere. Tall, dark, closely trimmed moustache.

'Albrecht!'

'Erlenbach, how are you?'

The handshake was warm, but Claus was surprised to see that Albrecht was still at the rank of captain. Yes, he was Colonel Lüdershausen's right hand still.

'But you, you've done really well', he told Claus. 'The General Staff was most impressed with the way you dealt with Lenin and those others'.

I didn't deal with them at all, thought Claus. 'All I did was accompany them'.

Albrecht clapped him on the shoulder. 'Don't be modest, Erlenbach. I've seen the reports. And how are you liking your new job?'

They talked for some minutes of prospects in an army limited to 100,000 men, with only 4,000 officers permitted by the Allies. 'I'm damned lucky to have been kept on at all', confessed Albrecht, 'and I've probably the colonel to thank. I was sure they'd go through the medical records to see which ones they would put on the list for discharge'.

A chance remark about a fallen comrade revealed that the two had mutual friends. Before they parted, Albrecht said: 'Let's have a drink together some time'.

They did. That same evening. Albrecht was exceptionally congenial company, and the two found that they were well suited to each other. It became their practice, a couple of times a week, to go for a glass of wine or cognac at the end of the working day. Occasionally they dined together.

At weekends, Claus often went shooting in the Schorfheide, that stretch of moorland and forest full of deer and wild boar little more than an hour's drive from Berlin. Albrecht, whose first name was Rolf, was a family man, but whenever domestic obligations allowed, he would join Claus in a hunting trip. Off they would go at daybreak or even before, guns, ammunition and bags with them in Claus's open Mercedes. It was usually dark before they returned to Berlin, always with more game than their two households could consume. Neighbours and colleagues became used to receiving Monday morning gifts of fresh meat for their pantries.

Having become very friendly with Albrecht, Claus was a frequent visitor at his comrade's home. Albrecht's wife Julia was a small, dark haired woman with unusually bright eyes and a high degree of intelligence. She made Claus feel more at home with the Albrechts than he was at Haus Schwaben when the only company was his father. What's more, Julia could discuss matters outside military affairs with a considerably greater store of knowledge than either Claus or her husband.

Towards the end of 1919 another old colleague of Lenin's arrived in Berlin from Moscow. This was Viktor Kopp, a member of the Cheka who had shared Lenin's pre-war exile in Vienna and had come to Germany nominally to discuss the repatriation of prisoners of war.

It was April 15, 1920, when Kopp called at the Foreign Office hoping for an interview with Germany's new Foreign Minister, Adolf Köster. The minister was not present, and the reception watchdog did some telephoning. 'Baron von Maltzan will see you, sir. He's the Head of our Eastern Section'.

Five minutes later, Kopp was seated in Maltzan's office. He needed to see the minister as a matter of urgency, to discuss the future course of German relations with Russia.

This was Thursday, and Maltzan, nicknamed Ago from the initials of his Christian names Adolf Georg Otto, suggested that a meeting could probably be arranged for the following Monday or Tuesday.

Kopp was not inclined to wait. 'Do you think', he asked Maltzan, 'that there is any chance of forming a coalition between the German Army and the Red Army for a joint campaign against Poland?'

The armistice not eighteen months behind them, and here was Kopp talking about engaging in further military adventures! And only two weeks earlier, on March 31, Germany's army had been reduced to a mere 100,000 men, the maximum strength stipulated at Versailles.

Maltzan was a diplomat, but he knew how to bite. 'May I remind you', he asked Kopp, 'that we need the meagre remainder of our army to maintain order in our own country? Apart from this, the amount of propaganda which the Soviet Government is systematically promoting in this country through radio and leaflets, and insulting the Head of State of the Reich as a "hangman's assistant" rather makes any such proposition illusory, don't you think?'

Maltzan had hit home. Kopp was discomfited. 'You must understand that our propaganda is in the habit of using very strong language', he pleaded. 'Any such excesses shouldn't be taken too seriously'.

Ten days after Kopp put out his feelers to Maltzan, the question of war was settled. Polish troops attacked Western Russia.

Kopp called at the Foreign Office again. 'What we want', he told Maltzan, 'is a common frontier with Germany, south of Lithuania, roughly on a level with Bialystok. The Polish Corridor will have to go. I know your hands are tied by the Versailles Treaty and you're in no position to take the initiative in this matter, but we're free to force massive concessions from Poland. We're also going to settle the question of Upper Silesia to Germany's advantage'.

'You mean return Upper Silesia to the Reich?'

'Of course'.

It turned out to be all talk. Just weeks later, it was Polish forces, commanded by the French General Maxime Weygand, who emerged victorious.

Major Otto was derisive. 'The Red Army's just not good enough. And they want us to stick out our necks and go in with them'.

It was the first time that Claus had seen the slender figure, very erect, that crossed the ministry's main entrance hall that July day, but he knew instantly who it was. Newspaper photographs had familiarized all Germany with the ascetic features, the neat silver moustache, the monocle and the look of inscrutable wisdom.

This was General Hans von Seeckt, who had proved such a brilliant chief of staff of the 11th Army that he was loaned out to Germany's allies, first to the Austrian Army and then to the Turkish. He was now Commander-in-Chief of Germany's rump army. At his throat, Seeckt wore Imperial Germany's highest war decoration, the Pour le Mérite, called by everyone the 'Blue Max'.

Seeckt, in appearance the very epitome of the austere and inflexible Prussian, was in reality an imaginative forward thinker years ahead of his contemporaries. As much philosopher as soldier, Seeckt believed the humanities to be the most important element in a young man's education.

Everyone knew the story – was it true? – that even during the war Seeckt and the British Field Marshal Lord Kitchener had continued to exchange Christmas cards. The two had met and become friends some years before hostilities, and Seeckt was a believer in chivalry.

So too had Kitchener been. Before his death in 1916 the British Commander-in-Chief had stated his intention of pressing for a peace of reconciliation once the fighting was over. The politicians, Kitchener told Lord Derby, were likely to make a bad peace.

Well, they had that bad peace now, and the essential thing, Seeckt argued, was to act. Failure to act would be fatal.

Perhaps, said Seeckt – and he admitted openly that this probability was small – the European nations would in future allow themselves time for calm reflection before going for the other fellow's throat. If not, well, one had to be prepared. The biggest temptation to war, he believed, was a defenceless neighbour.

The commander-in-chief was certain of one thing: Germany had to keep out of hostilities of all kinds. The top secret memorandum which Seeckt was on his way to complete was headed 'Germany's next political tasks'. In it, he argued that cooperation with Russia was not only the best way to overcome the Versailles peace but would also help avert any domestic attempts at revolution. He urged social reforms, including the overhaul of land law, the establishment of works councils and nationalization of the coal and iron industries. Take the wind out of the Bolshevist sails, that was his idea. And above all, act. Become the driving force behind events, not the object of other countries' actions.

On foreign policy, Seeckt's warnings were unequivocal enough: never do anything giving Britain and France cause to declare war, and under no circumstances go to war against Russia.

Surely no German government would ever be lunatic enough to break even one of these golden rules, let alone both.

Avus

There were three of them: Hasse, Niedermayer and Lieth-Thomsen.

They arrived separately that September evening. All very natural. Three regular army officers visiting a comrade at his home. This could not arouse comment, even if anyone noticed.

General Paul von Hasse was Seeckt's second in command. Major Oskar von Niedermayer had been a secret agent during the war, carrying out subversive anti-British operations in Persia in an attempt to prepare a joint push of German and Turkish armies through into India. As field commander of German air forces, Colonel Hermann von der Lieth-Thomsen had seen all Germany's aircraft – those that had not been sabotaged by their crews before handover, that is – taken by the Allies.

The house in the expensive suburb was the home of Major Kurt von Schleicher, head of the Political Department at the Reichswehr Ministry. If ever a man had been born with the right name, said the cruel ones, it was he. The verb schleichen means 'to creep', and it was certainly a fact that the major, a born lobbyist, cultivated the very best connections.

Schleicher's fourth visitor that night was not a soldier. He was not even a German. He was Leonid Krassin, chairman of the Soviet Defence Council, and he had travelled to Berlin in total secrecy.

Radek of course knew that Krassin was here. It was a secret from everyone else, but Radek knew. Radek had been the broker for this meeting, and the very fact that it was taking place at all showed the important stage which negotiations had reached.

Three of them, plus Krassin.

Claus had been invited to the party, but did not set eyes on any of the arrivals. He heard the cars, and that was all. This was a meeting at just about the highest level, and Claus was not a participant in the talks. His task was to patrol the villa grounds to the rear and both sides. A policeman, that's all Claus was tonight.

The perimeter hedges were thick as well as tall, offering a variety of nooks where he could stand in total blackness and watch for any unauthorized movement made towards the building.

It was the first time since the war that Claus had worn his Luger semi-automatic pistol. He was no longer used to the feel of it, and for a while in the car on his way here had found the weight at his hip awkward.

Not that either Claus or anyone else expected him to have to use the weapon. It was simply a common sense precaution. If he were going to do guard duty, it would be an absurdity to have no means to hand for dealing with any possible intruder.

For the men inside the house, the agenda was simple. It had, so to speak, written itself.

The intervention in Russia by foreign forces had brought home sharply to the Soviet leadership the weaknesses in its gigantic Red Army. Krassin did not admit this in so many words, but while the Communists possessed enormous numerical strength, they had little military skill. Germany, on the other hand, was rich in martial talent, yet denied both modern weapons and the means to train in the latest battlefield techniques.

The foundation for a marriage of convenience was, it appeared, already laid.

In Russia there were no Control Commission inspectors snooping into every factory and workshop for evidence of forbidden weapons being manufactured. If Germans would build up Soviet arms industries, guns could be manufactured for Germany inside Russia. Shells, too.

Thank you, the Germans would prefer to build their guns themselves. Could they do that in Russia? The Russians could manufacture the shells.

Junkers wants to build aircraft in Russia. We should like to make tanks there, too.

Come to Moscow and talk to our men.

It was irresistible.

64

Claus did not need to draw his pistol, never so much as saw the shadow of an intruder. Krassin went back home in as much secrecy as had cloaked his arrival.

It had all started at the beginning of the year. Thick frost was on the windows that winter of 1921. Claus's desk was laden with a fresh intake of files. Sort them into rough order of priority, that was always the first thing. He made a start.

Major Otto came in. He stood looking at Claus without speaking. This was not Otto's style.

Claus paused. Where was Otto the ever amiable?

'I'm losing you, Claus'.

Oh God! 'I'm being discharged?'

'You're being transferred. A new department. Special Group R. Oberst Nicolai'.

Everyone knew about Walther Nicolai. During the war he had been head of Army Intelligence.

'What's Special Group R?'

'Nobody knows. And no one's supposed to know. If it's Nicolai, it will be more secret than we are here. It's a new department set up by the chief, that's all I know'.

The chief. That was Seeckt.

'When do I go?'

'Immediate effect, I believe. Orders will be on their way'.

Otto looked at the mass of documents on Claus's table. 'You'd better clear away here. Nicolai will be keen to get you started'.

It was another wrench, just like leaving Baron von Romberg. It was impossible not to like the cheerful Otto. On the other hand, to work with the celebrated Colonel Nicolai would be the dream of many a young officer.

Claus's transfer order arrived that morning. Otto was right. Immediate effect.

Special Group R was being established in a group of offices sealed off from neighbouring departments. Nicolai was issuing his staff with special passes which they would need in addition to the ordinary ministry pass essential for entering the building. A large safe was to be the repository for the group's paperwork, and files would be drawn only when needed, signed for, and checked back in.

'Our job here', Colonel Nicolai told Claus, 'will be to handle all negotiations, transactions and cooperation with Russia'. So that was what R meant. 'A lot of people have been doing lots of different things, and from now on everything, going in either direction, will have to pass through us. It's up to us not just to coordinate traffic and make sure there's no senseless duplication, but above all to keep the lid on things. None of this is for public consumption, and there are far too many loose characters out there'.

Nicolai turned in his chair and gazed out of the window. 'Take that chap Kopp. He's back in Moscow now, and he's having talks with Trotsky'. Nicolai was still an ace in the intelligence game. 'Ten to one he'll be turning up in Berlin any day, and we don't want him doing what he did last time'. That was urging senior German officers first to destroy Poland and then to cross over the Rhine. 'When Kopp arrives we'll be channelling his activities. There'll be no more wild talks with anyone'.

Leon Trotsky was Lenin's War Minister, credited with being the creator of the Red Army. Trotsky wanted help in rebuilding Soviet forces, and as Nicolai expected, Kopp was soon back. By April, he had already found firms willing to build submarines, cannon and aircraft for Russia.

'Blohm und Voss, Krupp and Albatros now, as well as Junkers. You see what I mean? This thing is just going to go on, growing bigger and bigger'. Nicolai was first and always a security fanatic. 'We can talk to all these people as much as we like, try to hammer security consciousness into their heads, but the more who are involved, the greater the risk that someone is going to develop a loose tongue'.

66

'But it's in their own interests to keep it quiet', argued Claus. 'They don't want trouble with the Allied inspectors any more than we do'.

'I don't trust civilians. We can't control them like we can our own people. All it takes is one man having one drink too many'.

This was all too true. There had been people from industry included in the mission which General Hasse took to Moscow. Hasse was looking for ways to circumvent the Versailles restrictions, and found that the Russians were looking for, and talking about, something much more far-reaching. Like Kopp, General P.P. Lebedev, Chief of the Soviet General Staff, raised the issue of Poland.

Hasse had to sidestep, as Maltzan had sidestepped at the Foreign Office, but he did not return to Berlin empty handed. Shell and grenade manufacture was to be undertaken at Soviet plants under German technical supervision. Krupp was preparing a venture similar to that of Junkers, and a joint German-Soviet poison gas factory was to be established.

Special Group R sprang into life. Its title was simplified to Department R, and Schleicher persuaded the Chancellor, Dr Joseph Wirth, to place a secret fund of 150 million marks at its disposal.

'We need a business front', decreed Nicolai. They created one, a company whose function was to develop and manufacture in Russia those arms forbidden at Versailles: aircraft, bombs, tanks, armoured cars, heavy artillery, poison gas, anti-tank and anti-aircraft guns.

Let the Allied Control Commission inspectors – all 1,120 of them – roam Germany in search of breaches of peace conditions. Germany would commit her violations deep in the vastnesses of Russia, far from prying eyes.

The thought of putting one over on Germany's enemies certainly afforded satisfaction, but it was physical action that Claus both missed and craved.

When he was just seven, Claus had been taken by an uncle to motorcycle races which started on the outskirts of Stuttgart and followed an uphill route to the Solitude Palace. The sight and sound of the fastest NSU and Adler machines had thrilled the boy, but because of his years in Russia he had never since seen any other motor sport event.

Now a twelve-mile loop of high-speed road, intended for both motor racing and high speed testing, was being built on the edge of Berlin. Called the Avus, the circuit was inaugurated on a September weekend with two full days of car racing.

Claus went along on both days, and knew that he had found the outlet that he needed. For Claus, seeing how fast he could whip a car through bends had always been the whole fascination of driving. During the coming winter, he would have the motor of his Mercedes tuned and the vehicle converted into racing trim. Then next year...

Others had more serious plans for the future. Representatives of the Soviet military had their first meeting with Seeckt in December, and used the occasion to raise the question of joint war with Poland. Seeckt declined to make any commitment.

Radek saw Seeckt again in January, and resurrected the subject of Poland. What Moscow wanted was a firm commitment of German support in exchange for granting the Reichswehr facilities to circumvent the Versailles limitations.

In February Radek brought up Poland a third time, with a definite proposal that Germany and Russia should attack Poland in the spring.

This was early 1922, and in less than two years at least five approaches had been made to Germany for war against Poland: by Kopp on behalf of Trotsky, twice by leaders of the Red Army and twice by Radek in Lenin's name.

If this were to be kept up, one day motor racing and everything else was likely to suffer an abrupt interruption.

The domesticity which Claus enjoyed with the Albrechts more than once brought pangs of regret, reminding him of his foolishness in letting the girl at the hospital disappear from his life. How often had the glimpse of a girl in the distance sent Claus blundering in a fire of self-deception towards a stranger who would turn out to have only a superficial resemblance? Regret was pointless, and Claus would not waste time on sorrow about something which could not be changed.

68

Yet once, when Albrecht wondered aloud whether it wasn't time for Claus to be married, Julia must have caught the expression on Claus's face. Her look told him that she knew, and he in turn understood that Julia would be silent.

Claus was burying his feelings, practically his whole being, in his work. That work was demanding, but Claus would have had it no other way. Where once the notion of a ministry appointment would have appalled him as a total waste of youthful time and energies, he could now appreciate the importance of Department R activities, even those involving nothing more martial than paper. For the first time, the opportunity of helping to restore Germany's ability to defend herself appeared to him as a privilege.

Among the junior officers – the ones who had to do the practical work rather than the high level negotiating – Claus was easily the best Russian speaker. He was neat and competent, executing instructions swiftly and accurately, with a marked absence of fuss. In addition, Claus had a charm in his speech and manner which most Russians found irresistible. As a consequence, he almost automatically became Department R's man of choice for all personal dealings with Russian visitors. Whenever Soviet officials or Red Army men were expected in Berlin, Claus was despatched to meet the arrivals and escort them to their rendezvous.

Krupp signed a contract for the erection of a factory at Rostov-on-Don, and no time was to be wasted in building a Junkers works to manufacture forbidden aircraft in secret.

Things were certainly moving, but had any army, Claus wondered, ever had to work under such conditions? Officers posted to duty in Russia were discharged from the service before leaving Germany, and travelled in civilian clothes. Once back in the Reich, the men would naturally be taken again onto the Army strength. These elementary precautions would enable the Germans to be explained as 'invited observers', 'advisers' or simply as 'private visitors', should their presence at a military installation in Russia come to the attention of the Western Allies.

Manufacturers and the military were the pioneers of German-Soviet collaboration. It was the Treaty of Rapallo in spring 1922 which finally brought the politicians into the picture. Germany and Russia wrote off their mutual debts and agreed to accord each other the status of 'most favoured nation'.

The news caused worldwide shock. Almost every country condemned the Rapallo treaty in the bitterest manner. Fuel was added to the flames by a Central News Agency report according to which the Germans had appeared triumphant, announcing that they would defeat the Allies and create a new Europe.

Denunciation of the Rapallo Treaty was shrill enough. How much more penetrating still would have been the screams, Claus wondered, had the world overheard Soviet President Georgy Chicherin admit to his German partners that it was because of her plans for aggression against Poland that Russia had been in such a hurry to sign the agreement?

The Treaty of Rapallo signified formal recognition of the Soviet state by Germany. With full diplomatic relations now established, communications were simplified at a stroke. Private homes need no longer be co-opted as safe houses for negotiations.

Count von Brockdorff-Rantzau, the man who had refused to sign the Versailles peace, went to Moscow as Germany's Ambassador.

Now that Germany had an embassy in Moscow, Seeckt set up an office there, to conduct all negotiations with the Soviet authorities on behalf of Department R. It was Claus who coordinated the traffic. Cooperation went ahead fast, and Claus's hands were at once full.

Away from the ministry, he filled most of his time with supervising the preparation of the Mercedes for its racing debut. Wringing more speed out of the motor was, for the expert mechanic whom Claus engaged, chiefly an affair of raised compression ratio and altered valve timing. Modifications were made to ignition and carburettor, and a satisfying amount of power was now available. The next step was to save as much weight as possible. Claus had a completely new body made out of aluminium.

Three days before the next Avus races, the aluminium body was still not ready. Claus fumed and harried.

The body appeared on the afternoon before the race, and the final bolt was not tightened until late at night.

Claus could not fall asleep. He was on his feet again at four o'clock, impatient for the start.

The wait for the new body had been worth it. With its rear end shortened into a swan's tail shape, the car was now noticeably lighter and had a lower centre of gravity. It proved much easier to hurl through bends, though on the Avus this was of less importance than sheer speed. The new circuit was little more than a high speed test along two straights joined at either end by 180-degree curves.

Claus emerged from the paddock onto the track on the morning of the race more excited than he had been since his first taste of battlefield action. For the first time he was on a race track, somewhere at last where there were no limits to how fast he might go, no traffic heading towards him the other way, no vehicles popping out at him from side streets, no halt signs, no junctions. All were going the same way and he was finally completely free. The only restrictions to his speed were the parameters of his own ability in the corners and the technical limits of the car. Now he would really go! This was what he was born to do.

Claus's first lesson was how much quicker the really fast cars were than his own. Claus had his motor wound up to its maximum, and still the big boys, in the big cars, hurtled past his Mercedes from behind in a monumental blast of sound. Fortunately, entries were divided into classes according to size of engine, and in any case, rocketing round the banking flat out was absolute heaven. Nothing could detract from the joy and the exhilaration of the turns.

Fritz von Opel, in a monster of a vehicle, set the fastest time. Claus enjoyed the enormous satisfaction of finishing fifth in his class, and set off for Württemberg the following week in high elation. Originally a two-wheeled affair, the Solitude races were now to include cars for the first time. Solitude was where Claus had first seen a speed event, and he was keen to tackle the demanding course.

71

The test was tougher than he had expected. Despite teeming rain, some 50,000 spectators had turned out, and there was never any question of abandoning the races.

Twice Claus went into a bend too fast on the wrong line, and had to do some hasty, and in the wet risky, braking. This was his second lesson in racing: first find the line through the bend that will enable you to come out of it with the fastest possible start down the following straight, and only then begin to work up speed on that line. Claus had been going about things the wrong way.

Nevertheless, he finished fourth. Claus showed that he could control the sliding Mercedes in the worst conditions, pushing it to the limit of tyre adhesion and almost, but not quite, turning the vehicle over. The important thing was that he was learning.

A month later a new circuit was inaugurated in the Eifel hills, with eighty-six bends along a route just over twenty miles long. Five laps of this course had to be completed. Driving over these same roads before the event, Claus was unaware of any dangerous bumps in the surface, but at racing speeds these appeared to raise themselves out of nowhere. What had appeared as faultlessly smooth road revealed itself in the race as a monstrous switchback of humps and hollows intent on flinging his car into the air and from side to side. Claus had to fight not just to take the Mercedes through each of the bends with a minimum loss of speed, but also to keep the leaping vehicle straight and on the road.

Of course, Claus told himself, it was the same for everyone. At the finish, he was delighted to have achieved another fourth place.

When Claus woke in his hotel room next morning, his arms and shoulders were stiff and aching from wrestling the car through those five laps. It was, he reflected, the motor sport counterpart of that other stiffness which affects the lower back and the thighs when one rides a horse for the first time after long abstinence.

Once the Mercedes was put back into road trim, Claus set off on the long journey back to the Reich capital still stiff and still aching, but with a joy and satisfaction to drive out any and all discomfort. Claus was now completely committed to motor racing as his off-duty sport. It had replaced shooting as his major interest, and he now went less frequently into the Schorfheide with his guns.

Where his duties at the ministry were concerned, Claus was finding himself more and more involved in making travel arrangements. Several missions going each way between Germany and Russia during 1922 demanded weeks of organization and generated a rich variety of paperwork.

A Soviet military delegation arrived in Germany to discuss flying, and Claus was called in as interpreter. In August a concord was concluded defining the extent of the military cooperation. The Germans were to be given facilities for developing forbidden weapons, testing these under battle conditions and conducting tactical and weapons training. Flying, chemical warfare and exercises with motorized troops were all included. Russia was to receive an annual rent for the bases used, plus a share in the technical and tactical results.

Even Brockdorff was staggered by the daring and scope of the plans. In them he saw a danger to Germany's relationships with Britain and France.

Seeckt was scathing of Brockdorff's reservations. He was convinced that whatever Germany did would make no difference to French policy either way. France's aim was the total destruction of Germany, 'pûr et simple'.

Erika

If it hadn't been such a glorious afternoon, Claus would never have decided to take a walk through the Tiergarten before driving home. Just a few steps from the Bendlerstrasse, and it was as if one had left the city altogether. Greenery on every side, shrubs and trees damping out what noise there was from traffic. Classical statuary added to the impression of having passed into a more civilized world than that of the twentieth century.

Claus had the brisk gait that was natural to an Army officer, and on occasions like this he had to make a deliberate effort to slow down and enjoy his surroundings at leisure.

It was curious, really. Ever since he had first seen her, the image of the girl at the hospital had accompanied him, on walks like this, in the evening at home and frequently while he was busy at the ministry. He thought of her while he lay waiting for sleep, and he would see her beatific features and enchanting smile in the morning.

Yet the odd thing was that for once he wasn't thinking of the girl now, so that when she appeared walking towards him his reaction was to welcome the return of his familiar dream. An instant later Claus realized that the picture was real. She was hatless, and there was no doubt that it was the same girl.

Claus stopped in mid-stride. He could not believe it. Probably he was staring. The girl saw him, and it was clear that she too remembered.

'Good day'.

She was holding out her hand. Her smile showed that she was as surprised as he.

The girl was quicker at recovering. Before Claus had grasped that this was reality, the two were walking together through the park. It wasn't that the girl had taken the initiative, exactly; just that Claus had fallen in with her automatically. Whatever way he had been going before, he was not going that way now. At once there was a natural intimacy between them, a spontaneous warmth. It was as though they had been born to walk and talk together.

Tail high, a squirrel ran across the path in front of them and disappeared up a tree trunk into heavy foliage. This was one of the things that Claus liked about Berlin. One quarter of the capital's surface area was either woods or lakes. There was so much greenery, such a variety of water and forest accessible within the city, and even right here in the middle of the government quarter one could enjoy a small taste of the countryside.

The girl's delight in their surroundings, in the animals and the birds, was as evident as his own. By the time they sat under a striped umbrella at a small round table outside a café, Claus felt as though the girl had always been part of his life. She laughed easily, and had a directness and an intelligence such as Claus had not experienced among the young women of his circle. The only exception, perhaps, was Julia Albrecht.

They lingered over the coffee.

'I thought you lived in Magdeburg, and I should never see you again'.

Oh no. The girl was a Berliner, a primary school teacher. At Magdeburg she had been visiting her aunt, and the aunt had died in her arms while she was talking to her.

That was why the girl had not left the hospital along with everyone else at the conclusion of visiting hours.

Claus had not been in uniform when he went to Magdeburg, but the girl was not surprised to learn that he was an Army officer. She would have been surprised had he been anything else. 'I would have known that from a hundred yards away', she told him, 'from the way you hold yourself'.

Her name was Erika Wolf.

Erika. Claus said her name to himself as though he were tasting it, savouring the sound like a child lingering over a delicious sweet. Erika.

They talked of music and of books, discovered that they had many tastes and interests in common. Erika lived with her mother in the working class district of Wedding. Her father had been unfit for military service and had died at home, shortly before the end of the war, from diabetes.

Erika spoke of her father's death without bitterness. It was something, she acknowledged, that could not be helped. Even had there been no Allied blockade, the course of his illness could not have been stopped. Wartime measures were one thing; her anger was reserved for the Allies' post-war conduct. Continuing the blockade was murderous, and how could they claim that Germany bore the sole blame for the fighting, when the course of events leading to hostilities showed otherwise? The trouble was between Austria and Serbia, not Germany and anyone else. Yet the Russians had rushed to mobilize, sending three million men westwards while Germany was still trying to negotiate a diplomatic solution. Germany had not been anxious to enter someone else's quarrel, and the Russians should have kept out of it as well. The French, of course – well, what did one expect? Any excuse for a fight suited them. They had been trying to run Europe for the past eleven hundred years, ever since the death of Charlemagne.

No woman Claus knew, even within his own family, spoke with vehemence on such matters. Politics, and foreign affairs in particular, were always considered to be men's province. Women just knuckled down and made the best of whatever circumstances the men had created. It was as though war, shortages, hunger, violent death and crippling injury were acts of God, trials to be endured and beyond woman's capacity to alter. Erika on the other hand appeared to believe not only that things could be changed but also that she could do something about changing them. Claus had not known that any girls like that existed.

It was when he suggested a second cup of coffee that Erika was reminded how long they had been sitting, and sprang up. She had expected to be home an hour ago and had exercise books to mark that evening, ready for the next morning's lessons.

Claus hurried with her out of the Tiergarten to the parked Mercedes, restored now, until the next race, to its everyday trim.

Erika asked to be dropped at the corner of her street. They exchanged addresses and promised to meet at the weekend. Driving on home to Charlottenburg, Claus felt as though he wanted to sing out loud to the world.

Erika had not wanted to be collected from her home, and on Saturday afternoon they were to meet at the Romanisches Café, right in the commercial heart of the city and next to the Kaiser Wilhelm Memorial Church. Claus arrived twenty minutes before the agreed time, taking a seat at a small table where he could watch the entrance.

As he waited, the doubts began to come. At first it was mere impatience, then concern, and finally fear. Why had Erika not asked him to call at the address she had given him? Why in any case had she left his car at a street junction and then disappeared round the corner? Surely it was so that he could not see which house she entered. Was the address she had given him genuine, or a made-up one? Perhaps she hadn't gone into any house in that street, at all. Perhaps she lived in a different part of the city altogether.

He would give it ten – no, fifteen – minutes after the time they had agreed, then he would drive straight to the house whose number she had written down for him. He would find no Wolf among the names alongside the bells. He knew it. He was certain of it.

The afternoon was bright, the atmosphere in the fashionable establishment carefree. All the same, Claus sank ever more deeply into gloom and despair. His mouth went dry. She wouldn't come. She wouldn't come.

Erika walked in through the door, and it was as though a great light had been switched on. Claus could have leaped into the air and shouted for joy.

She wore a blue dress of some lightly shimmering material, and a simple chain round her throat. It was the mark of a woman properly brought up not to overdress and certainly never to overload herself with jewellery. Erika's taste was, to Claus, perfection.

He had already drunk one cup of tea with lemon, and now Claus ordered tea and a selection of pastries for them both.

They sat and talked for an hour, Erika confirming and deepening with every word Claus's impression that she was the most erudite, the most companionable, the most angelic creature in the entire world.

The arrangement to meet had been made hastily, without any idea by either of them of what they were going to do. Did Erika want to go to a theatre?

'We couldn't talk, then. I'd sooner we were just together'.

So they strolled along the Kurfürstendamm, with its stores and theatres, its cafés and its bars. Outside the restaurants the tables were protected from the sun either by striped awnings or by huge individual parasols. All Berlin seemed to be out and filling the thoroughfare, yet Claus noticed no one. The only person who existed for him was the girl at his side. They walked first down one side of the great street, then back along the other.

They talked of a hundred different things, of books they had read and had still to read, of the theatre and what Max Reinhardt had done in his ground-breaking and spectacular productions. Erika had only read about Reinhardt's work, not seen any of it for herself, but Claus had been to The Death of Danton last November, and she begged him to tell her all about it. Describing visual effects and costumes was not exactly Claus's forte. He had neither eye nor memory for details of that sort, and knew only that the overall effect of the work and its impression on him had been tremendous.

'I'll take you to the very next Reinhardt production', Claus promised.

'Will you?' Erika squeezed his arm. They had shaken hands, but other than that this was their first physical contact. It was the most natural thing in the world.

'Of course'. They would consult the What's On pages in the newspapers. 'Just tell me when you want to go'.

Opposite the Kranzler-Eck they were passed by an open light carriage drawn by a single chestnut horse. In the heart of the city, these were becoming rarer. There were of course still plenty of horse-drawn delivery vehicles on the streets, but nearly everyone who could afford the upkeep of horse and carriage now had a motor car instead.

Erika clutched his arm again. 'Oh Claus, isn't that beautiful?'

Her admiration was for the animal, not the carriage. Erika had herself never had an opportunity to ride, but she loved the beauty of horses.

Claus told himself what a joy it would be to teach her to ride. And to teach her about wines, too. Erika knew nothing about wines, and Claus imagined himself showing her the new vineyard at Falkenstein and in a few years' time the press, the fermentation process and the bottling with Falkenstein labels.

'Do you like detective stories?'

Yes, Claus admitted that he liked them, though he had so far read very few, one of them about a man called Sherlock Holmes who smoked a pipe like Karl Radek's and whose logic had appealed greatly to him.

'Only one?' Erika had read every Sherlock Holmes story published. 'You must read the rest. There are dozens of them'.

Claus promised that he would.

How many miles had they walked? How many hours had they been immersed in each other's company and conversation, learning how much they had in common, what animated them, what they rejected?

The day was beginning to turn chilly. Sudden concern for Erika gripped him.

Did she need to go home yet? No. They returned to his car, and Claus drove to a quiet Italian restaurant he knew, off Friedrichstrasse. It was clearly a new experience for Erika, who was fascinated by the variety of dishes. They dined slowly and fully.

How marvellous that the girl had walked so far, and totally without complaining, seeming indeed as fresh afterwards as at the outset. All the young ladies of Claus's circle alleged tiredness after half a mile.

80

What a refreshing change Erika was! She would even be able to tramp with him across the fields at Falkenstein.

Claus cancelled the loose agreement which he had to go shooting with Albrecht next day. Instead, he met Erika again, and they toured the Pergamon Museum, with its treasures from the world of antiquity, sections of temple facades, arched gateways and massive reliefs. The two of them stood fascinated before King Priam's treasure, brought back from Troy by Heinrich Schliemann. Beakers in solid gold, vases of silver, a magnificent golden dish, bracelets, necklaces and chains of gold, some of them inlaid with pearls.

Too late they realized that they had not allowed enough time for a complete tour. Several days would be required to give the exhibits the attention which they deserved. Work to expand the building was taking place, and Claus wondered that there could still be so much more to be accommodated.

They met every weekend after that. Long walks in parks and through the woods at Grunewald were a favourite occupation. Occasionally they went rowing on one or other of the Berlin lakes, taking advantage of what was left of the late autumn sunshine. 'We'll save the museums and the theatres for the winter', they promised themselves.

His father, Claus knew, never had any time for what he called the empty-headed type of girl, the sort who seemed to him all too frequent. He would therefore love Erika, who was all brains and common sense, and was obviously of strong character too. Claus would invite her to visit them at Haus Schwaben. Then, perhaps, a trip home with her to Falkenstein...

She beat him to it. 'My mother asks would you like to come and have tea with us next Sunday'.

Claus was surprised, but Erika only laughed. 'Naturally she wants to know what sort of a fellow it is I've been running out to spend each Saturday afternoon and Sunday with. You might be completely disreputable'.

Where they lived was not the worst part of Wedding. It was indeed one of the better apartment blocks, just off Seestrasse, with a baker's shop on the ground floor.

The apartment was small, smaller than Claus had expected, but it was as neat and sparkling as the proverbial Dutch kitchen.

A single glance at Erika's mother told Claus that in her youth she would have been as beautiful as her daughter was now. He recognized, too, that it was not just the years which had done their worst, but hardship and overwork. Grey hair could not have been staved off, but sunken cheeks, deep forehead lines and sallow skin stretched taut were not unconditional requirements of the middle years. Nor was the permanent expression of worry which the woman wore. It was apparent that the deprivations of the war years and the necessity of working long hours in a factory, alongside nursing a mortally sick husband and raising a small daughter, had aged a once lovely woman many years too soon.

'Frau Wolf, I am delighted to meet you'. Claus was pleased that he had decided to dispense with the stiffer form of greeting used in more formal circles. The eyes which met his were nervous, the eyes of a woman unused to receiving anyone grander than a tradesman, and it was obviously important to put her at ease without delay.

The woman's dress was immaculate, grey hair faultless in its arrangement, unmarked hands astonishingly well kept despite the five and a half days spent each week at a milling machine. It was the hands which revealed all. Clearly this was not a woman who had taken care over her hair and washed, ironed and put on a good dress just to receive a visitor. This was a woman who kept herself and her home as pristine as could be, all the time. Respectable working class; wasn't that the backbone of the German nation?

Claus was no snob. He had seen too much of the virtues in the workers on the Falkenstein estate to have any false ideas about their character and value. Work was something at which the ordinary German was a master. At the front, too, Claus had more than once known the everyday, uneducated man set an example to his 'betters' in both character and effort.

82

The meal was superb. There was a danger at first, it seemed, that Frau Wolf would spend her time waiting on Claus and Erika. They put a stop to that at once.

'But you must join us, Frau Wolf'.

'Yes, sit down, mother'.

Did Erika know that Claus could put her mother at her ease if only he were given the chance? The thaw, at any rate, was rapid.

From Haus Schwaben stock, Claus had brought his hostess a bottle of wine and some leberwurst. Both were items of Falkenstein produce, the wine a pre-war vintage but no more than an ordinary Trollinger. With the woman so obviously shy, almost intimidated by her guest, there was no point in deepening what she would see as the gulf between them by announcing that the items were from his family estate.

Before he left, Claus managed to induce a smile in his hostess. Deep inside it he saw that same loveliness as when Erika, too, smiled. How sad, he reflected, that this woman could allow herself to smile so rarely.

'My mother said that her heart was in her mouth when she knew that you were coming', Erika told him when they met on the following Saturday. She clung to his arm and reached up to give him a gentle kiss on the cheek. It was their first. 'But you won her over. Thank you, darling'.

He gripped her hand. 'I'm not an ogre'.

'I know you're not. And she knows it now, too, but she's not used to gentlemen'.

'But your father – he wasn't a working man, was he?' She had told him that her father had been a teacher, like herself.

'All the same, we are from different worlds, you know'.

Those worlds should have been melted into one by the war. 'Your mother – does she have to go on working in that factory?' It was not class consciousness, but concern for the woman's health and well being.

'I'm afraid she does. It started in the war, when my father became too ill to work, and women were needed in industry'.

'Of course. There was no way round that then, but now, surely..?'

'Claus, we need the money. I don't earn enough'.

'But isn't there something else she could do, that would not be so demanding – physically, I mean? With shorter hours, perhaps, if such a thing were possible'.

'You're right, Claus. I see the change in her myself. I'll try to persuade her to look for something different'.

Things could not have looked more promising. 1923 would be the best of years. There was talk of new motor racing circuits, of more meetings on the calendar. Claus would race again at the Avus, at Solitude, in the Eifel and everywhere that a race was organized. The lightened and tuned-up Mercedes had proved itself, Claus had confirmed his own innate ability. He could fling the car through bends with a minimum loss of speed, judging – so far without error – just how far he could push things before his tyres lost adhesion and the vehicle turned over.

Claus was determined to do better than he had so far. Over the winter some further improvements would be made to the car's performance, and he would make 1923 a great year of racing. Another year or two after that, and it would be time to think about marriage.

Just a few good years, then he would give up racing and concentrate on domesticity. It would be unfair to Erika to continue to race once he had a wife and, presumably, children.

Claus was utterly besotted with Erika, obsessed with her to the point of irrationality. He knew it, and didn't mind a bit.

Erika had brought him joy of a depth which he would never have been able to imagine. He thought of her constantly when he was awake, he dreamed of her when he was asleep. It was as though he had known her always, as though she had been there from his birth. Which of course was silly, since in any case she was four years younger than he.

Yet what did silliness matter? All that was important was the knowledge that life without Erika was now unthinkable, unimaginable.

His mother had noticed a change in Claus when he arrived at Falkenstein before the Solitude event. Unerring maternal intuition had told her that the glow of excitement which surrounded him was not attributable solely to anticipation of the race. Yet she said nothing and asked no questions. Claus would bring the girl to meet his family when he was good and ready.

A month later, he did take Erika to Haus Schwaben to meet his father. As expected, the two took to one another well, but Erika was surprisingly subdued and his father remained non-committal. 'A lovely girl, and a very sensible one', he remarked, without asking Claus any of the questions he had expected to face.

It was not until some weeks later that Erika admitted having found herself in awe of her surroundings. It was this, then, which had repressed her natural sparkle and prevented her making the impression on his father which Claus had expected. Erika told Claus frankly that she had been shaken on discovering the difference in their stations. Oh yes, she knew that Claus was an officer, but when he had said that his father was at the Foreign Office she had imagined him to be a clerk of some sort, not one of the leading men. As for their house, she had not expected the grandeur of the villa (Claus himself thought that it was modest), nor that she would be waited on at table by the Erlenbachs' housekeeper just as though they had been out at a restaurant.

Well, Erika would grow used to that soon enough. She would herself make the most charming mistress of the house, and be an ornament to Falkenstein, too. All who visited them there would believe that she had grown up in those surroundings.

Meanwhile, there were races to be driven, and races, it was hoped, to be won.

The French put an end to all such ideas early in the new year. The Reparations Commission decided that Germany was in default in her payments for the twelve months just finished – by December 31 had paid 98.4 per cent of the total reparations due during 1922.

France seized on the late 1.6 per cent as an excuse to send in 40,000 soldiers to occupy the Ruhr area.

Britain protested at the heavy-handed French action on such a trivial excuse, pointing to the enormous payments and deliveries made already by the Reich under great difficulties.

Russia, too, declared her support for Germany – taking the opportunity to warn Poland that any attack on either Silesia or East Prussia would be considered a blow against the Soviet state.

'Moscow', commented Claus, 'seems to be looking for any excuse to invade Poland'.

'They're certainly behaving', agreed Nicolai, 'as though they already had formal military alliance with us'.

For their part, the French were behaving as though – well, the bare facts spoke for themselves.

In all, 133 Germans were killed by occupation troops in the Rhineland and the Ruhr. Another 180,000 were simply evicted from their homes and deported to unoccupied parts of the Reich.

More than four years after the end of the war, 3,150,000 Germans were now living under armed occupation.

These events forced the Reichswehr to an important conclusion: that the creation of means for Germany to defend herself needed to be forced at a faster pace. The ministry set up a so-called 'Ruhr fund'. The secret monies concealed under this code name were to finance the speeding-up of Germany's rearmament. Should the worm ever turn, their high-handed occupation of the Ruhr could yet prove a bitter 'own goal' for the French.

Falkenstein was already having an almighty struggle to climb back out of the red, and now the French occupation made the Reichsmark collapse at once.

Before the war, there had been four marks to the dollar. By June 1923, a dollar was worth 74,750 marks; on July 1, 160,000 marks; in August one million marks and by November 4,210,500,000,000 marks.

86

Sixty-two firms were now working round the clock printing paper money.

It was pointless trying to buy postage stamps. These had no value from one day to the next, and so were no longer printed. Letters from Claus to his mother had to be taken to a post office, where they would be franked by hand with the rate for that day.

A magazine whose cover price had already shot up to 1,500 marks in July cost 200,000 marks in October and 50,000,000,000 marks in November.

Was it any wonder that as soon as they received their wages, people would hurry straight from their work into the nearest shops, fearful that the currency would sink still further in the next few hours and that their money would buy them less? Money was no longer carried in wallets, but in briefcases or even in baskets. Lifetime savings were wiped out overnight. Neither Erika nor her mother now left their apartment without a folded shopping bag in a coat pocket. Any food that was available to buy, and whose price was within reach, was on principle bought at once. Tomorrow – or even later that same day – it might not be affordable.

Keeping accounts and paying the staff at Falkenstein was becoming meaningless.

Neither at the Avus nor in the Eifel was there money available to stage races. That year's events were cancelled at both circuits.

The organizers made an effort at Solitude, though. An estimated 100,000 spectators turned out, 105 cars competed, and new supercharged Mercedes models reached well over 100mph on the straights. Claus simply did not have the power to match. He was compelled to force his car through every bend faster and faster, taking things right up to, and sometimes over, the absolute safety limit. Several times he all but slid off the edge of the track, twice the car began that rolling motion which was the prelude to turning over. It was, he believed, impossible to have pushed the car any harder without disaster, yet at the end he could finish no higher than sixth. This had been, Claus believed, his best drive to date – but what a struggle against the fast boys!

It was apparent that his own car, despite all the tuning, had become uncompetitive overnight. Claus would buy one of the new Mercedes two-seaters fitted with a supercharger which could be operated by the flick of a pedal. This would be readily convertible into racing trim and still provide transport for everyday needs.

But when would he be able to afford it?

A pound of butter which Claus saw in a shop window was marked at 6,000,000,000,000 marks. This made him realize how lucky his family was. They at least had produce from their estate, whereas Erika and her mother, and many millions more, were threatened with the starvation of the wartime years.

The mood on the streets was one of utter hopelessness. Groups of grey-faced working men and women stood around on corners, hungry, helpless, angry. Communist agitators staged meetings almost every day.

By chance in the course of a trip to the Hanover area, Claus had seen people without food storming fields and digging out green, immature and often poisonous potatoes. Such events had led to potato fields being placed under police guard, with the harvest then stored in police station cellars for equitable distribution.

Each week, Claus took a basket of provisions to the Wolfs. If only it were possible to do the same for every needy household!

Yet soon he realized that even helping out just the Wolfs was shortly going to be beyond him. From being a matter of occasional conversation, the future of Falkenstein now became the principal evening topic of discussion between Claus and his father. It was no longer a question how soon the estate might become profitable, but whether Falkenstein would survive at all.

It was clear that Germany's currency had become meaningless. Money was now no more than figures on a piece of paper. After centuries as the Erlenbach family home, Falkenstein would finish up in the hands of a bank. Claus and his parents would spend the rest of their days at the house in Berlin.

If they could even hold on to that.

Bliss

Claus had never heard of Dr Hjalmar Schacht. The newspaper report that Schacht had been appointed National Currency Commissioner meant nothing to him.

It was different with that fellow Hitler. Claus read all the details of the affair in Munich with great interest and some bewilderment. This was action. This was something that he could understand.

Hitler had attempted to take over the government in Bavaria and been stopped by Reichswehr soldiers. Seventeen of Hitler's supporters had been shot dead, and others wounded.

This was all part of Seeckt's credo. The Army's function was to protect the nation and the legal government. Seeckt had sent in troops to put down Communist insurrections, and with total impartiality now sent them in against nationalists as well. Hitler's attempted putsch had been a threat to the state and Seeckt had seen to it that it came to a bloody end.

What Claus couldn't understand was that Ludendorff, the Army's former Chief of Staff, had gone in with Hitler. That had been quite wrong. A German officer did not involve himself in politics. He could advise, of course. Indeed, in certain circumstances it was his duty to give advice. But he must not commit a political act.

Hitler and Ludendorff would be facing trial, and quite rightly too. Meanwhile, Schacht was working a quiet miracle.

Hjalmar Schacht was a director of the German National Bank and a doctor of philosophy. He had studied at no fewer than four different universities to prepare an analysis of 'British mercantilism'. He had both enormous practical experience and vast theoretical knowledge.

To end the nightmare inflation, the Minister of Finance took Dr Schacht from his bank, invested him with special powers and created him Reich Currency Commissioner. Schacht waved his wand, out of his top hat came the 'Rentenmark', and with the Rentenmark came something like the old pre-war stability. The Rentenmark had an exchange rate of 4.20 to the dollar and, like the gold mark, a value of 1,000,000,000,000 Reichsmarks.

The gold mark, in which reparations payments had to be made, was not subject to the paper money inflation. It had the real value of gold, to which many currencies had been tied until the war.

In the middle of this financial chaos, the German Government granted Russia a trade credit of 75,000,000 gold marks. If there was one country which could not afford to extend credit, Claus told himself, it was Germany. If there was one country which itself needed all the credit it could secure, that country was Germany. Yet despite all the pressures of reparations payments and a domestic inflation of unimaginable proportions, Germany was leaning over backwards to accommodate the Russians.

'We owe it them', was Nicolai's dry comment, and it was certainly true that the Soviet Government had meanwhile set German rearmament well on its way.

It was agreed that the Junkers factory near Moscow should manufacture 300 aircraft annually, of which Russia would take sixty. The Russians would provide the raw materials and labour force, Germany the machinery and technicians.

The blow fell when Dr Gustav Stresemann became Chancellor. Stresemann let it be known at once that he wished no military collaboration with Russia. He was prepared to tolerate only economic cooperation.

Faced with the new Chancellor's opposition, Nicolai had to devise a means to conceal the collaboration. He disguised future expenditure as straightforward economic aid to Russia.

Krupp was starting experiments in modern farming methods over a vast area in the south of Russia. The firm's engineers were developing agricultural machinery, but inevitably also manufacturing artillery and ammunition. Krupp's Russian 'Werk S' was turning out 30mm infantry weapons, and a cannon was produced which fired a 10.5cm shell over a range of twelve miles.

90

Germany's firepower was increasing, and the Russians were anxious to make it clear that ideological differences were of no practical significance when it came to alliance. All that mattered was that the two countries were pursuing the same foreign policy objectives.

Viktor Kopp had once protested to Maltzan that Soviet propaganda was not to be taken seriously. Now Brockdorff-Rantzau had a similar tale to tell. When Brockdorff met Chicherin in Moscow, along with the entire Soviet Foreign Affairs Commissariat, the ubiquitous Karl Radek was at pains to stress that 'the Soviet Government could work well with a reactionary German government'. At this, Chicherin put in: 'Mussolini is now our best friend'.

The Fascist leader Benito Mussolini, dictator of Italy for the past year, was giving his country's Communists short shrift. And he was now the Kremlin's best friend! Did the Soviet leadership even believe in Communism at all?

Behind the closed doors of Department R, the workload was increasing. Work was begun on an aerodrome at Vivupal, outside Lipetsk. Repair workshops and engine test beds were built, and a hospital as well. This aerodrome was intended to function with complete independence and to be shut off from the world outside. Here, German servicemen were to be trained as flyers.

Now, with the retirement of Colonel Nicolai from Department R, Claus found himself once again parted from an older mentor. Claus was learning not to become too attached to individuals.

Except of course for Erika. Thanks to Erika, Claus was as happy, he thought, as it was possible for a human being to be.

Claus called at the apartment in Wedding almost every weekend now, chiefly to take Erika out, but sometimes simply to sit with her. More than once he spent an entire evening sitting contentedly in the Wolfs' tiny apartment, helping Erika mark a huge stack of her pupils' exercise books. Even this simple task was a joy to him. To be next to Erika, this was all that mattered to him in the entire world. They would spend hours in each others' arms, and Claus felt that he could sit and gaze at Erika for ever.

Hers was a frank, open face, almost baby like in its roundness, with bright eyes set wide apart and a nose which seemed to set a standard for neatness. There was a way that the girl's nose wrinkled lightly when she laughed which Claus found totally captivating. It did not happen when she smiled; only during a full blooded laugh.

Claus had not known that such happiness could exist. The rapture which enveloped him, which filled his hours and his dreams and swept him in a haze of enchantment through each day, was at its most intense whenever he parted from Erika and headed homewards. Burning still in the afterglow of companionship, Claus would sense his affection expanding to embrace the entire world. He would see the city around him, its buildings huge and small, its lights and its homes, would picture all the people behind the walls and behind the windows, and be overwhelmed by an upsurge of love and compassion for them all. There were sad people out there, lonely ones too, and Claus wished, wished with all his being that everyone could be blessed with the same happiness as he. All of humanity had a right to that divine joy.

Encouraged by the new financial stability – Falkenstein's security was meanwhile assured – Claus bought one of the new supercharged two-seaters in time to run it in and prepare it before the 1924 racing season. The car, to which Mercedes had given the complex type designation of 10/40/65, proved surprisingly good at threading its way through the ever thickening Berlin traffic. At the same time, the supercharger when required could provide a more than sixty per cent increase in power. Technically, the car was an amazing advance over anything else on the roads. It was the first model one could buy with an overhead camshaft engine, the first with a supercharger and the first with synchronized brakes on all four wheels. Technology was simply streaking ahead.

Apart from the racing, Claus was looking forward to finding out whether he could beat the time taken by the train from Berlin to Falkenstein.

When he did drive the new car for the first time to his family seat, he took it relatively easily. Claus was on his way to the Solitude races, and the car was laden with spares and tools.

As though to compensate for the atrocious weather of the previous meeting, this time the Solitude event was blessed with boiling heat. The new Mercedes was a flier, and with the advanced four-wheel system Claus could leave his braking until the last possible moment before entering a bend. He was beginning to develop a technique of braking late, changing down through the gears as he did so, and accelerating all the way through the corner right from the point where he turned into it. In other words, he reached the lowest point in his speed immediately before beginning to turn. Until now Claus had, like most drivers, been still braking while already halfway into the turn, changing down a gear only at that point. His new technique enabled him to come out of a bend that much faster, giving him a flying start along the next straight. Acceleration, he discovered, also made the car altogether more stable throughout the turn. Claus did not drive rounds bends, but through them.

Claus found his new car and his new driving style a great success. All the same, there were larger, extraordinarily quick rivals among the entries, and he had to be content with fifth place.

The torrential rain was back for the Eifel race, where the distance was doubled to ten laps. Claus made a bad start, losing precious time by stalling his engine on the line. The setback made him all the more determined to pull up in the field once he was under way. For more than five hours Claus battled the Mercedes through storms and hail. He could barely see the solid objects which lined the course, the walls, the trees and houses, and did not even notice when a grandstand which had been built to hold 3,000 spectators was destroyed by the weather.

Claus's reward was second place. If he could have just one win before he retired and settled into married life...

Meantime there were weekends without races, but with outings into the Brandenburg countryside.

Claus took Erika everywhere in the open white car. When the country roads were empty and he could see far enough ahead, Claus would indulge himself with that quick snap of the accelerator which activated the supercharger. Up would go the revs, they could feel themselves being pushed in the back by the shaped leather seats, and the countryside would flash past in a blur and mix of colours. These bursts never lasted for more than a minute, and Claus was careful not to put Erika at any risk.

In any case, where Claus was concerned, going quickly in a straight line was never the point of motoring. His whole enjoyment came from forcing a car through bends as fast as it could be pushed without leaving the road or turning over. Probing the limits of what was possible, that was the whole challenge for Claus.

Well, he couldn't do that with Erika aboard. Carrying precious cargo meant toning everything down; with Erika beside him he did no more than ease his way through the curves. And he had no time at all for those others on the road who blasted along as quickly as their motors would carry them whenever they were on a straight, then braked unnecessarily approaching even simple bends. Straight-line heroes, Claus called them, and to him they would never be real drivers. Anyone could go quickly on a straight.

Once Claus drove with Erika to the Baltic coast, where they walked on the beach and looked across to the island of Usedom. On their way back to Berlin, the clouds opened. By the time Claus had stopped the car, fished out and assembled the hood carried when not racing, Erika's hair was hanging down in little ropes. Her cotton dress was clinging to every part of her body and drops of water were falling from the tips of her nose and chin. Claus was appalled that he had not seen what was coming and acted in time, but Erika only laughed. 'I'll dry off', she assured him, and she did.

That year they toured most of Brandenburg, its lakes, its hills, its forests. They walked among birches drooping low over fresh streams, discovered springs bubbling over multicoloured pebbles and sat together on hillsides below regiments of dark green pines.

There was no doubt about it. Erika was the most engaging of companions. The two of them laughed together a great deal, they seemed to know instinctively what the other was thinking, feeling or needing. Sometimes Claus would sit cradling Erika in his arms for an hour or longer, neither of them feeling any need to speak. At others Erika would demonstrate the fieriest of passions, clinging to him with

94

an ignited energy which swept him away with its boundlessness. Or she would exhibit the most exquisite tenderness, stroking his face with fingertips more gentle than Claus could have imagined possible, kissing him lightly time after time, on his forehead, his nose, his cheeks, his throat, his chin, even his eyelids, and at intervals with swelling necessity on his lips.

In her attentions, Erika could not have been more affectionate. At the same time...

It was curious, but Claus could not avoid a feeling that Erika was somehow holding herself back. It was as though she were afraid to let go and give herself completely, as though something stopped her saying, as he without hesitation would say, Yes, darling, I am yours for ever and ever to the end of my life, unreservedly.

Had some man at some time let Erika down, given her – what was it that Dr Freud called it? – a complex? If the poor girl had been made wary of men due to the misconduct of another, well, she could surely be cured of that over time. Claus would just have to be patient, and all would come right in the end. Meanwhile, the thing was not to rush the girl.

Erika was fascinated when Claus revealed that he had spent some childhood years in Russia. 'Have you read anything by Alexandra Kollontai?' she wanted to know.

'Not by her, but I've read of her. She's just become the world's first female ambassador'.

'Yes, Russian ambassador to Norway. And before that she was the world's first female government minister. Isn't it wonderful?'

Claus was unsure what could be wonderful about it, but Erika admitted no doubt. 'Claus, don't you see? Industrialization has changed the world. Wives and mothers used to have to stay at home to produce all kinds of things, bake bread, make jams, pickles, preserves, butter, God knows what. Now these things are manufactured for us in great production centres; all we have to do is buy them. The family no longer produces; it only consumes, so it is no longer necessary for a woman to stay at home to do these things'.

'We have had bakers for centuries', Claus countered, 'even in the smallest villages. Wives haven't always had to bake the family's bread'.

'Yes, but don't you see? All these other things as well are being produced in quantity now, leaving the woman free to play her part in society the same as any man. This is what Madame Kollontai has shown us'.

'And what about bringing up children?'

For the first time since they had met, Erika showed impatience. 'That doesn't have to condemn a woman to staying at home. Didn't you have a nanny?'

'A governess'.

'Well, every child will be able to have a nanny or a governess in future. There will be crêches for the children while their mothers play their part in society. The old type of family has had its day, Claus. You've seen it now, with the war – mothers having to go out to work in factories. This has meant a triple load for the woman: breadwinner, housekeeper and mother all at the same time. This will not do. The old idea of an indissoluble marriage based on the servitude of women must be replaced by a free union of two equal citizens'.

'Servitude?'

'Yes. No more conjugal slavery. Instead, there has to be a free and honest union of two people whose children are the responsibility of the state. This is, after all, the twentieth century'.

Claus could not understand any of this. He knew well how to conceal his feelings, but some of the terms Erika was using were almost too big a shock.

'If… if we were married, would you want our children brought up by the state? Wouldn't you want to look after them yourself?'

'I don't think that I shall ever marry'.

It was like a dagger of ice through the heart.

'I am a teacher. I intend remaining a teacher. Society does not need me to stay at home. There is no need for me to do what earlier generations of wives did. I am more useful to society as a teacher'.

That seemed to settle it, even before he had put the question.

It was work, work for Claus from now on. The files in Department R's safe were multiplying, and the variety of tasks demanding a solution kept him from dwelling on Erika's strange ideas.

So too did the weekend motor racing. The number of events in the calendar was increasing, and Erika's refusal to marry had, as it were, given him a reprieve. He had no need now to retire from the track, and 1925 was to give him his busiest racing season yet.

The course at Solitude was rebuilt to produce a circuit of fourteen miles, with races up to ten laps. Bugattis appeared, and Lancias, and there were new, faster Mercedes types. Claus was forced to work harder than ever behind the wheel, and could finish no higher than seventh.

Perhaps his most important lesson came in this race: not to try to follow the big boys too closely. One of the new Mercedes models overtook him on a straight, and Claus hung his own car on to the tail of the faster vehicle going into the next series of bends.

It was very nearly his undoing. The other car had better steering and better brakes, and Claus, following into the first bend at the same speed, was unable to drive through and out of the turn in the same way as the faster man. His nearside wheels left the road, sending up showers of dirt. Only by a massive effort of muscle and concentration could Claus retain control. He tried the same thing, hanging on to the man in front through the next bend too, and through the next – with the same result. In the end Claus realized that he would just have to let the faster car go. He must find his own pace, the maximum speed at which he could go through bends in safety, and not worry about what the men in the factory-entered latest models were doing.

All the same, the new course layout included bends which Claus found greatly satisfying to take at full speed. This was living!

The next race in which he drove left Claus with none of this elation. Over the longer circuit in the Eifel, the event was won by an Italian driver and cost three lives. One of the crashes occurred just behind Claus's Mercedes while he was travelling at full throttle. Claus knew nothing about it until after the finish. At the moment when it happened he was aware only of the road pouring towards him, the rushing wind in his ears and the necessity of changing down and braking in time for the next bend.

Afterwards, Claus was surprised to find that the three deaths affected him more immediately than the thousands he had seen on the battlefield. In war he had learned to distance himself from what was, after all, only to be expected.

To die in war, that was – could one say natural? No, that didn't sound quite right, but death was in the nature of the thing. Death in the course of a sporting endeavour, on the other hand – well, admittedly there was nothing unknown about that. Hunting accidents, falls during mountaineering and the like – these were commonplace enough. Why, though, did they always seem more tragic than death in battle?

There was something sensual about indulgence in speed. Claus recognized his need for that sort of exhilaration and knew that he was its slave. At the thought that he might be developing any other kind of addiction – to alcohol or tobacco, for instance – Claus would have reacted in self-abomination and given up the practice immediately. He would have been shocked by the idea that any craving might become his master.

Claus did not smoke and now allowed himself to drink only once the racing season was over for the year. He would take a glass of wine or cognac up until the New Year and then enter a period of strict abstinence. Motor racing demanded concentration and dedication, and Claus was prepared to give the sport both.

He was giving no less to his dealings with the Russians. When Red Navy chiefs wanted help in creating a submarine fleet, Claus saw to it that they were sent blueprints. German Admiralty men went off to visit Soviet naval bases, and Claus warned them what to expect.

'You were right', they told him when they came back. 'The Reds wasted no time telling us how we should go to war together against

98

Poland'. The Soviet Navy, it seemed, was now offering to blockade the Bay of Danzig on Germany's behalf to protect East Prussia.

Lieth-Thomsen put in a requirement for aircraft, and Claus sent a man to the Netherlands to purchase fifty Fokker D-XIIIs, the fastest fighters in the world. The Netherlands had been neutral during the war and was not a party to the Versailles peace. All the same, Claus took no chances. He instructed the front man who made the purchases to tell Fokker's that the machines were being bought for South America. The fighters went to the new secret German flying school at Lipetsk, where German manufacturers were soon to develop their own aircraft.

Department R had a string of plans on hand, but Stresemann's hostile attitude was forcing a certain amount of restraint. Schemes which had already been planned with Moscow to an advanced level could not now be forced onwards at the pace both sides had foreseen. The brakes were on, and it was becoming as essential to hide things from Stresemann as from the Western Allies and the Control Commission.

The German Communist Party had no such inhibitions. It renewed its campaign to 'burst the fetters of Versailles', and then went further. 'Union of Austria with the Reich' was the Communists' next demand. Their Russian partners, Claus reflected, had things a lot easier. Every move they made in collaboration between the two countries had the encouragement of the Kremlin. German military men on the other hand were forced to act without the knowledge of their own government.

That government now gave Russia a further credit, worth 300,000,000 gold marks.

In Germany, soldiers practised tank manoeuvres using wood-and-canvas mock-ups mounted on tricycle undercarriages and pushed about by men on foot – but this was all for the benefit of the watching, mistrustful Western Allies. Fifteen hundred miles to the east, near Kazan on the Volga, the German Army's secret tank and gunnery school was training with the real thing. At this establishment, codenamed Kama, German manufacturers were running a 'Heavy Vehicle Experimental and Test Centre'. Until the Germans had developed their own panzers, the Red Army placed two types of Soviet tank at the disposal of its guests.

North of Saratov on the Volga, German Army specialists were operating an illicit school of gas warfare, codenamed Tomka, and a joint Soviet-German company, Bersol, was created to manufacture poison gases in a sparsely populated region east of the Urals.

In every one of these undertakings, Claus had the feeling that they were not only putting one over on the Allies, but were outsmarting their own government, as well. This was scarcely a comfortable feeling for an officer whose most deeply ingrained instinct was obedience to orders. The only way that Claus found to justify matters to his conscience was telling himself that it was a soldier's function to protect his country from the follies and neglect of his own people as much as from the onslaughts of her external enemies.

Motor racing took a huge step forward in 1926, when the first German Grand Prix was run on the fast Avus circuit. Expectations were high, with entries from French and Italian drivers, and new Mercedes cars to take on the Bugattis, Alfa-Romeos and Talbots.

Erika had not accompanied Claus to any of the race meetings which had involved travelling away from Berlin. These would have involved overnight stays, and Claus rejected anything which could compromise Erika. Some other drivers took their wives with them, and of course there were always other young women around the race tracks who were not drivers' wives, but Claus had until now treated his races as though they were men-only events.

The Avus was different. The circuit was right here on the outskirts of Berlin, running down towards Grunewald. Erika could accompany him into the paddock on the morning of race day and be home again that night.

The weather was atrocious. Rainwater flooded the track and with obscuring mountains of spray flung high from every wheel, visibility was as good as non-existent. To be following another car was to be driving blind. Only with a clear road in front could one see anything at all, and that was blurred to the point of making it impossible to know where exactly on the track one was. What was more, in the few years of its existence the surface of the Avus had already developed significant ripples. In places there were bumps up to four inches high.

Claus made a flying start. He was away from the line ahead of everyone else, but of course the Avus, with its long straights, favoured the faster motors. The first of the powerful works cars came past him after only a couple of hundred yards. One after the other, the big boys thundered by, throwing up huge blinding tails of water. Five of them had gone past, then the field seemed to settle down. No one else overtook him, and a fierce determination took hold of Claus. Sixth place. If he lost no time at all on the bends, he ought to be able at least to hang on to that.

Claus went into the banked turn absolutely flat out. Supercharger and motor were screaming to bursting point, the Mercedes was flying as fast as it ever had or could. Ears near to deafness in the wind, Claus was concentrating overstrained eyes through the obscuring curtain of spray, feeling more through his grip on the wheel than he was able to see. His wheels hit a massive bump, and the Mercedes shot into the air, slewing round as it went.

For an instant, Claus thought that he and the car were going to be launched over the top of the banking into space.

It was the other way. Down shot the Mercedes into the saturated ground on the inside of the track. The front of the car buried itself, Claus was catapulted head first over windscreen and bonnet. Earth and sky chased one another round a couple of times, then an elephant kicked him with all of its weight in his rear end.

He was unhurt. Landing with such force in a sitting position had given his spine an almighty jolt, and he would doubtless be stiff for some days, but spinning head over heels as he had meant that he could just as easily have been head down when he hit the ground. It had been a fifty-fifty chance of a broken neck, and Claus had been lucky.

The Mercedes could not be moved from where it had landed. Walking back to the paddock, Claus could feel the stiffness setting in, and weren't both of his ankles beginning to swell? Well, he wasn't going to let Erika notice anything beyond a smile.

Before Claus arrived, another Mercedes shot off in a bend, demolishing a scoreboard and a timekeepers' hut. The driver was killed, along with a scoreboard official and two young men in the hut.

Erika greeted Claus in the paddock white-faced. She flung an arm round his neck and hung onto him as though he might fly away into the air if she did not restrain him down on earth.

'It's all right, darling', Claus told her, but still Erika clung to him for the best part of a minute while the rain continued to fall on them both.

Only seventeen out of forty-six starters completed the race. Erika held on to Claus's arm until the finish, letting go only when Claus set off with his mechanic to attend to the retrieval of his car.

Things were not as bad as they might have been. The Mercedes had suffered only bodywork damage which could be easily repaired in time for the next meeting.

Claus was delighted that the car had survived for further races. It was a reaction which Erika could not understand. All that mattered to her was that Claus had come through. A car was nothing, an object, an artefact. It was replaceable. Claus was irreplaceable. So, indeed, was every human being.

That night, Claus and Erika held each other in an embrace that promised to have no end. It did end, of course, but not before they had sworn to each other a score of times how deep and enduring was their love. Erika clung to him as she had never done before. Claus sensed that her intensity signified relief that he was still alive.

Erika kissed him on the lips, a quick, urgent kiss, wrapped a hand round the side of his head and entwined her fingers about his ear. Claus looked into her eyes and could see that she was going to be serious.

'Why is it', Erika asked, 'that we appreciate how important things are to us only when we lose them? Or when we nearly lose them?'

There was no answer that Claus could give. He kissed Erika fully. Not briefly as she had kissed him, but lingeringly and with unmistakeable affection. When he broke off, Erika stroked his face.

'It's important you, isn't it? Racing, I mean'.

'Yes, but I'll give it up if you want'.

Erika had seen the fire in his face during the practice sessions at the Avus, his eagerness before going out on to the track, the glow which animated him when he came in. 'No you won't. If you gave it up for me, you would resent me for it ever after'.

'Darling! How could I ever resent you?'

'Oh, you might not at first, but later on, when we are older, you might look back and wonder what you might not have achieved if only you had kept on. You would blame me for hindering you'.

'Don't be silly. I would do anything in the world for you, and gladly'.

Erika shook her head. 'You won't give it up. Not yet. You'll give it up when you are ready to do so, and not before. I won't ask you to give up anything that matters to you. I don't believe that anyone should do that. What is important to you is a part of you'.

She kissed him then, as lovingly as he had kissed her.

It was true. Claus had not realized it himself, but Erika – was it simply woman's natural intuition, or due to her own personal insight? – had divined the situation correctly. Motor racing was indeed now a part of him.

Thank goodness, Claus had often said to himself, that he had been born into this age of motors. What, he wondered, would have been his principal indulgence in an earlier age? Horses, obviously. Flying over obstacles at full stretch, that had been a boyhood pastime, but even the fastest gallops offered nothing like the intense gratification of high-speed motor racing.

On horseback one experienced wild excitement, and generations of Erlenbachs had had to be content with that. Yet no equestrian thrill was to be compared with that of hurling a car through bends at the very highest speed that was physically possible. Those moments on the track were exhilarating beyond description, but there was an added dimension: the detached inner satisfaction of precision driving, of

103

pointing a car onto that exact line through a bend which would effectively straighten out the road and necessitate the least possible drop in speed.

Claus certainly did not want to abandon racing, but would of course do so without hesitation if Erika wished it. What, after all, was love, if not the willingness to make sacrifices for another?

But it was not just motor racing; Erika too was part of him. It seemed to Claus, when he thought about it, that each man's life, his time, his thoughts and his energies, were dominated by three things: his work, his hobbies and his girl. From what he had observed, there were, sadly, millions who had no luck with any of these. To have found contentment in one area of life was perhaps the average. Those who had been fortunate in two were indeed happy men. To be blessed in all three – well, that sounded like the stuff of fiction, yet, incredibly, it was true for him. Even in his work Claus had been granted an immeasurable privilege. He was helping to strengthen his country's defences, and there was surely no more gratifying occupation for any man.

Claus had lost no time in introducing Erika to the Albrechts, and the four of them were by now regular weekend companions. The domesticity which the two of them shared on their visits to the Albrecht household would, he hoped, in time soften Erika's attitude towards marriage. The Albrechts had two small children, and Erika played every conceivable kind of game with them. The children adored her. Now Julia was pregnant again.

'Aren't you going to marry the girl?' Julia asked Claus one afternoon when Erika was not present. The note of reproach in her tone suggested that she thought Claus were merely stringing Erika along.

'Goodness knows I've asked her often enough. She just doesn't want to marry'.

'But that's absurd! She obviously adores you. I've never seen two people so obviously right for each other'.

'I know we're right together, too, but she just won't'.

'What do you mean: she won't marry you, or she won't marry at all?'

'She doesn't want to marry at all. She calls it domestic servitude. It's old fashioned, she says, and not for her'.

Claus's unhappiness was too evident. Julia touched his arm, and her tone was soft.

'Let me talk to her'.

Claus set off for the Bendlerstrasse next morning happier than he had felt for months. Julia, with her great common sense, would surely make Erika understand that these silly anti-marriage ideas were just so much nonsense. Erika was so good with children, it was inevitable that she would one day feel the urge to have some of her own. When she did, she would surely realize that the only way to give them the necessary care was for their parents to be conventionally married. All this talk about the state bringing up children in future, it was just so much ridiculous and impractical nonsense. For goodness' sake, Erika was anything but stupid. She must see it for herself. These were just the sort of silly ideas that appealed to people when they were young, but with the years people usually became able to recognize such absurdities for what they were. It was just a matter of time, and Erika would come round.

Activity at the ministry was becoming hectic. Shells and grenades for Germany were being turned out at no fewer than four Soviet production centres. In 1926 alone, the bill to Department R for munitions manufactured in Russia amounted to more than 150,000,000 gold marks.

So much activity called for a great deal more than inventive paperwork. A safe means had to be found for guns, shells and all other clandestine materials to be brought from Russia to the Reich. They were sent by sea, in packing cases labelled as 'machine parts', direct from Leningrad to the German free port of Stettin, on the Baltic. The same route was used for material travelling in the other direction. Particularly sensitive shipments, or those which on account of size or shape could not be brought through Stettin in disguise, were sailed across the Baltic via other harbours, using small vessels crewed by German officers.

The most bizarre solution which Claus had to find arose on the three occasions when a German flyer was killed in an accident at Lipetsk. Each time, the man's body was brought back to Germany in a packing case labelled as containing 'machine parts'.

Shipments of arms from Russia meant that by the time the Allied Military Control Commission was wound up in January 1927 the Army held in clandestine arsenals seventy-five heavy cannon, 600 field guns, 400 mortars, 12,000 machine guns and 350,000 rifles over and above the officially permitted stocks of arms. Weapons in store were already sufficient to equip an army of 300,000 – three times the size of the existing legal force. Control Commission inspectors never discovered these secret stores, and Department R had every reason for satisfaction.

Nürburgring

For Claus, personal matters were far less pleasing. Julia had spoken to Erika at length about Claus, marriage, motherhood, domesticity and everything associated with the subject. Erika remained obdurate.

Oh, she loved Claus, would love him until her death, but she would never marry. This was a matter of principle. Marriage was outdated, and she would not be a party to continuation of the obsolete. Someone had to make a stand. If no one did, progress would never be made.

'It all depends', Julia responded, 'on what one means by progress'.

'Erika', Julia explained to Claus, 'sees herself as a pioneer. This is missionary zeal, Claus. She has fallen for the ideas of Alexandra Kollontai, and against that kind of fanaticism one is helpless. All you can do is resign yourself to it. Accept the situation. Live with her by all means, but the more you press her about marriage, the more deeply she will dig in her heels'.

'Live with her? Without being married? I couldn't ask her to do that'.

Julia reached out to his arm. 'Oh, Claus, you are so old-fashioned'.

'I don't care if it is old fashioned. It's what's right. If I were to live with her without marrying her, I should feel that I was simply using her'.

'But Claus, that would be her choice, not yours'.

Claus shook his head. 'I couldn't do it'.

Julia knew Claus too well to pursue the point. He would always, at any cost to himself, do only what was compatible with his notion of honour. 'Anyway', she consoled him, 'who knows? Maybe one day she'll change her mind of her own free will, without your saying anything'.

There really did seem nothing else for it. As Julia advised, he would refrain from further attempts to cajole or persuade Erika, and simply wait for her to see sense.

Yet who was this Alexandra Kollontai who put such damned silly ideas into girls' heads? 'Servitude', Erika had called marriage, and 'conjugal slavery'. Had Claus's mother ever given him the impression that she was a slave or in servitude? And Inge. His sister was as happy as could be since her marriage. One had only to look into her eyes. Claus would just like to know with what right this Kollontai had got hold of and perverted the mind of an otherwise normal, healthy and wonderful young woman.

Claus thought of Erika constantly. Whether he was clearing documentation for a 'machine parts' shipment, authorizing a transfer of monies from the 'Ruhr fund' or arranging for officers on their way to Russia to be discharged temporarily, one image would spring out of nowhere into his thoughts. Department R work was top secret, demanding care and plenty of concentration. Yet no matter how totally Claus was immersed in whatever he might be doing, the same picture would arise somewhere in his mind. It was not an intrusion, could never be that. Rather, Erika's delightful face provided a warm and comforting background to the task in which he was otherwise absorbed.

Berlin was a lively place now, and there were plenty of diversions. Besides its proliferation of night clubs and cafés, the capital held forty theatres, three opera houses and numerous concert halls. There were cinemas, too, and Claus succeeded in securing tickets for the premiere of Fritz Lang's futuristic masterpiece Metropolis. He was fascinated by the astonishing images in the film, but unsure what to make of the story. In any case, it was far too long. Erika, though, was enthusiastic.

She tugged on his arm. 'Don't you see it, Claus? It's we two. He's the son of an industrialist and she's a worker's daughter'.

'My father's not an industrialist'.

'No, but the idea is the same. They're from different classes, but nothing can keep them apart because they love each other, and it's because they do that the two classes are reconciled in the end'.

Claus could not see the least resemblance. What the film maker had been trying to say was, to him, a mystery.

'You're so old-fashioned, Claus'. Erika took his face in her hands and kissed the tip of his nose. 'But that's part of why I love you so much'.

Claus was out of his depth.

He had meanwhile read up about Alexandra Kollontai and discovered to his horror that the Russian diplomat was an advocate of what was called free love. And Erika was a disciple of hers!

'It's all right', Erika assured him when he confronted her on the subject. 'It's not compulsory'.

Then, realizing how seriously Claus was taking the subject, she slid her arms round his neck and kissed him with a lingering and escalating passion. 'It's you that I love, Claus, and it always will be. There can never be anyone else'.

All the same, whenever Claus thought about Kollontai and her damned ideas, he became livid both at her and at Erika's folly in adopting them. This was, though, only while they were apart. As soon as he saw Erika again, he found it impossible to feel any anger at all.

Nowadays, the cream of the literary and artistic world was said to meet at the Romanisches Café. Claus and Erika went there still from time to time, but for the excellent fare, not to see the Bohemians, and it was a fact that they never saw anyone there whose face they recognized as that of a celebrity. Perhaps, suggested Erika, members of the creative set gathered at the café only while they were struggling to be discovered; once they had 'arrived' they no longer found it necessary. It was beneath them now, perhaps.

If that wasn't human, Claus didn't know what was.

There were Otto Klemperer's Sunday morning concerts at the Kroll, too. The two of them attended these as often as they could. Once they went to the Nelson Theatre on the Kurfürstendamm, where the American negro dancer Josephine Baker was a big hit. All Berlin was talking about her, and it seemed essential to go along and see the performance for oneself.

The energy and sheer athleticism displayed in the show were impressive, but Erika dismissed Miss Baker's act as 'exploitation of the negro', and expressed her disappointment.

Claus simply found the whole thing far too primitive for his taste. Like so much that was being passed off as art nowadays. The most atrocious paintings, something like the sort of thing he had seen his schoolmates produce at around the age of ten, and sculptures that had no shape of anything at all. Beauty was being abandoned in favour of the grotesque, and if it wasn't a search for beauty what, Claus wondered, was the point of art at all, and how could mankind expect to advance without it?

The Albrechts had their third child now, a son whom they named Thomas. Claus was delighted to be asked to become the boy's godfather. 'I wonder', he remarked to Albrecht, now a major at last, 'if he'll become a soldier, too'.

The circuit used so far for the Eifel races, the course where two years earlier there had been three fatalities, was replaced in 1927 by a specially built track centred on the Nürburg, an old castle on top of a steep hill. With its 174 bends on each eighteen-mile lap, this was a course that was going to take some learning. But what a circuit! What a contrast to the roads used previously for the Eifel event! The very latest in road building technology had been employed, to produce the smoothest surface Claus had ever seen. Races here would not be one never-ending wrestle against a machine threatening every moment to be flung from the road; they would be a test of speed, steering, road holding and reliability, as motor races should be.

Claus was full of admiration for the exacting course, yet against the newer, factory-entered cars he was never able to pull any farther ahead than the middle of the field. All the same, this race was his most gratifying and electrifying yet. In the longer events, individual races within a race frequently developed out of nowhere, and almost from the start Claus found himself duelling against another Mercedes with comparable performance. What the other drivers were doing suddenly no longer existed for Claus and his rival; they had their own private battle and they made the most of it, each risking everything trying to out-brake the other as they hurtled into bend after bend. Frequently the

110

two were wheel to wheel alongside each other, never at any point were they more than a couple of lengths apart. First Claus was in front, then the other driver. At the finish, coming out of a desperately taken final corner, Claus had the length of his bonnet in front, and no more.

The two drivers slapped one another on the back and congratulated each other heartily. Never mind that the Mercedes factory entries had taken all the leading places; these two had enjoyed the most exciting afternoon in their own young lives. Wringing the most out of the vehicles they were in; that was what they had striven to do, and that was what they had achieved.

Claus came away knowing that next year he would master a lot more of the Nürburg course.

If he raced next year.

His Mercedes was being left behind by the rapid advances in newer models, but was it worth switching to one of the latest and most expensive developments? At any time, Erika might change her mind about marriage, and Claus was determined that then he would adhere to his resolution to give up racing.

Meanwhile he was accumulating irreplaceable memories and experiences. At Solitude, Claus managed to take third place in a race won by a Bugatti. It was a performance which attracted some attention, since there were many faster cars in the field and Claus finished in front of several out-and-out racing models.

There were already two Soviet officers attached to the Reichswehr Ministry, and their number was now increased to three. These had no access to Department R, with which they had no dealings. The men were in Berlin to learn the organization of a general staff. All three were German speakers, but were obliging enough to give Claus frequent opportunity to speak Russian with them. Claus enjoyed their company, and from time to time dined with them at a Russian restaurant off Alexanderplatz. For Claus, the borsht in particular recalled schooldays at St Petersburg, but on the whole he preferred to limit the frequency of these social excursions. The Red Army men drank far too much vodka for his liking. In drink they became noisy, and Claus suspected loose tongues. The Russians slapped him on the back or the shoulder, frequently put an arm round him and called him 'Tovarich Erlenbach'. Claus could never quite accept the description of comrade, though he did enjoy singing again those Russian folk songs which he had learned as a boy. All in all, he found the conduct of these men disturbingly incompatible with what was expected of senior officers.

Lenin was dead, and the vast Soviet empire now had a new, undisputed sole ruler: Josef Djugashvili, who had adopted the name 'Stalin', meaning Man of Steel.

Stalin's realm was enormous, but still basically an agricultural country. The new dictator at once set about transforming Russia into a modern industrial state comparable with the most advanced on earth. German engineers were already busy creating Soviet industries out of nothing, and in particular expanding those serving armaments production. Railway engines, motor vehicles, electrical equipment and machinery of all kinds went from German factories to produce a modern Russia. In return, Russia supplied Germany with those raw materials she lacked – principally oil, minerals and grain.

Claus's duties had until now involved a great deal of paperwork, a certain amount of discussion and almost no travel. The summons from above was, he thought, on a routine matter. He was wrong.

Major-General Werner von Blomberg, the Army Chief of Staff, was planning to tour all the German forces' establishments in Russia during August and September 1928. Claus was to go with him as interpreter, aide and general dogsbody. The general's unofficial adjutant, as it were. At once Claus became excited by the prospect. He had left Russia with his family in 1912. How had the country changed since then? The inequalities which Claus had known pre-war were, according to the Bolsheviks, no more. Yet reports which reached his desk showed that overall the country was worse off than under the Tsar.

Claus had not before met Blomberg, a tall man whose amiability was legendary. Where Seeckt was aloof, withdrawn and silent, Blomberg was all congeniality. Claus liked him from the outset.

The Chief of Staff spent four days in Moscow, which despite obvious official efforts to show it from its best side appeared to Claus a depressed and depressing place, the antithesis of what he had known pre-war. When Blomberg held talks with Red Army commanders, Claus shared the task of translation with a Russian interpreter.

The experience was illuminating.

Straight away at their first meeting, before any of the practical matters on hand had even been mentioned, Marshal Klimenty Voroshilov, the Soviet Defence Minister, opened discussions with the words: 'Not only in the name of the Red Army, but on behalf of the Government of the Soviet Union as well, I should like to state that the Red Army is ready with every assistance in the event of a Polish attack on Germany. Can the Soviet Union count on Germany in the event of a Polish attack?'

It was clear that Blomberg was staggered. He answered that this was a question of fundamental state policy, for which only the politicians were responsible.

Voroshilov was not content with this. The question, he stressed, was a decisive one for the Soviet Union. He asked again how the German Army stood on the matter. If required, he said, Germany could count on Russian help. It was unnecessary to say what form this help would take.

Blomberg could only give the same answer as before.

From Moscow, Blomberg went on to inspect Kama, Tomka and the Lipetsk flying school. During these journeys, Claus looked about him for signs of change or improvement in town and countryside. It was a futile effort. Transport was provided by the Russians, and the visitors were whisked directly to their destinations without any detours. It was apparent that their hosts wished the Germans to see only what they needed to see or what they themselves wished them to see.

Near Gomel, the visitors attended aerial exercises, and at Kiev the Red Army's autumn manoeuvres. Here there was much that was impressive, and Claus forgot the negative impressions he had brought from the capital. At a training ground near Voronezh, he watched with Blomberg as German flyers worked together with Russian artillery, directing the gunners' fire from the air. The cooperation was first class and the Russian batteries' fire excellent.

By the time they returned to Germany, Claus could see that Blomberg had been very nearly overwhelmed by the friendliness, cordiality, hospitality and general helpfulness of the Russians. Claus himself found his impressions of the trip blotted out at once by the ecstasy of reunion with Erika.

Respectable Berlin was asleep when Claus drove away from the Wolfs' apartment. At this hour on a weekend night, embarrassed wives who had themselves spun out the entire evening sitting over no more than two small drinks would still be coaxing and supporting their overloaded husbands homewards.

But this was Monday. In a few hours the alarms clocks would shrill the heaviest slumberer into consciousness, and another day of repetitive toil would begin. Tonight the pavements were empty, and the white two-seater had the dark roadway to itself.

As always when he left Erika, Claus was floating in a heaven of euphoria. His driving was automatic, a skill exercised only by his subconscious. There was nothing to demand Claus's attention as he turned right into the dark side street. At the front of the Mercedes, the circle with its three-pointed star swept along the black fronts of the houses like the sights of a traversing field gun.

It was instinct and experience, nothing more, which made him react at once to the shape which emerged from a doorway just round the corner on the right hand pavement. Claus knew that partial crouch, the tensed bending of the knees, the purposeful forward hunch of the shoulders.

The man was raising a pistol, and he was pointing it towards another figure farther ahead on the same side of the road. Even as Claus rammed on the brakes and knocked the gear lever into neutral, a small spurt of orange flame accompanied the over-familiar crack.

Claus hurled himself out of the open vehicle towards the gunman, who had turned at the sound of the car. Ahead, the figure on the

114

pavement had fallen, and the pistol was now brought round towards the leaping arrival.

The gun went off a second time as Claus flung himself onto the man. Down the two of them went, with Claus on top and grappling at the man's gun hand.

It was a gun hand no longer. Caught off-balance in the act of turning, the gunman had collapsed under Claus's weight like a wet cardboard box, and lost his grip on the pistol. The weapon had flown out into the roadway.

The man was winded, and for a moment Claus wondered whether the heavy fall onto the stone paving slabs had not stopped his heart.

Only when he began to pull the man's belt from his trousers to lash the fellow's hands behind his back did Claus realize that he himself had caught a bullet in the shoulder. At the moment of throwing himself on the assassin he had felt nothing.

Lights had gone on at house windows, and police arrived with reassuring swiftness. The man who had been shot farther along the street was still alive, though with a bullet in his back. He was rushed to the Charité Hospital.

It was a hospital bed for Claus that night, too. This time he had no clean wounds from a bullet which had passed right through. The projectile had smashed into two bones and stayed there.

The operation to remove the bullet was skilfully performed, but could not be hurried. 'And now', the surgeon told Claus after showing him the deformed and bloody lump of metal, 'you will have to be patient and keep still while those bones knit together. We don't want you losing movement in your shoulder, do we?'

No, Claus did not want that. The thought of being invalided out of the Army was appalling. And to be forced to leave because of a wound incurred elsewhere than on the battlefield! All because of some ghastly criminal!

At all costs Claus must regain full fitness as quickly as possible. His shoulder, upper arm and part of his chest were in plaster, and he would

115

do nothing to hinder the healing process. Thank goodness at least that it was his left shoulder that had caught it.

Two plain clothes policemen, accompanied by a constable in uniform, were waiting to interview Claus as soon as he was brought from the operating theatre.

No, he couldn't keep the bullet as a souvenir. It was now an exhibit in a case of attempted murder. Might even be murder, if the other man who had been shot with the same gun did not pull through.

Claus made a detailed statement of what he considered a very simple affair, was thanked and praised by the detectives and fell into a long and dreamless sleep.

When he woke, his father was sitting in a chair regarding him with his customary dispassionateness.

'I haven't told your mother', he told Claus. 'She'll have to know some time, of course, but I see no point in worrying her and having her come rushing up to Berlin while you are still in hospital. Once you are back on your feet you'll obviously have some leave and then you can go home for some convalescence. It will be time enough for her to be told about it then, once she sees that you have come through it all right'.

Claus was sure that his father was right. By going home, of course, his father meant to Falkenstein. The prospect of a rest in the country, Claus had to admit, was appealing – except for the thought of leaving Erika behind.

He had made no arrangement to see Erika again before the weekend. With any luck, he would be out of the hospital by then, and he hoped that she would not hear beforehand of what had happened. Once he was properly clothed and on his feet he would be able to meet people and make proper light of matters. Until then…

Of course the ministry had been informed of the reason for his absence, and Claus began to worry that Rolf Albrecht, with the best intentions, might call on Erika with the news. In any case, the shooting would be reported in the newspapers, and it was possible that he could be named. Would Erika see it? Either way she could come rushing in to the hospital, and Claus would prefer that she did not see him in this condition, and start making a fuss.

It was not Erika who arrived to visit Claus, but three strangers in sombre-looking suits and plain ties.

More policemen?

Two of the visitors, heavily built types, remained standing and said nothing. It was the third man, in a grey suit and carrying a floppy trilby hat, who shook Claus by the hand, pulled a chair close to the bed, seated himself and did all the talking.

The man gave his name as Himmler. It meant nothing to Claus. Nor did his explanation that he was head of the Schutzstaffel of the NSDAP and that the man whose shooting Claus had seen was one of his men.

'It is certain, Hauptmann', Himmler was telling him, 'that but for your intervention the gunman would have gone up to our man and finished him off with a shot to the head. Thanks to you he is alive, and the doctors believe that he will make a full recovery'.

Claus had always found it a good policy to keep quiet when he did not understand the topic under discussion. By shutting up and listening carefully, it was always possible to fill in gaps in knowledge without revealing one's ignorance.

Claus shut up now. Inside three minutes he understood that the Schutzstaffel, or SS, was the section of the Nazi Party which provided a bodyguard for the party leader, Adolf Hitler. The gunman whose arrest he had effected was a Communist, from the Red Front Fighting League.

The shooting made sense to Claus now. Though he took no notice of political developments beyond those which impinged directly on his Army duties, he did read the newspapers. Shootings between Communists and Nazis were a weekly occurrence on city streets. Let them kill one another off, was his father's comment, and Claus concurred.

'The NSDAP is indebted to you,' Himmler was saying. 'The Führer' – this, Claus gathered, was how Nazis habitually referred to Hitler – 'will be coming to Berlin shortly. If the Red Front could get near enough to assassinate him, they would try it. Meanwhile they are doing everything they can to weaken the SS.

'Hauptmann, the SS will soon become the fighting force of the National Socialist Party. It will be a military order of Nordic men. In due course it will represent the élite of the nation, and as such the SS needs men like you.

'There is a place on my personal staff for a man of your experience and proven courage. Hauptmann, resign your Army commission and join me at SS headquarters'.

Claus was thunderstruck. At moments like this, he envied those of his colleagues who smoked. When faced with an awkward question, the smoker could always gain time for thinking of a response by taking a long drawn-out puff and exhaling slowly. He could even take out a fresh cigarette from a case and take his time lighting it up.

Claus had no such means of procrastination to hand. He simply stared at Himmler for some seconds, studying the pale face, the weakish chin, the thin moustache, the blue eyes behind the small-lensed glasses.

'I'm sorry', was the best that he could find to say. 'I appreciate the invitation, but I am a soldier and must serve the state. I cannot serve one party alone'.

'I respect your decision, Hauptmann, quite as much as I regret it. It confirms what I had never doubted, that you are a man of honour. I am sure that you are making a mistake, but' – Himmler rose – 'one day you may see that the National Socialist Party and the German Reich are one and the same'.

Out came Himmler's hand. 'Thank you once again in the name of the Führer and the SS for what you did. Get well soon, and good luck in your future career'.

Well, that had been a shock out of the blue. To his knowledge, Claus had never met any Nazis before. He had seen the party's storm troopers, the brown-uniformed SA men, parading in the streets, heard disparaging tales of their rowdiness and read plenty about the violence between them and the Communists. The SS was a new concept to him,

118

and he wanted nothing to do with any kind of party army. The very idea was anathema to his concept of a soldier's role.

Yet Himmler had been ultra-courteous, surprisingly so. There was no denying that the head of the SS was mildness itself, the antithesis of the political street brawler.

What the man had not understood was that Claus had not intentionally saved the life of an SS man. He would have acted in the same way had he come across a Nazi firing at a Communist. Indeed, he had not had any conscious thoughts at all at the time, reacting purely out of instinct. The idea of a political shooting had simply not occurred to him. When he did think about it, afterwards, he had assumed that the incident was an attempted robbery or a quarrel between criminals.

By the following morning, Claus had put the encounter with Himmler and the absurd offer from his mind. What he had to concentrate on now was persuading his doctors as early as possible that he was fit enough to be discharged.

Everything else went out of his thoughts that evening, when he saw Erika hurrying towards his bed.

'Darling!'

At least it hadn't been Oh, my poor darling.

Claus had been afraid that if Erika saw him bandaged and plastered in bed she would fall over him with a maternal outbreak of pity and concern.

How could he ever have underestimated her? Of course Erika was far too rational and level headed to behave like that.

Claus was pleased after all that she had come. Erika leaned over and kissed him, not on the forehead or the cheek, but fully on the mouth. She cupped his head between her hands, Claus's right arm went round her back, and any pain in his shoulder vanished.

Erika broke away and seized the chair on which Himmler had sat that morning. She pulled it right up against the bed, sat on it as closely to Claus as she could and took his right hand in both of her own.

The girl was comfort, the girl was calmness, the girl was commonsense itself. Only when Claus mentioned that the gunman he had tackled was from the Red Front did a moment of alarm break through in Erika's eyes.

The whole country knew about the street battles between Communists and Nazis, and anyone would be shocked at being caught up in that murderous feud.

'It's all right', Claus told her. 'He wasn't a very good shot'.

Erika stayed with him, holding his hand and occasionally stroking his face, until a doctor came by to look at Claus's shoulder. She kissed him then, on the lips, and left.

'I can see why you are anxious to go home', the doctor told him, his eyes glued on the departing figure. 'Don't forget, though, that you mustn't do anything to risk cracking open those bones while they are still setting'.

There's no fear of that, Claus promised himself. Apart from his need to stay in the Army, there were still steering wheels to be wrestled.

Every evening after that, Erika was there. The Albrechts came too, and colleagues from Department R. A note wishing Claus a speedy recovery was delivered from General Blomberg, and a man from the public prosecutor's office arrived one morning to take a statement.

The shot SS man was out of danger, but the charges against the Red Front gunman would be more than that of attempted murder. There was laboratory evidence connecting the same man to two political killings from the previous year.

Claus was exhausted by the time the lawyer left, but made his usual effort to show how fit and active he was. Every day, from his second morning on, Claus had asked when he could be discharged.

His entry wound healed surprisingly swiftly, and the doctor made a playful attempt at sounding resigned. 'All right, Hauptmann. I suppose I can't keep you here any longer. You'll only make my life miserable if I try'.

The daily pestering had paid off. He was discharged next morning.

120

Claus stayed only two nights at the Berlin villa before taking the train to Württemberg. Painful as it was to part from Erika, he knew that his mother was expecting to see him now that she had been told about his wound.

Once at Falkenstein, Claus was pleased that he had come, though it was a mild shock to realize that his mother was beginning to show her years. She held herself just as straight, but Claus could recognize the effort that this was costing her. He reproached himself for having stayed in the capital for far too long. In future, he promised himself, he would visit Falkenstein at least twice a year.

It was a delight to walk once more those fields and woods which had been such a part of his childhood. The food, too – why, it was like being transported back to pre-war years. Dishes appeared from the Falkenstein kitchens which Claus had not tasted for years.

Far too quickly, in his mother's view, Claus boarded a train back to Berlin. It was time to have his plaster removed. As eagerly as he looked forward to this procedure, his anticipation was nothing to the excitement which animated him at the prospect of seeing and holding Erika once more.

She was waiting for him at the Zoo station. Claus forgot the warnings about risking a cracking open of the damaged bones.

Next day the plaster came off. X-rays revealed that the bones had healed to perfection, and Claus prepared to return to his duties.

A yellow envelope arrived at Haus Schwaben from the office of the Prussian state prosecutor. It contained official notification that Claus would not now be required to give evidence at a trial. The Red Front gunman had succeeded in hanging himself in his cell. He's done everyone a favour, thought Claus.

Day to day life changed when Claus's father retired and withdrew to Falkenstein. With increasing age, his parents were now less interested in spending time in the capital. The old pre-war pattern of the year had gone, the accustomed social season was a dimming memory. So many of the family's old friends from the Kaiser's day were no more. Claus was left as master of the Berlin house.

He found that he was settled. It was not the life Claus had imagined when he joined the Army, but he was conscious of doing something of significance for the Fatherland's future, and that was what mattered. One day, he told himself, he would be able to return to regimental duties. This was the pole star to which he had to cling. Alone in the house, doubts would come. Would he be too old for active service by the time the necessity for it arose?

Stresemann, no longer Chancellor but now Foreign Minister, had praised and thanked Claus's father at his retirement dinner. A lifetime of selfless service, Stresemann acknowledged, had been devoted to the interests of the Reich.

What use was such devotion, Claus asked himself, when Stresemann and the others who directed policy were timid and unimaginative? Securing Germany's future would require boldness. Claus could see no indication among his country's parliamentarians that they were ever likely to become the initiators of events. They seemed content to let the Reich drift, buffeted by the will, and at the whim, of other nations.

Reparations payments were crippling Germany, with no end in sight. A new schedule produced by the Reparations Commission demanded annual payments of 1,707,000,000 gold marks until 1988, inclusive – seventy full years, or an entire human lifespan, from the time the shooting had stopped.

'Anything I said about the Allies before', commented Erika, 'was not harsh enough'.

Germany was not forbidden to manufacture or possess machine guns, but she was banned from importing or exporting weapons of any kind. It was a particular delight for Claus to assist the firm of Rheinmetall-Börsig in supplying machine gun barrels to Russia, concealed among shipments of water pipes. This illicit trade was part of a true joint production. The weapons were completed by the Russians.

Germany's Defence Minister, General Groener, was by now anticipating the end of collaboration with Russia. The Reichswehr's 100,000 soldiers had been so thoroughly trained that they were capable of becoming instantly the officers and non-commissioned officers of any new conscript army. Graduates of Kama, Tomka and Lipetsk now became in turn instructors to a new generation of recruits.

In November 1930, Groener succeeded in persuading his Cabinet colleagues that the Versailles military restrictions should finally be flouted.

It would mean the end of Lipetsk, Tomka and Kama, and the winding up of Department R. When that happened, the last thing Claus wanted was another appointment within the ministry. He had done his stint, he told himself. Surely they couldn't deny him a posting back to his regiment. Or to any regiment.

Towards the end of 1931, a dozen Arado 65 fighters, developed at Lipetsk, were flown from Russia and stationed secretly on airfields at Nuremberg, Berlin and Königsberg. Once the 1932 summer class of pilots had passed out, the flying school outside Lipetsk was quietly closed down. The Russians kept the by now outdated Fokker D-XIIIs, while all the newer, German machines were flown to the Reich. From now on, the secret air force would grow on home ground.

And now year Claus was racing a seven-litre supercharged Mercedes-Benz SSKL, the same model that had won a thousand-mile race in Italy, the 1931 Mille Miglia.

Expectations

'Look at this. One of the cypher clerks had it'.

The date was January 2, 1933. Rolf Albrecht, showing grey now, handed Claus a copy of that day's Berliner Lokal Anzeiger. The paper was folded to display an article headed 'Germany 1933 – a look into the stars'.

This was a side of Albrecht that Claus had not before glimpsed. He had always regarded horoscopes as something for silly young girls and certainly never to be taken in the least seriously. Could any of this mumbo-jumbo ever mean anything?

Claus could envisage many things for the coming year, but his visions had their origins in experience, not in anything as baseless as a horoscope.

Developments in motor racing, for example. The past season had been very satisfying. His Mercedes SSKL was in permanent racing trim, and had proved its value in all events entered. Claus had saved as much weight as possible on the car, and recognized that lowering the centre of gravity as close to the road surface as practical would improve the road holding out of all recognition. Without basic redesign, this would prove impossible for the private owner. Claus had made appropriate suggestions to Mercedes, and was assured that new cars were already on the drawing board.

Then there was Department R. Having served their purpose, the department's installations in Russia had been wound up, and Claus was dealing with what he hoped would be for him the end of paperwork. Krupp had developed tanks at Kama, 300 pilots had been taught to fly at Lipetsk, aircraft were waiting for them at secret locations and the Army now had anti-tank guns and new artillery. To be posted to a regiment, that was what Claus hoped for in this new year.

The Lokal Anzeiger's horoscope was not concerned with personal fortunes, but with the future of the nation. Despite the continuing grip of worldwide recession, Germany, it was predicted, would recover from it 'better than other countries'. How, Claus wondered, could anyone foresee that?

'A general upswing, above all in prosperity'. It all seemed most unlikely. The Reich had by a long way the highest suicide rate in Europe, and Claus had himself seen a restaurateur on the Kurfürstendamm who was offering meals on easy payments.

'Unexpectedly favourable circumstances'. 'All the influences point to a new Germany'. 'We can see unmistakably that the trend will be upwards, once clever and energetic men take up new posts'.

'Who', Claus asked Albrecht, 'are the clever and energetic men?'

'Well, enough people have had a go at government and no one seems able to pull Germany round. It's time for someone else to be given a shot. It's probably either Hitler or, if things get much worse, the Communists'.

The idea was appalling.

Between 1919 and the end of 1932, Germany had had no fewer than fifteen different elected governments. Moscow's persistent wooing in pursuit of military commitment had led nowhere. The frequent changes in the offices of Chancellor and Foreign Minister were unsettling to the Kremlin. Pledges made by one government might not be upheld by its successor. The Russians needed stability in Germany.

The German people too needed stability. They were meanwhile undergoing yet another round of inflation as a consequence of the worldwide depression unloosed in 1929. Money was not being devalued at the same farcical rate as in 1923, but gross national product had sunk by forty per cent since 1929 and banks collapsed.

Claus could see the effects of all this for himself. Visits to Wedding brought him face to face with loose groups of grey faced men, workers without work, who lounged on street corners in attitudes of hopelessness and resentment.

Every day, 90,000 court orders for payment of debts were being made and 10,000 declarations of insolvency sworn. Bailiffs were distraining thousands upon thousands of goods without effect. Hungry

126

mobs stormed grocery shops and fuel stores. The number of unemployed was reaching seven million, with twenty-three million Germans living on public funds.

The Nazis had been the strongest party in the Reichstag for six months already, though without an absolute majority. On January 30, President Hindenburg accepted the inevitable and installed Hitler in office as Chancellor.

Nearly thirteen years had passed since Victor Kopp's first recorded approach in Berlin about war on Poland. For nearly thirteen years Moscow had made unremitting efforts to draw Germany into a war of aggression. Successive German governments and, crucially, the Army had consistently resisted these blandishments.

Now Hitler was Chancellor. The question which occupied Claus, which occupied not just Department R but the entire ministry, was whether Stalin had found a willing playmate.

That evening, Claus became caught up in a noisy, celebrating crowd on the streets. Column after column of SA men, the Nazi Party storm troopers, marched into the Government quarter through the Brandenburg Gate carrying flaming torches, then wheeled right onto the Wilhelmstrasse and past the Reich Chancellery. Everywhere, youngsters had climbed trees and lampposts and were clinging there for a clear view. Even the windows of the French and Japanese embassies were crowded with spectators. There was singing and a great deal of chanting and hooraying.

Claus went home in unusually thoughtful mood. At the Chancellery, lights continued to burn late into the night.

Hitler, a wounded and decorated veteran of the Great War, had been introduced to politics by the Army. In 1919 he was ordered by Army Headquarters in Munich to attend a meeting of the small German Workers' Party and report on its members, aims and methods. It was the same sort of thing that Claus had done when sent to observe Lenin's meeting at Zürich.

When the Army was compelled to reduce its numbers to 100,000, Hitler was discharged and became head of propaganda for the German

Workers' Party. General Ritter von Epp, commander of the 7th Infantry Division, provided a loan of 60,000 marks to buy a newspaper for conversion into the party's main propaganda medium.

Many of Claus's colleagues at the ministry declared that they despised the former corporal and his hooligan storm troops. Others insisted that Hitler was one of their own, an Army man. It was the Army which had put Hitler into politics. Surely he would do plenty now for the Army.

'It's better than the Communists', insisted Albrecht.

'That wouldn't be hard', Claus told him, 'but a great many people don't seem to like Hitler or the Nazis'.

'Well, I can certainly understand that, but Hitler should be good for us. He's an Army man from the ground up'.

Claus was not so sure. 'From what I've heard, those SA people seem to think they ought to become the Army themselves'.

'What?'

'That's what I've heard. Like the Red Army. A political instrument of the ruling party. It would mean we'd be scrapped. Or turned into SA men'.

'For that to happen', objected Albrecht, 'the Nazis would need to be the only party in the country'.

Well, that at least was reassuring. The Reich had some forty political parties.

It began on March 23, when the Nazis forced through the Reichstag a bill giving the new government emergency powers. Hitler at once set about installing himself, like Stalin, as sole dictator of his country.

First the Communist Party was banned, then the Social Democrat Party outlawed as 'a party hostile to the State and the people'. Other parties soon took the hint and disbanded voluntarily, one after the other. In the end, the founding of new political parties and the reorganization of old ones were forbidden. The Nazis were now the sole power in the state.

128

For his part, Stalin did his best to remove obstacles from Hitler's path. Via the Comintern, he had already dismissed the leader of the German Communist Party, Ernst Thälmann, for 'wrongful conduct'. Thälmann's offence was publishing an open letter calling on workers to unite in a 'fighting alliance against fascism'.

Claus had often felt that the Kremlin's conduct had a surreal, almost Alice in Wonderland quality to it. Now that it had come so far in pursuing a Soviet-German military alliance, the Kremlin was not going to allow anyone to rock the boat. Litvinov, the Soviet Foreign Minister, went out of his way to assure Germany's Ambassador, Dr Herbert von Dirksen, that differences in ideology were irrelevant, even complaining that National Socialist propaganda had so far 'failed to distinguish between Communism and the Soviet Government'.

So there it was. Official. Communism and Kremlin policy were two different things.

This admission would have shocked the adherents of Communism worldwide, had they heard it. German Communists in particular – now outlawed, some under arrest, others in exile, on the run or in hiding – would have been even more shocked had they seen the note which the Soviet Government sent to Berlin expressing the Kremlin's 'satisfaction' that Hitler had secured those very emergency powers which he was using to suppress Communism in Germany.

Lieutenant-General Alfred von Bockelberg, the Army's chief of weapons procurement, visited Russia for three weeks in May 1933, at the express invitation of his Red Army counterpart, Marshal Mikhail Tuchachevsky. Once again, Claus found himself acting as travelling aide and interpreter.

For a second time, as earlier when he had accompanied Blomberg on his Russian tour, Claus came face to face with Voroshilov. The Soviet Defence Minister played the old tune again. It was essential, he said, for their two governments to pursue the same foreign policy objectives. Alexander Yegoroff, the Red Army Chief of Staff, told Bockelberg that 'the coming war' would be a war of chemical weapons and 'a war of motors'. The winner would be the side which was the most technically developed and could put the greatest number of advanced weapons into the field. For his part, Tuchachevsky stressed several times that Germany should build a fleet of 2,000 bomber aircraft 'to make her way out of the difficult political situation'.

Claus's thoughts during the early part of the journey back to Germany were dominated by reflections on their Russian hosts' eagerness for action. He could not put Tuchachevsky and the bombers out of his mind. Nor could he forget that Yegoroff had not said 'if there should be a war', but had spoken directly of 'the coming war'. The Soviet leadership had clearly already made up its mind.

Then anticipation of seeing Erika again drove these dark considerations from Claus's mind. The nearer they came to the German border, the more intensely his thoughts revolved round Erika and the things they would do together.

How extraordinarily fortunate he was, to be sure! His was the most astonishing happiness.

Erika was highly sensuous and the most delightful companion. With Erika he was relaxed, contented, totally happy. It seemed to Claus that when they were together, irrespective of circumstances, everything was all right. On the other hand, away from her no matters, however satisfactory in themselves, could ever be completely right.

How many years had the two of them already wasted? It was time to break down that silly reserve of hers. As soon as he saw Erika again, he would tell her straight out that it was time for them to marry. And this time he would countenance no objection. Erika's mother, he knew, would be on his side.

It was late when Claus arrived at Haus Schwaben. As soon as they reached Berlin, he had gone straight to the ministry and locked his notes from the tour in the Department R safe. It was too late to call at Wedding, and the Wolfs, like almost every other working class household, had no telephone. Claus would spend the evening preparing his words, marshalling the arguments with which he proposed to change Erika's mind.

Having dined, Claus poured himself a Courvoisier. His proposal to Erika must overwhelm her. How many times had she told him that she

130

would never marry? He had never been able to accept this, and surely her attitude was not natural. Erika's mother was retired from the factory now, and Claus would suggest that once he and Erika were married Frau Wolf should give up the apartment in Wedding and come to live with them at Haus Schwaben.

It was a different Berlin, a different Germany, to which Claus had returned. Materially conditions were improving; politically the signs were less reassuring.

Already during those few weeks that he had been in Russia with Bockelberg, trade unions had been closed down, the assets of the union movement's central bank seized and union leaders arrested. The Social Democrat Party, its funds confiscated, had sent its leading members into the safety of exile abroad. Works by 130 authors who were anathema to the Nazis were placed on a proscribed list. A Hitler Youth ceremony of burning banned volumes in public caused many to recall the words of Heinrich Heine from 110 years earlier: 'Where they burn books, they end by burning people as well'.

Hitler had made a broadcast speech in which he swore that Germany did not want any more war, and had assured the Polish Ambassador that he recognized the existence of the Polish state as it stood. On the other hand, he had given an interview to Sir John Fraser from the Daily Telegraph in which he admitted that Germany's fate depended on the question of her eastern borders,

Unemployment was coming down, with the motor industry in particular taking on a great number of new workers. Companies were being encouraged to invest by granting tax relief on the purchase of new machinery, and Hitler had established an industrial injuries compensation fund. A billion marks had been set aside for public works, including the erection of housing estates, and new laws were set to secure the future of agriculture. Nearly all farmers were heavily in debt, and regulations were being drawn up to write off their obligations and see that farms were not broken up by being taken into the possession of banks and moneylenders.

Falkenstein was not encumbered, though survival had been a close call during the unimaginable inflation of ten years earlier.

Claus had still to learn of some of these developments. Though he was tired after his journey, anticipation of seeing Erika tomorrow and rehearsal of what he would say to her would, he knew, prevent him from falling quickly into sleep. He decided that before going to bed he would after all not postpone the task but look now at the mail which had accumulated during his absence. The glass of Courvoisier went with him into his study, where he went to work with a paper knife.

A bank statement and a grocer's bill were not favoured with attention, but there was a letter from Falkenstein and this time it was not his mother but his father who had written it. Claus read not just with interest but with positive enjoyment. He was amused by his father's remark that he found himself so busy in retirement that he wondered how on earth before he had ever had time to go to work at the Foreign Office. Evidently the old boy was fighting fit and enjoying himself. His mother, too, was well, and Inge was expecting her third child.

A magazine subscription renewal, an electricity bill. Nothing Claus would call bedtime reading.

One envelope did not bear a stamp. Nor was there a note of the sender's identity on the reverse. Odd.

His address had been typewritten, but the letter which he took out was unmistakably in Erika's hand. She addressed him as 'My darling'. Claus cursed himself for not having opened his mail earlier. For hours he had been sitting in the house, this precious communication from the woman he loved right there within easy reach. And he had not known.

'The fact that you are reading this means that I am in Russia'. Had he read this wrongly, or had Erika become confused? He was the one who had been in Russia. He read the first sentence again. Yes, that was what it said. 'The fact that you are reading this means that I am in Russia. I am giving this letter to a friend who has promised to deliver it to your house as soon as he receives word that I have arrived safely'.

Arrived safely?

'I am a Communist. Did you know that, darling? I sometimes thought that you must know it, but of course you never said anything. I have been an active member since 1920, and now that the Nazis have banned the party many of us have received instructions to save ourselves by escaping to Russia. I hate leaving Germany, and leaving you too, Claus, but there will be no future either for me or for my work as long as the Nazis remain in power. May that not be long! Then I can return and we shall be together again. I love you, Claus. I have always loved you, and I shall love you always, to the end of my days. It is only the cruelty of political events which separates us now, but never forget, my darling, that this is not a parting for ever. In Russia I and my comrades will be working to liberate Germany from the shadow which has overtaken it. Until then, my dearest darling, I shall be dreaming of you always, and be with you always. Do, please, always remember that. Just one thing, my darling. If you go to see my mother, please be careful. The Nazis are sure to be watching to see who her contacts are. She did not know that I was a party activist, and I told her only on the night that I was leaving. She was distraught, as you will imagine, and I know that she would be pleased to see you, but you must also think of yourself. You could put yourself in danger, and oh, my darling, I do want you to be safe. Live for me, as I shall live for you, and we shall see one another again in freedom. All my deepest love go with you, my dearest darling. A thousand kisses from your Erika'.

At first reading Claus could not take this in. Was it some kind of joke? But no, the handwriting was indubitably Erika's. He read the whole thing again, this time slowly, consciously allowing the significance of each of the words to sink in.

When he had finished, he sat for a full half hour without moving.

At some point he must have roused himself and gone to bed, yet never afterwards could he recall having done so. When the alarm clock woke him next morning he had an overwhelming feeling of emptiness which at first he could not understand.

Not until Claus was on his feet did he remember the letter. Realization hit him like a severe blow to the abdomen. For an instant he stood immobile.

It was a lifetime of soldierly habits which saved him. There was duty to be performed. Despite feeling as though in the grip of a great sickness, he readied himself automatically for the day and arrived at the ministry a few minutes ahead of time, as usual.

Claus had recorded exact details of all the people with whom General Bockelberg had talked in Russia, and also of the institutions they had visited. He had summarized every one of the general's discussions. These notes provided the factual framework for the exhaustive report of his tour which Bockelberg now compiled.

The day's duty over, Claus drove straight to Seestrasse. Damn any danger! If people were watching, they could make what they liked of his visit, but he was going to see Erika's mother, and that was that.

As he stepped out of the two-seater, Claus almost bumped into Frau Wolf. She was carrying a wicker shopping basket and walking with head down.

Before he realized what he was doing, Claus had gripped the woman by her upper arms. She saw his face, and all but collapsed onto his chest.

'Let me take your basket'.

Two tortured eyes looked up at him. 'No. Don't come home with me. There's no point getting yourself into trouble'.

'Nonsense!'

'It isn't nonsense. One of Erika's friends warned me. You can take my basket, if you like, but we'll not go to my apartment. We'll go for a walk in the opposite direction'.

There could be no argument when a determined woman simply turned away from one and began to walk back the way that she had come.

They had gone perhaps a hundred yards when they reached a café. Claus steered the obviously distressed woman inside.

They sat at a table for two at the back of the establishment. Claus positioned himself so that he could watch everyone passing and detect whether anyone displayed particular interest in them. In the hour that they remained, he saw nothing and no one to cause any anxiety.

Unsurprisingly, Erika's mother was tearful. The trouble with that sort of thing was that it was easily catching. Despite all his efforts, and Claus had always felt himself to be a master of self-control, he soon felt his own eyes burning with hot moisture.

Less explicable was the need, which the woman evidently felt, to apologize for her daughter. 'I don't know why she did it. She didn't get any of these ideas from me. Or from her father'.

There was only one way to deal with a mother's natural distress. 'Frau Wolf, if Erika was in danger, she's safe now. That's all that matters. We have to be thankful for that'.

'Is she safe?'

'Of course she is. The Russians will look after her. They'll regard her as one of their own. It's better than going to prison here, isn't it?'

It was not easy to convince her. Surely they couldn't keep people in prison just for being Communists? Not for very long, anyway. Not unless they had actually done anything criminal, like that Dutch fellow who had set fire to the Reichstag. Erika would have had nothing to do with anything of that kind. She was just a believer in an idea, that was all. Even if she were arrested, a short absence in prison would be better than not seeing her at all. She would never come back from Russia, surely? Never.

'She's alive and well, Frau Wolf. Just keep on remembering that'.

It wasn't the way that Claus himself was capable of feeling about it, but he had to give some comfort to a grieving mother. After all, this honest, hard-working woman had already lost her husband, and now her only child had gone. And yes, she was almost certainly right. Erika probably never would come back. The poor woman now had absolutely nobody. She could only wither away until dying alone, probably years ahead of her time.

'Don't come to the house. If you need to contact me, write to this lady. She is quite safe, totally apolitical. She worked with me at the factory, and will pass on any note'. The address which Frau Wolf gave him was in the Meyershof, one of those massive tenement blocks which

135

had given Wedding its bad name for overcrowding. 'You can suggest where and when to meet – for preference well away from Wedding'.

Despite Claus's protests that the basket was much too heavy for her, the unhappy woman insisted on walking home alone. Claus remained seated for a minute after she had left the café, then he too went out into the street. In the doorway he paused and scanned the thoroughfare in both directions. There was no obvious watcher and no one following the bowed figure which was already a hundred yards distant. No one was stationed in any of the doorways opposite.

Claus went home numbed. He stayed that way for weeks, little more than an automaton.

Erika a Communist! And she had never even put a single question to him after he returned from visiting Russia with Blomberg, though she must have been bursting with curiosity. That, Claus assumed, was what party discipline meant. Secrecy was certainly something which he understood.

Each morning Claus rose, bathed, shaved, dressed and went to the Bendlerstrasse as though he were a robot steered by a distant controller. At the ministry he performed his tasks as if sleep walking. At night he lay awake until the early hours, seeing Erika's face, feeling her touch, hearing her voice, wondering again at that little wrinkle in her nose when, in his indelible memory, she laughed.

Oh Erika, Erika!

It was at such moments, at three, four o'clock in the morning, when human resistance is known to be at its weakest, that the absurd ideas would come. He would resign his commission, he would emigrate to Russia, he would ask the Soviet authorities to reunite him with Erika. They would spend the rest of their days together, just as Erika had said, but not in Germany.

Always, in the morning, he knew that he could not do this. He was a soldier. A soldier served his country. He had served the Fatherland all his adult life, and could not desert her now. Personal happiness was nothing; the future of one's country was everything.

136

Voroshilov had been keen to renew the joint poison gas venture, but Reichswehr declined, and the last of Department R's interests in Russia was abandoned. This brought Claus's thoughts from his personal misery to the necessity of securing a posting to regimental duties.

The final act in the historic collaboration was a naval matter. Krupp's Germania shipyard at Kiel had designed a submarine for the Russians, with motors supplied by the Schiffsmaschinenbau AG at Bremen. The vessel was now completed. It was handed over, and entered service in the Red Navy as the S-13.

Before the Russian officers attached to the ministry returned home, they invited Claus to dinner, toasted him repeatedly in vodka as 'our comrade Claus Erlenbach' and presented him with an plaque carved to commemorate their collaboration. The illustration showed the S-13, marked with the words 'Made in Germany', firing a torpedo at a ship named Versailles. The Versailles was breaking in two. In Russian, the inscription read 'Ten glorious years of Soviet-German comradeship'. The 'Made in Germany' tag was a little misleading, since Krupp had been compelled by the Versailles ban to have the vessel built by subcontract at The Hague. All the same, it was a German ship.

For once, Claus drank too much. It was late when he returned home. His written application for a posting to regimental duties had been submitted that afternoon.

The rejection of this request weeks later upset Claus less than he had feared. No doubt he was still numb from the loss of Erika. Whatever the reason, he received his orders with detachment. He was to stay at the ministry, where his new task was to collate and evaluate reports from Germany's military attachés at her embassies worldwide.

This fresh assignment brought promotion to major and a move to a larger office. The promotion was long overdue, and in the normal course of events would have been his some years ago. It came to him now, he knew, only to confer some sort of equality of rank in his dealings with embassy staff, personnel at the Admiralty and the like.

Claus gave the plaque presented him by the Russians a central place on the wall of his new surroundings. Those years of cooperation with the Russians were, he reflected, the most important of his life. It had been, as his father had said, a matter of honour to do whatever was necessary to end the condition of defencelessness into which the Versailles peace had plunged his country. Claus felt privileged to have been allowed to play a minor part in these undertakings.

In Department R, there had been a small pool of orderlies to do the clerical work. Claus now had his own orderly in an anteroom.

His new status did not reflect any higher level of spending at the ministry. For now, the government was keeping the defence budget at the same level that its predecessors had set. With almost seven million out of work when Hitler took office, there was considerably less money coming into the Treasury than at any time in the previous history of the republic. Companies making losses instead of profits did not pay any tax, and neither of course did the unemployed. On the contrary, the millions out of work, far from contributing to the Treasury, cost the government money.

Already, though, there was a small drop in unemployment. The government policy of encouraging firms to risk investment and take on workers was an obvious success. Could there be anything after all to those crazy predictions about an economic upswing?

In October, Hitler took Germany out of the League of Nations. The league, it was generally agreed, was a waste of time. It had done nothing for Germany and showed no sign of doing so. The organization had been founded with a promise of implementing general disarmament, yet none of the major countries had disarmed. Tanks and artillery which Germany had surrendered as part of the 1918 ceasefire had not been destroyed but taken into the armies of her enemies. The Poles for instance now had German tanks, while Germany was forbidden to have anti-tank guns. And the Poles had twice since 1919 mobilized their forces along German borders, without any Hitler in office and without any moves by the timid German governments.

Now the Reich was beginning to stand up for itself again, and at the ministry there was a noticeable quickening to everyone's step, a brightening of the eyes, a sense of walking a whole inch taller.

Others, particularly outside Germany, saw withdrawal from the League as a warning of war to come.

Litvinov, on the other hand, was quick to confirm Moscow's support for the German action.

At Falkenstein the 1933 vintage was in, and with Germany already showing signs of recovery under the new régime, there was promise of prosperity at the estate for the first time in twenty years.

Claus had driven recklessly in all of his races that summer, and he knew why. With Erika gone, he was careless of his neck. What did it matter if he died now? What reason did he have to go on living? Anyone else could do the same work at the ministry that he had been performing. Better a quick death doing what he enjoyed most; it was, after all, the only delight he now had left.

At the Nürburgring Claus had really overdone it. He tried to overtake not just one but no fewer than three other cars going into the banked Karussell hairpin. Leaving his braking absurdly late, he dived past all of them on the inside, travelling simply too fast for the 180-degree turn. His heavy Mercedes shot up towards the top of the banking. Claus had to brake with all the force that could be applied, and the car all but went completely out of control. While he was struggling to keep the vehicle on the track, all three cars which he had just overtaken shot past him, and so did another two. Claus knew that he had been in fifth position; in one hot headed move he had tried to sweep right up into second place. The consequence was that instead he went down to seventh.

With the season over, Claus was able to give these events the reflection that they deserved. He had been stupid. Criminally stupid, even. Carelessness with his own life was one thing; it was quite another to risk other people's lives, and that was what he had been doing. At the Karussell that time he could have caused an almighty pile-up, killing four or five other drivers. Apart from their own lives, those drivers had families. Parents certainly, wives perhaps, and maybe children.

There could be no justification for killing others because of his own unhappiness. He would race more responsibly in future.

Julia

There was no doubt that the eyes behind the pince-nez were on him. Claus could feel their gaze as keenly as though the man were in front of him and not across the room. What on earth, though, was Himmler doing here?

This was a purely Army occasion, a reception given on a senior general's retirement. Yes, some top men from the Admiralty were present as well, but the sight of Himmler flanked by two aides was unprecedented in these surroundings. Was the SS now to be considered respectable?

Himmler's presence was the second surprise of the evening. The first had been when Major-General Walther von Brauchitsch went out of his way to speak to Claus. Brauchitsch had recognized Claus as the officer who was also a racing driver, and asked him about his plans for the following season. The general knew something about motor sport; his own nephew Manfred was one of the leading Mercedes drivers against whom Claus raced regularly.

It was during his short conversation with Brauchitsch that Claus became aware of eyes that were fixed on him. At the periphery of his vision was a dark shape.

The general wished Claus good luck for the future, and turned away.

Claus finished the champagne in his hand. Turning to place the empty glass on an orderly's silver tray, he allowed himself a glance across the assembly. Sure enough, the still figure looking at him from among a convivial group of generals was Heinrich Himmler. Blomberg, affable as ever, seemed to be entertaining the group. At Blombreg's side, Claus recognized Walther von Reichenau, who seemed to have become the Army's liaison man to the Nazi Party. Was Reichenau responsible for Himmler's presence?

Before the reception ended, one of the SS aides appeared at Claus's side. His black uniform, Claus noted, bore the insignia of a

Standartenführer, the equivalent rank to colonel. 'Major, the Reichsführer would be pleased if you would call on him tomorrow. Prinz Albrecht, ten o'clock. The Minister has given his consent'.

Reichswehrminister, that was Blomberg now. Was his acquiescence necessary before an officer could be investigated?

Of course SS and Gestapo knew all about Claus's long-standing devotion to Erika, his liaison with a woman whose activities (whatever they had been) would certainly be interpreted as hostile to the state, if not treasonable. They knew that Erika was in the Soviet Union, while he himself held a sensitive defence post. Claus was tailor-made for suspicion. What did it matter that he had known nothing even of Erika's political convictions, let alone her actions? Who would believe that?

It was to Himmler himself that Claus was summoned, and if Himmler was to do the interrogation, they evidently regarded him as a high level case.

On one thing Claus was utterly determined. He would say nothing against Erika personally and tolerate no criticism of her. They could deplore her actions – goodness knows what he himself wouldn't give to undo the situation – but Erika, whatever her errors of judgement, was the finest person he had ever encountered, and nothing, nothing, could alter that. Claus did not share her views, but then he himself was totally apolitical. Ideologies and dialectic meant nothing to him. He was a soldier with a sworn duty to defend the state. He would perform this duty no matter what government his country had – yes, even if it had a Communist one. He would tell Himmler that if necessary.

A year ago just the functionary of a political party, Himmler was now the head of an organ of state, with the title and rank of Reichsführer SS. It was as though a lieutenant had gone in one leap to being a field marshal.

Himmler in uniform, Himmler behind a mahogany desk, Himmler with black-uniformed SS men guarding his door and on every floor of the building – this was a different Himmler from the visitor in the plain civilian suit who four years earlier had sat by Claus's hospital bed. The quiet manner and the scrupulous courtesy were still there, but there was no mistaking the man's authority.

142

The eyes which had looked at him in hospital through those small lenses were still without expression. 'Please sit down, Major. And first, I should say congratulations on your promotion'.

Courtesy could be a mask. What had Shakespeare said? There's no art to find the mind's construction in the face.

'Major, I have to tell you that Heydrich is taking considerable interest in you. Any day now you may expect a summons to Heydrich's office'.

Besides being Himmler's deputy, Reinhard Heydrich ran the Sicherheitsdienst, or SD, the Security Service which he had modelled on the Soviet Cheka.

On his desk, Himmler had a folder directly in front of him. If that's my file, Claus thought, I wonder what they have in it about Erika that I don't know.

'So, Major, these days you no longer work with just the Russians. You now deal with intelligence from all over the world'.

The reports which Claus analysed did not exactly amount to intelligence, but he did not contradict the assertion.

'You have been an assistant military attaché. You have worked more or less at the centre of Army administration for' – Himmler opened the folder before him – 'fourteen years now. You have plenty of all-round experience, some at high level, and have worked with many senior commanders'. The eyes seem to look right into Claus. 'Though your closest connections are in Russia'.

There was only one thing to do. Look back at Himmler directly and without wavering. 'It depends on what you mean by connections'.

'Well, you have met Voroshilov on more than one occasion. Radek, too, and Tuchachevsky'. The eyes were still without expression, but the beginnings of a smile were appearing round the mouth. 'You know other people in Russia, Major, of whom I have only just heard'.

Claus did not, could not reply. He waited, his eyes on those behind the pince-nez.

143

Himmler raised a hand, removed his glasses, and leaned forward. 'Over the years you have acquired a mass of specialist knowledge – valuable knowledge, it must be said'.

A small cloth appeared – was it a handkerchief? – and Claus watched as busy fingers polished the lenses of the pince-nez. Back they went onto the nose, and the SS chief smiled. 'Major Erlenbach, I told you once that one day the National Socialist Party and the German Reich would become one and the same.

'That day has arrived, Major'.

And if I don't serve the Nazi Party, I am not serving Germany, thought Claus. Is that what he's trying to say?

Himmler smiled. It was a faint smile, but a smile. 'As I told you, Heydrich has been looking at you very carefully. You are, in fact, high on his list'. The eyes were resting steadily on Claus's now. 'I should add that you are also high on mine, and I thought I would get in first.

'I asked you once to join me on my personal staff, and you refused with the most honourable of reasons. I have not forgotten what you told me while you were recovering from the wound you incurred in saving the life of one of my men. As a soldier you could not countenance serving a party; your duty was to serve the state. At that time you could not have given me a better and more honourable answer.

'Major, I now repeat my offer. The SS is the backbone of the National Socialist state, and we need men with your knowledge, experience and integrity of character. There is a senior post here for you, and I should be pleased if you would accept it.

'Heydrich is setting up a foreign department in the SD, and you are one of the foreign specialists he is keen to recruit. The SS does owe you a debt, and if you join my personal staff you will be beyond Heydrich's reach'.

For a few seconds, Claus was speechless. Is that all Himmler wanted? No interrogation? No accusations? No arrest? Not a word so far about Erika, only a hint.

He could not sit there dumb for ever.

'Reichsführer, you overestimate my abilities. I am not a high-powered administrator, but just an ordinary soldier. The ministry is not where I want to serve. Now that the army is being expanded, I hope to return to regimental duties. That is why I joined the Army in the first place, not to sit at a desk. With all respect, Reichsführer, if I joined you, I should just be exchanging one desk for another'.

Himmler leaned a little forward. 'Believe me, Major, I do understand. During the war, I felt exactly the same. I was desperate to join the action and had to fight for a long time against my parents before they would let me become a cadet. But it is a question of age, Major. Since then, we have all become older, and regimental duties are best left to the younger men'.

Himmler's smile this time was a full one. 'As an SS officer you will be able to continue to satisfy your need for physical action on the race track. You have no need to fear that you will not be given the necessary leave. You have my word that you will granted every facility to pursue your racing career alongside your duties'.

Did Himmler want the SS to have a driver from among its own ranks to be seen competing in the more important races? Was that what Himmler was after? Claus as an advertisement for the SS?

'Also', Himmler went on, 'the Army is not exactly rewarding you handsomely for your years of service and devotion. Join me and you will have immediate promotion. On my staff you would begin as a Standartenführer. After that...'

'I'm sorry, Reichsführer. I'm an Army man. I shall stay with the Army and take my chances about the future'.

'I am sorry, too, Major. But of course I respect your loyalty'. Himmler rose and offered Claus his hand. 'The Army is very fortunate. I hope that your career works out as you wish'.

The whole thing was incredible. Surely Claus's connection to Erika made him politically unacceptable. How could he be considered for SS or SD? Was it possible that they knew nothing after all? They certainly acted as though they were omniscient, but perhaps they were a less efficient bunch than they thought themselves. Either they knew nothing of his connection to Erika, or they simply didn't care, now that Erika was out of the country. Logically, though, if they did know of the relationship, they should be keeping an eye on him. Well, if a job offer came from Heydrich, he would tell the man what he had told Himmler.

There was no approach from Heydrich. There were only long, long days at the ministry and even longer nights without Erika.

When Claus's orderly rang through from the anteroom it was to announce: 'Major Albrecht'.

'Send him in'.

Before the door from the anteroom opened, Claus was up out of his chair, his arm ready to reach out for his old friend's hand.

Albrecht's appearance took Claus aback. Never had he seen his comrade pale, and certainly never shaken. He was pale and shaken now.

Claus came round from behind his desk and grasped the other's hand. 'Rolf! What is it?'

'I'm leaving the Army'.

'Retiring? I thought you were going on for another four years yet'.

'I've decided not to wait'.

'But why? Sit down. Have a drink'.

Claus fished the cognac from his cupboard and poured two glasses. 'Why on earth?'

Albrecht emptied his glass in one. His eyes reminded Claus of a spaniel he had once seen wounded accidentally during a shoot. 'It's Julia'.

'Julia? She's not ill, is she?'

'No. But I'm leaving because of Julia'.

It made no sense. 'What can Julia have done?'

'It's nothing she's done, but what she is'.

Now it really made no sense. 'What do you mean, what she is?'

'Julia's Jewish'.

'But Rolf, she goes to church'. Sometimes on a Sunday, when the two men were going out afterwards for some shooting, they had all gone to church together, the Albrecht family, Claus and Erika. Erika had been a tactful non-believer who accompanied the others out of politeness, but Julia was a keen churchgoer.

'She's a Christian. Her family's been Christian for generations. But it doesn't make any difference. She's Jewish in blood, and that's all that matters. Like Mendelssohn'.

Though a Jewish family, the Mendelssohns had been Christians, and now Mendelssohn's music was banned. Yet how could anyone say that his works were any different from anything composed by Schubert, say, or anyone else? Claus couldn't understand the ban, and had heard how the conductor Furtwängler had written a protest letter to Hitler. Or was it to Goebbels; wasn't he in charge of the arts now?

Claus refilled his friend's glass. Civil servants, he knew, had been retired early if they were Jewish. And even teachers. It was all part of the Nazi government's policy, and an order had just come through applying this regulation to the forces as well.

'You're not Jewish, are you, Rolf?'

'No. It's just Julia'.

Even if Albrecht were Jewish, the order wouldn't apply to him. Those who had done front line war service were exempt. And Albrecht had not just served; he had been both wounded and decorated.

So far Claus had not heard of any Jewish officers falling victim to these new measures, but then he didn't know any Jewish officers. There had been plenty of them during the war, but none that he knew had stayed on in the forces until now. Somewhere, he presumed, there must be some, but in any case there was no mention of wives in the order.

'But why must you go because of Julia?'

'It's this edict that's just come down. It must be a matter of course for a German officer to choose his wife only from among the Aryan peoples'.

'But you're already married'.

'Yes, and I'm going to stay married. What they mean is, divorce Julia or leave the service. And I'm not going to divorce Julia'. Albrecht's face had become as white as the papers on Claus's desk. He swallowed his second cognac. 'They're not throwing me out. But I'm going, anyway'.

Divorce Julia? Of course he wouldn't. But were they going to dismiss civil servants and teachers who had Jewish wives, as well?

'What will you do?'

'No idea. I'm going home to discuss it with Julia. I didn't want to retire yet, and certainly not just when the country is looking up'.

Yes, and it had been Rolf who had expected so much from the upturn. Poor Albrecht! Claus could do little but sympathize. And poor Julia! He promised to visit the Albrechts that evening.

Claus had never suspected that Julia was Jewish. But what did it matter, anyway? A woman like that was an asset to any man, and Rolf was an asset to the Army. The two of them were of value to the country. It made no sense to exclude either from public service.

At the Albrechts' home that evening Claus found his comrade depressed, Julia philosophical. 'I'm trying to tell him to make the best of it', Julia explained. 'I'll soon get him used to the idea. He'll have his pension, and we'll just set about enjoying a nice quiet retirement'.

They drank to that.

The telephone call came early next morning. Claus's father had died in his sleep.

There had been no period of decline, no illness, no suffering. The heart had done enough, and it stopped.

Claus was familiar enough with death, but this was unexpected. It was not until he saw his father in his coffin, pale yet strangely youthful, that he realized the finality of what had happened. There was so much for which Claus was indebted to his father, whose rules for conduct were an invaluable and indelible legacy.

In everything he did, it was his father's definition that guided Claus: A gentleman is one who causes no distress to others.

The Foreign Minister, Baron Konstantin von Neurath, attended the funeral at Falkenstein, and there was a telegram from Hitler. Blomberg, now Reichswehr Minister, sent Claus a handwritten note of condolence.

Claus returned to Berlin with recent images vivid in his mind. His mother, dignified as ever at the funeral. Inge, doing her best but not quite succeeding in suppressing all tears.

Claus had lost Erika. He had lost his father. He still had the Albrechts.

And he certainly had motor racing. Since his driving had sobered up from the wildness of the previous season, Claus had achieved a number of respectable placings, giving works entries several hard fights and twice finishing ahead of drivers in more advanced machines. What was more, he had become a reliable and responsible driver, considerate of his machines, safe and consistent. His performances at the Avus and the Nürburgring in the early part of the 1934 season attracted an approach from Alfred Neubauer, a former racing driver for the Mercedes factory who had more or less invented for himself the role of team manager. For Neubauer, being in charge of the Mercedes works team was a way of staying in the game despite the fact that other drivers were faster than himself. Now Neubauer was promising to catapult Claus into the higher ranks of the motor racing world.

Mercedes had won the last French Grand Prix before the war – and in what style! The Stuttgart factory had taken the first three places in 1914, and now, twenty years on, was to enter the French event again. It was time to show again the superiority of German engineering. Not only Mercedes, but the new Auto-Union cars as well, now had something no one had seen before: independent four-wheel suspension. These cars were going to hug the road like no others, and their drivers would be able to take them through the corners that much faster.

Claus was invited to join the Mercedes team as a test and reserve driver. Neubauer intended to take two cars to the fast Montlhèry circuit a fortnight before the race for some intensive testing and practising. If Claus could secure leave for the period…

149

Of course he could. There was never the slightest difficulty about that sort of thing. The Army encouraged its officers – and other ranks, as well – to engage in representative sport. This would be the first time that Claus had driven on a track outside Germany, and he would have an incredible amount of horsepower at his disposal. Under his control would be one of the most powerful machines yet devised. Claus was growing more and more excited at the prospect as he drove to the Albrechts' home to tell them about it. The trees lining the avenues of Berlin were at their freshest, and it was one of those sun-filled Sundays which always made the capital so pleasurable for him.

Claus found his friends more sombre than he had yet known them.

'We're going to America'. At first he thought they meant for a visit.

'Julia has relatives in New York. They've offered us a home. All happened rather suddenly, I'm afraid. The offer came out of the blue. Neither of us really wants to go, but Germany will be no place for the children to grow up'.

'But this is not the time to go. The country's on the way up'.

'Not for us, it isn't. There'll be no future for half-Jewish children. Julia doesn't want to leave Germany any more than I do, but we must think of the children. Jews are being pushed out of all the professions. What future would they have here?'

'But this nonsense can't last'.

'Unfortunately it can'. It was usually impossible to disagree with Julia. Invariably, she was better informed than either of the two men. 'Have you read the Nazi Party programme?' she challenged.

Claus had not. Neither had Rolf until she had drawn his attention to it.

'Article Four: Only Germans can be citizens of the Reich. Only persons of German blood can be considered Germans, irrespective of religious adherence. Therefore no Jew can be a German'.

'But you...'

'Wait. It goes on. Article Five: Anyone who is not a citizen is to be allowed to live in Germany only as a visitor and will be subject to the laws governing foreigners. That means me, and if they consider the children are not of pure German blood, then it means the children too'.

'But how can the children be foreigners?'

'Well, will they consider them to be of German blood? What do you think? And Article Six: Only citizens have the right to a voice in the government and laws of the Reich, therefore only citizens can be appointed to any public office. And according to the Nazis, remember, citizens means people of pure German blood'.

'But Julia, surely they can't really mean that? When did a political party ever stick to the points in its programme?'

'When it was the only party in the state'.

'But surely that's the very situation where it doesn't need to keep any promises'.

Julia fixed Claus with a look he had not seen from her before. 'Do any of those points sound to you like promises? No, of course they're not. They didn't bring in any votes. They're not promises; they're threats. And does Hitler strike you as the sort of man who will not do what he says? I'll tell you something odd. A paradox, if you like. Democrats don't usually deliver what they promise, but I have a feeling that Hitler, who is anything but a democrat, will be the first Chancellor to do exactly what he said he would. He didn't put these things into his programme in order to win votes, but because he believes in them absolutely.'

Claus looked from Julia to her husband. 'I'm afraid I don't know very much about what Hitler says'.

'And you haven't read Mein Kampf, either?'

'I'm afraid not'. Everyone had heard of Hitler's book, and copies of it were to be seen everywhere, in bookshops, on office desks and even on private bookshelves, but Claus knew no one who had gone so far as to read it.

'I've read it', said Julia, 'and it's frightening'.

Albrecht had no doubts. 'Julia's right. Look at what they did to me. They wasted no time. The Army was told to get rid of certain personnel and did it, even if in my case it was only a hint. I could have insisted on staying on, but what future would there have been? They mean what they say all right, and we can't afford to take any risks with the children'.

Julia's relatives owned property in New York. They had promised Albrecht not only the tenancy of an apartment, but the prospect of a position in a commercial firm.

'But it isn't easy to get into America, is it?'

Julia as usual knew all the facts. 'The annual quota for immigrants from Germany is 57,000-odd, and we've had assistance from the HIAS – that's the Hebrew Immigration Aid Society'

'Never heard of that, I'm afraid'.

'Well, you wouldn't have. It was started when there were lots of pogroms in Russia, to help Jews with the formalities for entering the States. In our case, of course, it helps that I have relatives there. I put our names down, and HIAS did the rest. We just need to wind up things here now'.

It was going to be yet another parting from people to whom Claus had become attached.

He had not seen Julia this solemn before.

'It's the people staying behind that I'm sorry for', she told him. 'I think we're getting out just in time. It's going to be harder later on. Do you know how many Jews there are in Germany? More than half a million. That quota of 57,000-odd is going to be filled every year, with lots of poor devils desperate to go and simply no place for them'.

'I can't believe things will be that bad. Not every Jew will want to go. Far from it'.

'I should like not to believe it, but I'm sure this government is serious. Being treated as foreigner in one's own country. If you had children, would you take the risk?'

There was no counter to Julia's good sense. Claus was after all Thomas's godfather, and he felt some joint responsibility. All he could do was promise to visit his friends in America once they were settled there.

Only weeks later, Claus accompanied the Albrechts to the port of Wesermünde. On that day he could have been at Montlhèry with the Mercedes works team, but in the end had declined Neubauer's invitation. It had been the opportunity of a lifetime, but there would be many more races, and Claus had only one lot of friends like the Albrechts.

On the pier of the Norddeutscher Lloyd Line, Julia was in tears, Rolf grave and pale. The two men embraced, Julia kissed Claus and hung on to him as though he were the incorporation of the Germany she could not bear to leave. The children showed no signs of distress. For them, embarkation on the 51,600-ton Bremen, with her eleven decks, was an adventure. On her maiden voyage in 1929, the Bremen had, after all, gained the Blue Riband for the fastest crossing of the Atlantic.

Somehow, one never could find the right words to say on such occasions. In the end, one just had to turn away. Though Albrecht was a striking figure, he and his small family group were swallowed up quickly among the more than two thousand passengers boarding for New York.

Claus watched the Bremen heading for the open sea until he could no longer distinguish his friends at the rails. All at once he knew, knew with complete certainty that he would not see the Albrechts again. The knowledge alarmed him. Not the knowledge itself, but the fact that it had come to him out of nowhere. Claus had never had any premonitions or other experiences of the kind that are called psychic, and he found such spontaneous certainty disturbing. How could anyone possibly know something that had not yet happened? All the same, he knew, and that was inexplicable.

Claus returned to Berlin with a sense of loss which staggered him by being almost as keen as that he had felt at the death of his father.

It was all such a ghastly pity. There was no doubt at all that the country was being pulled out of the humiliation and misery that had

153

followed on Versailles. Surely his friends were wrong about things. If only they had stuck things out. Albrecht had his pension, no one was starving, and these measures against the Jews, surely they were just temporary steps until the country was properly back on its feet again.

Yet how could Claus quarrel with his friends' decision? The future of their children must always be the first concern of all parents. The Albrechts must be credited with knowing what was best, and they, unlike Claus, had no centuries-old family estate to keep them in the Reich.

All the same, people like the Albrechts were a loss to the nation, and from what Claus had heard, some of its best brains had already left the country. How could that help the general upswing?

There was no question that the positive trend was continuing. Unemployment was coming down sharply. The grey faces, the gaggles of lounging and discouraged men, were no longer to be seen on the streets. There was bustle and a general feeling of self-confidence in the air. Prolonged unemployment had a profoundly demoralizing effect, and by conquering it in no time at all Hitler appeared to have restored both the individual's and the nation's self respect.

Opportunities were being created for the ambitious, but for Claus there were no more invitations to drive a works Mercedes. No one was given a second chance to say no to Alfred Neubauer, and there were other, younger drivers, who would give years off their lives for the same chance that Claus had spurned.

Not for an instant did Claus regret that decision. What would have caused him years of regret would have been if he had failed to see the Albrechts off into their exile. They were saying farewell to their homeland, possibly for ever, and their departure must have been a poignant experience for them. Not to have supported his friends at such a moment, merely to indulge a personal passion, would have seemed to Claus the depth of selfishness.

The Albrechts had become special to him, and loyalty was fundamental, to friends just as to one's family, one's regiment, the Army itself and to one's country. No, missing Montlhèry was not important. There would be other races, plenty of them – and even if there weren't, what would that matter? He could not possibly have let the Albrechts make the journey to Wesermünde alone.

Let Neubauer go into a huff. Of course he was not used to being turned down; an invitation to drive for Mercedes was the motor sport equivalent of canonization.

Claus would in any case go on racing his SSKL. It was far from being a Grand Prix car, but in its permanent racing trim was now a good number of miles per hour faster than when it was first built. For everyday transport, Claus was still using his older supercharged two-seater, the 10/40/65.

In April 1935 Hitler extended the Kremlin a trade credit worth 200,000,000 marks – the third which the Communist régime had received from Berlin. After all, without the Russians Germany would have none of the new weapons with which she was now able to astonish and frighten the world.

The Luftwaffe, with sixteen squadrons already based at German airfields, was established officially that spring. Then Hitler reintroduced conscription with the aim of expanding the Army from ten to thirty-six divisions.

Foreign military attachés were surprised to see how many armoured cars, tanks, guns and aircraft were on display during Armed Forces' Day at the 1935 Nazi Party Rally at Nuremberg. With the great mass of the public – abroad as well as in Germany – Hitler enjoyed the credit for this swift creation of a new Wehrmacht. Few were aware how much Germany's military regeneration was due to the willing assistance of the Soviet Union.

Such assistance was given less eagerly to brother Communists. A revolt by some military men against Spain's Popular Front government led to the outbreak of civil war in July 1936. The Popular Front, which included Communists, appealed to Stalin for help. He was in no hurry to give it and appeared to do so with some reluctance. Arms were supplied only against cash payment in gold, and then in the name of the Comintern, not of the Soviet Union.

155

Germany and Italy on the other hand had no hesitation in sending troops to fight on the side of the rebels, who were commanded by General Francisco Franco. The world watched in fascinated horror as two ideologies – deadly enemies, it was believed – fought one another by proxy in Spain.

Stalin was now desperate to rescue his chance of the alliance which he had so long sought. He despatched Ambassador David Kandelaki, who had been Russia's envoy in Norway, as the head of a delegation to Berlin. Kandelaki introduced himself as an old school friend of Stalin and delivered messages in Stalin's name urging renewed talks for closer relations with Germany.

Claus was given the job of listening to what Kandelaki had to say. He saw through the story of the 'old school friend' at once. It was obvious that Kandelaki, though a Georgian like Stalin, was about ten years younger than the Soviet dictator. Claus initiated some research. He discovered that Kandelaki was an old Chekist who had made a name for himself with his ruthless cruelty as early as 1918. In this sense, Claus reflected, he was certainly a man from the same school as Stalin.

The whole farcical episode, Claus concluded in his report, showed just how seriously Stalin was pursuing military alliance.

Fulfilment

Was it on the Havelsee where Claus was rowing, or was it the Tegelsee? Wherever it was, there could be no sight more reassuring than the strength and gracefulness of his strokes as they slipped between the water birds or glided beneath the overhanging foliage near the banks, few pleasures more warming than to snuggle down in the cushions opposite him while the sunlight tipped his face and hands with liquid pale gold.

Or they would be resting on a bed of needles under the great trees of the Grunewald, she tucked into his arms to watch the huge shadows moving ever faster with the unstoppable dipping of the early evening sun.

At such moments – oh, would they but last for ever! – a cocoon of warmth enfolded her and she would know the rapture of ultimate fulfilment.

Then Erika would wake, and the bare walls of her room would stare at her with empty gloom and hopelessness. Claus, Berlin and the warmth would vanish as if someone had wiped them away with the single sweep of a cloth.

Training herself to suppress conscious thoughts of Claus was one thing; the subconscious longings which came in sleep were beyond mastery. Delightful as these dreams always were, afterwards they only made reality the harsher.

It was pointless to live in the past. What mattered was tomorrow. In Comrade Stalin's hands the future was safe, and tomorrow everything would be better, for everyone.

It had never been in Erika's mind that she would remain a primary school teacher for all of her working life. At some point she would secure a post teaching children of secondary school age, preferably those on the brink of university.

Thanks to the Soviet Union, this ambition had now been fulfilled.

They had given her an apartment – well, it was just one cramped room, really – and a position teaching advanced German to seventeen- and eighteen-year-olds at a special school for the gifted. It was a dream appointment. These élite educational institutions were something which other countries would do well to copy. They were, in Erika's view, supreme proof of the superiority of Soviet society and an ideal which it was necessary to spread right across the globe.

All of Erika's pupils were, by definition, exceptional; otherwise they would not have been at that school. Inevitably, though, there were always a few who stood out above the others, forming an inner élite among even this élite. At the moment Erika had two, a boy and a girl, who read Goethe and Schiller and Heine and discussed these writers' works in German as easily and exhaustively as though it were their mother tongue.

It was a principle that only German was spoken during Erika's classes. The curriculum was not restricted, which meant that almost any subject could be covered. Erika taught the literature, geography and history of the German-speaking countries and encouraged discussion of these topics, along with exploration of Marxism and Leninism. Karl Marx's book Das Kapital was a standard work; practically the first thing Erika's pupils did was to read this work and discuss its truths in lively day-long sessions.

What the authorities wanted was people who could converse easily on any subject in German. Elsewhere, there were similar classes to train advanced speakers in English, French, Spanish and Italian. To Erika, it was apparent that these higher level courses were not just part of an ambitious education system, but had been founded to fit activists for specific functions. Her own pupils, she assumed, would in a year or two become 'illegals' in Germany, Austria or Switzerland.

Erika had heard about the Bulgarian Georgi Dimitroff, who in the pre-Hitler era had lived undiscovered for years in a Potsdam apartment while he coordinated subversive activity among German Communists. Dimitroff had become something of a hero after being arrested by the Gestapo and tried for allegedly organizing the Reichstag fire. He too was in Moscow now, having been simply deported by the Nazis. It would be a privilege if Erika could help a young Communist develop those skills which would one day enable him or her to become a second Dimitroff, an even more successful Dimitroff, one who would, perhaps, bring down the Nazi régime. It was evident that the party had known well what it was doing when it advised her to leave Germany. The work that she was doing here was infinitely more valuable than anything she could ever have hoped to accomplish at home. They had told her that she should escape the Nazis for her own safety. Yet what was personal safety, when it was the cause, not the individual, that mattered?

Leading members of the German Communist Party were housed in Moscow's prestigious Hotel Lux. Erika had seen none of these prominent personalities since her arrival in Russia, though meetings with low-level exiles like herself were frequent. All were comrades in the great struggle, and Erika was happy to work with them. The only uncomfortable moments were caused her by a weedy pseudo-intellectual named Preiss, an individual of pasty complexion and dull eyes behind black-rimmed glasses, who walked in slouching fashion and never displayed a single original thought or initiative. Preiss was the archetypal unquestioning slave who made dictatorship so easy.

This tiresome fellow had already been a nuisance to her in Berlin. At party meetings Preiss had always contrived to sit next to Erika, invariably offered to accompany her home, persisted with ridiculous suggestions for outings together and seemed unable to absorb her firm assurance that she was committed to another.

Even so, in Germany it had been a fairly simple matter to deter and avoid Preiss. Now the fool seemed to think that their common exile must automatically bring himself and Erika together. Scarcely a week went by without her receiving an unwelcome visit and absurd sexual importunities. It was unnatural, according to Preiss, that a woman should live alone. 'You need someone', he protested.

But not you, Erika was tempted to shout. Even though parted from the man she loved, Erika remained devoted to him. If fate would not bring her and Claus together again, either in the Soviet Union or in a liberated, Communist Germany, then she would remain unattached. There could be no one else in her affections.

Despite her enmity towards the régime which Claus was now serving, Erika could not help reflecting on those sound qualities of his which made such a contrast with the ineffectual, pathetic Preiss.

She wondered, too, whether she now spoke Russian as well as Claus. He had told her of his school years in Russia, but she had not heard him use the language. By now, she hoped, her facility with the tongue might well be on a par with his.

In the early days, it had not helped that she spoke German all day with her pupils. Inevitably, this had slowed down her progress with Russian. The fastest way to master a new tongue was to immerse oneself in it completely, and this she had been unable to do. Outside school she spoke Russian as much as she could, in shops, on public transport and with her neighbours, but was usually too tired at the end of the day to do much more than go home, mark exercise books and go to bed.

With time, though, mastery had come. She had forced herself to work through and understand the articles in Pravda and Isvestia, and reading was always easier than understanding the spoken word. It had taken two or three years before she could understand everything said on the radio news. It was as much a matter of attuning one's ear to the sound as anything else. From the first, Erika had been able to phrase a question with faultless grammar, such as: Could you please tell me from which platform the ten o'clock train for Leningrad departs? She could say this without error, but understanding the answer given her was in the early days a quite different matter.

Erika had taken to visiting the cinema in the hope that this would help. To begin with, the pace of the dialogue had left her floundering, and she had found it easier to follow the old silent films of Sergei Eisenstein, such as October and Battleship Potemkin. It was a help to see the dialogue written, and there was always a time interval to digest what one had read before the next title came up.

Two anti-Nazi works by exiled German Jewish authors had been filmed in Russia, and Erika had seen them both. Professor Mamlock and The Oppenheims both dealt with the anti-Semitism of Hitler's régime, and Erika was enthusiastic about them.

160

One event was promised for Soviet cinemas: the British actor Charles Chaplin had made a film in America satirizing Hitler. To Erika, news of this film, called The Great Dictator, showed that the rest of the world was at last beginning to wake up to the dangers of the Hitler régime. This was encouraging, since so far only Communists had stood up to the Nazi dictator. Erika was looking forward keenly to the film's arrival in Moscow.

Erika had set herself the task of reading all of Lenin's works in their original language, and had already made a good start on this. She no longer envied Claus his early opportunity to learn Russian, as she had when she first arrived. She had also disciplined herself not to think about him too much. Erika had to abandon those wild fantasies she had that one day Claus would arrive from Germany to share his life with hers in the great work of building up the socialist paradise.

She had managed to suppress the longing to be with Claus, and for them to have children together, only by reminding herself that these children would be brought up not by the two of them but in a state crêche. For all Erika told herself that rearing and education by the state was the correct socialist ideal, she could not face the idea of losing any children of her own. The only way to deal with such conflict was to put all such thoughts from her, firmly and for ever. She must discipline herself to accept what the party taught in this, as she had accepted everything else. It was actually a relief that the possibility of children with Claus was for the present out of the question. Such a dilemma was now unlikely to arise.

Claus, of course, had known only the old imperialist Russia. Were he to come here now he would, Erika was sure, share her enthusiasm for the progress that was being made today in creating a society free from oppression.

What made Erika particularly proud of taking part in this great task was the fact that, while the other powers were giving in to Hitler, Russia alone was standing up to the Nazi dictator.

Then came Stalin's speech to the Communist Party congress.

It was March 1939, and Britain and France were watchful of Hitler after his annexation of Austria and forcing of the German-populated

161

Sudetenland from Czechoslovakia to the Reich. Now Stalin told congress that the Western powers were trying to push Germany into war against Russia, 'but the Nazi leaders have given them the cold shoulder'. Stalin added that he could find no visible reason for a possible conflict with Germany.

'No visible reason' for a Russo-German conflict. Then what on earth were Erika and her fellow exiles doing in Soviet Russia, which they looked on as the world centre of opposition to Hitler?

What was worse, it looked as though Hitler had taken Stalin's words to be a hint, a green light for further adventures. He had now moved in to occupy the remainder of the Czech state.

The Spanish Civil War ended with victory for Franco. Adherents of Communism all over the world had looked expectantly to the Kremlin, waiting for their great leader Stalin to put an end to the European drift to the right. Yet Stalin had already stopped support for Spain's Republicans. Even for ready cash, he would supply no more arms. Spanish Communists who had gone to Russia for military training were not allowed to return to their homeland. They ended their days in Siberian labour camps.

In Berlin, Thursday, April 20, 1939 was a memorable day. Among those congratulating Hitler personally on his fiftieth birthday was a Papal Nuncio. After the receptions, the biggest military parade in German history began along the new Ost-West-Achse. This new ceremonial thoroughfare, comparable with the Champs Elysee or The Mall in London, had been opened only the day before.

A huge grandstand was erected both for Hitler to take the salute and to accommodate numerous guests. For three and a half hours they marched or rolled past, the infantry and the panzer units, the gunners and the signals teams, the naval crews and the airmen.

The Berliner Illustrierte produced an extra edition dedicated to the Führer's birthday, and postage stamps were available franked with the day's date. For Claus, though, the occasion was memorable from a quite different cause. Orders took effect that day for him finally to leave the Reichswehr Ministry. He was posted as regimental adjutant to a new mechanized infantry formation stationed in East Prussia.

At last he could be a proper soldier again! And if he had accepted Himmler's offer, he would have missed this chance.

The Nazi Party and the German Reich, Himmler had told him, would become one and the same. Well, it seemed that the man had been right after all. Claus hadn't wanted to believe it, and had certainly not liked what he had seen of either the SS or the SA. The trouble was, he had seen too much of them. They were everywhere in the nation's life now. One couldn't go down the street without seeing a figure in one or other of the party uniforms.

All the same, the nation was doing so well, how could anyone possibly criticize? It was only the anti-Jewish measures which had disturbed Claus, and he had since learned to put these to the back of his mind. Politics were none of his business, and letters from the Albrechts confirmed how happy they were in America and how much the children were flourishing. Why, it looked as though the régime had actually done his friends a favour. One day, Claus really would take some leave and sail for New York to visit them.

Erika had been gone for six years, and the pain had ebbed. It was inexplicable, and he cursed himself for it as if he were somehow guilty of treachery, but the fact was that he no longer saw Erika in his memory with the accustomed clarity and the expected pain.

Now Claus's excitement at his new posting smothered the last of any yearning.

The image of Erika had stayed with him for far too long. The girl had blinded him to all others for what he knew now was a ridiculous period. It was only earlier that same year that he had finally abandoned his dreams of meeting Erika again through some fortuitous fluke of destiny such as an assignment to Russia which would bring them together. A life without marriage was something to which Claus was now resigned. Immersion in his work had helped him through the difficult years during which his obsession with the girl had threatened to tear him apart. Then events in Germany had developed at such a pace that they began to absorb his complete attention. There had been little time for wasting thoughts on what might have been or might yet be.

163

Claus knew that he was finally free of Erika's thrall when he came out to the old two-seater that he was still using for everyday transport, looked at it, and decided that it would have to go. The car represented the last physical and emotional link to his lost love, would forever be bound up in his mind with Erika and the journeys they had undertaken together. There was no time to arrange for the car's disposal now, and it would have to stay in the garage at Haus Schwaben.

Instead, Claus would take the SSKL with him when he reported to his new regiment. He had finished with racing now, and the SSKL had been restored finally to road trim.

Official trips during his years at the ministry had several times taken Claus into an Army barracks. Each time, he had needed to make an effort to suppress his yearnings for life in a regiment.

This time, his arrival at a regimental headquarters represented the achievement of his every dream and personal wish. Sweeping in through the great gate, he was aware of both an upsurge of joy and an inward sigh of fulfilment.

The regiment, Claus learned at once, was to be equipped with SdKfz251 armoured personnel carriers, a design which had emerged from a prototype developed at Kama. To date, none of these vehicles had arrived, so that the regiment was still training on foot, as had the Reichswehr in pre-Hitler days.

There was no hurry about motorization. For now, Claus had his hands full with all the everyday tasks concomitant on the establishment of a completely new unit.

The commemorative S-13 plaque presented to him by the Russians went with him to his new posting, but this time Claus did not hang it on his office wall. He placed it instead in a position of honour in his quarters.

Claus found the East Prussian landscape charming, with its lakes and its forests of birch. Though it was so different from his hilly and sunny Württemberg, he felt immediately at home in this part of the Reich. One of Claus's new regimental comrades had relatives who lived on an estate near Mohrungen, within driving distance of their barracks. 'You don't know this part of the country at all, do you, Erlenbach?', he asked. 'I'm going to visit my uncle and aunt on Sunday. Come with me. You'll like the place and them. They keep a good table, and there's fine shooting'.

The two comrades set off by car at dawn. Claus was introduced to his host and hostess, and with an hour to spend before lunch his comrade took him on a brief tour of the estate. As they left the house, Claus saw a young woman emerging from a room at the end of a passage. It was no more than a glimpse, and Claus did not pause in accompanying his fellow officer out of the building, but in the moment of that brief sighting Claus knew that he wanted to spend the rest of his life with that girl.

Would she still be there when the two men returned to the house, or was she a visitor on the point of leaving? Preoccupation with this question distracted Claus throughout his tour of the estate. They went first to the stables, where Claus could see at a glance how fine was the bloodstock. This was no surprise, since East Prussia was, after all, noted for the quality of its mounts.

Two horses were selected and saddled, and the brother officers set off. After lunch they would go shooting. The prospect no longer excited Claus. All he could think of was the girl in the corridor.

She was there when they went in to table, and was introduced to him as his comrade's cousin, Marion. The girl was still in her twenties, blonde and blue-eyed with a certain overall resemblance to Erika, but of less than medium height.

Her parents noticed at once that the girl was taken with their guest, and clearly approved of him themselves. They intervened in the conversation in such a way as to encourage their daughter to address herself directly to Claus. 'Marion, tell Major Erlenbach about the time you...'

When the table had broken up, his comrade put an arm round Claus's shoulder and laughed. 'The first thing they asked me was whether you were married'.

165

They cancelled the shooting. Instead, Claus spent the afternoon talking to Marion. The girl had an amazing sense of humour, was well read and demonstrated something which Claus felt was more valuable than the sheer intelligence which she also undoubtedly possessed: clear common sense. This, heaven knew, was despite its name rare enough. There was something else, besides. Claus realized that unlike most young women Marion did not speak of herself. Where the conversation of so many he knew tended to revolve round their own needs or wants, the word 'I' appeared to be absent from Marion's vocabulary. It was of the problems of others, and of ideas, that she spoke. Claus found this the most admirable characteristic he had yet encountered in a fellow being.

Three weeks later, they were engaged. Marion was twenty-eight, fifteen years younger than Claus. How she had not long before been snapped up, Claus could not imagine. There must, he told himself, be something wrong with the young men in that part of East Prussia.

'I have high standards', she teased him. 'You're the first one to match up to them'.

They would marry before the end of the summer.

Claus was overwhelmed by his unexpected bliss. What was the line in that Franz Lehar song? The sweet golden dream that one lives only once. Claus had believed firmly in the 'only once'. Now he knew better. It was incredible, it was simply unimaginable, but the fact was that he was experiencing inexpressible ecstasy for a second time.

Elsewhere, a marriage of a quite different character was being planned. Stalin dismissed his long-serving Foreign Minister, Maxim Litvinov, who was Jewish, and replaced him with the non-Jewish Vyacheslav Molotov, considered more acceptable to the Germans.

Moscow's Ambassador, Astachov, put out feelers in Berlin with an indication that there had been a special significance in Molotov's appointment – a significance which would work out to Germany's advantage. Did the two régimes, asked the Kremlin, entertain similar views on the future of Poland?

It appeared that they did, and a telegram from Moscow soon arrived at the Berghof, Hitler's house near Berchtesgaden. The Kremlin would be pleased to receive a German plenipotentiary.

There was a condition. Stalin insisted that any pact must be accompanied by a secret protocol designating the two countries' spheres of influence. A pact would be valid only if the secret protocol were signed at the same time.

Molotov sent a draft of the pact to Germany, and in return Hitler gave Stalin yet another trade credit. This was the second from Hitler and the fourth which the Soviet régime had received from Germany in the space of sixteen years. As in 1935, it was worth 200,000,000 marks. The Soviet Union was to supply vital war materials, in particular petroleum, phosphates for explosives, platinum, timber, cotton and feed grain.

Hitler, too, had a new Foreign Minister, Joachim von Ribbentrop. Germany's supplies were now guaranteed, and Hitler despatched Ribbentrop to Moscow to sign the pact.

The secret additional protocol on which Stalin insisted divided the spoils of war in advance. Signed by Molotov and Ribbentrop on August 23, this secret addendum divided Poland along the line of the rivers Narev, Vistula and San, as well as allocating Lithuania to Germany. Latvia, Estonia and Finland were left to the Russians.

Where south-eastern Europe was concerned, Moscow stressed its interest in the Romanian province of Bessarabia. Germany, despite its dependence on supplies of oil from Romania, declared its 'complete disinterest' in this territory.

In the course of a jovial celebration after the signing, Stalin loosed a tirade against the British. 'If Britain rules the world', said Stalin, 'then that is due only to the stupidity of other countries'.

The champagne flowed.

After his return to Germany, Ribbentrop reported enthusiastically to Hitler on his first class reception by their new allies. In Moscow, he had felt exactly as though he were among old party comrades.

167

Ribbentrop had grasped what the men in the Kremlin had realized years before: that in their thinking and actions, there was nothing to distinguish between Nazis and the Soviet leadership.

All the same, what on earth was Hitler thinking of?

For war production, Germany needed nickel, supplied by Finland. Above all, she needed oil, and for oil she depended on Russia and Romania.

Yet Stalin had secured without quibble Germany's assignment of Finland to the Soviet 'sphere of interest', as well as a declaration in writing of Germany's 'complete disinterest' in a strategically vital area of Romania.

It was always a mistake to be in a hurry when signing anything.

Erika and the hundreds of other German exiles in Russia were more than bemused at the rapprôchement between the two régimes. The news took their breath away.

In a world evidently prepared to capitulate before Hitler, the Soviet Union, they believed, offered the only hope of destroying the hated Nazi régime.

With the announcement of the German-Soviet pact, it was as though the entire universe had been turned onto its head in an all-enveloping surreal nightmare.

Throughout the Soviet Union, all books containing anti-Nazi material had to be removed from libraries immediately after the pact was signed. 'Immediately' meant immediately. Library staff were forced to work special overnight shifts to dispose of the offensive works before libraries were opened next morning. The films Professor Mamlock and The Oppenheims were withdrawn at once.

They won't show The Great Dictator now. The thought shot through Erika's head, and she was at once surprised and annoyed with herself. Where had such a frivolous reflection come from, and how could she be so superficial as to think of something as unimportant as that, when far greater matters were at stake?

168

Press and radio had reported the signing of a non-aggression pact. Did that mean that Soviet Russia had promised not to intervene if Hitler continued his imperialist expansion? Would the Red Army do nothing to stop the Nazi career of crime?

Erika's need to go outside was overwhelming. So long as she remained in her room, she would be unable to master the turmoil in her thoughts. It was the school holidays. Almost all the staff had gone away into the country, and there was no one handy with whom she could discuss her fears. Erika reached for her coat.

Of the many people on Moscow's streets, everyone else at least seemed to be going somewhere. According to age and fitness, they bustled or struggled along, each with an obvious purpose. Erika on the other hand simply wandered without plan. The socialist paradise had not yet progressed so far as to include much motor vehicle traffic, and Erika was able to cross streets in a way which would have been frankly suicidal in Berlin.

Moscow's avenues were broad, its architecture fine. On any normal day in late summer it would have been a delight to roam the capital's thoroughfares and its side streets. Today, Erika's mind and emotions were too overburdened for enjoyment. She could only walk and walk, disjointed thoughts chasing themselves round in endless circles as she struggled to construct a coherent explanation for the Kremlin's conduct.

Comrade Stalin must know what he was doing, but how could teaming up with Hitler, of all people in the world, advance the cause of socialism? There was no explanation, however abstruse and fanciful, which fitted any kind of logic.

The sun was losing height, the air turning cold. How long and how far had Erika been walking? She was in a part of the city unfamiliar to her.

By the time Erika regained her apartment, it was dark. She was hungry, but her mind was settled. She knew what she must do. It was not up to her to question the actions of the party leadership. Erika must leave it to Comrade Stalin. Whatever Comrade Stalin did, it would be for the best.

169

It was on the following afternoon that Claus stood with Marion to recite his marriage vows before the altar of the Protestant church at Mohrungen where his bride had been baptized. Claus, like most Württembergers, had been brought up a Catholic. The simpler service of the Lutherans was new to him. Claus had no strong views on religion, and was content that their children, when they had them, would be brought up in Marion's faith.

Before the marriage licence could be issued, Claus and Marion had been required to attest that they were both of pure Aryan blood. This proceeding recalled to Claus all the pain of the Albrechts.

Despite her years, Claus's mother made the long journey by rail from Falkenstein, through the Polish Corridor, to attend her son's wedding. Inge, her husband and children accompanied her. At least they had the Berlin villa for a halfway stop.

Claus had been given only a 48-hour leave. Something was afoot, and his honeymoon must be of the briefest. Claus was lucky, his CO had said, to have been given any leave at all. 'Go now while you can', he told him, and Claus left the barracks several hours before he was due at the church.

They went to the coast. The weather was glorious, the Baltic Sea that kind of blue which, when Claus had seen it on postcards, he had always suspected to have been artificially coloured. They took long walks and sat for hours on the beach, but did not swim.

'Your mother is a darling', Marion told him. 'And making such a journey at her age! Southwest to northeast of the Reich. It's scarcely possible to travel any farther and still be in Germany. She was so relieved, I suppose, at seeing you married at last. She must have despaired that it was ever going to happen, and just had to come to make sure that it was really true'.

'Wanted to see what sort of a witch had got her hooks into me, more like'.

Marion's teasing was one of the things that endeared her to him, and through it she had revived his sense of fun. It seemed to Claus that he had barely smiled since Erika had disappeared, and that was six years ago. Now he smiled a lot. Laughed, too.

Marion had brought him back to life. She snuggled against his chest while he held her, and wanted to know all about Falkenstein. So far he had told her little. He showed her photographs and described the vineyards and the fields, the woods, the hills and the house. One day Marion would be mistress there, but perhaps she would prefer to live in Berlin, a halfway house, as it were, to her own family?

For now, Marion would remain at Mohrungen with her parents, Her home was within easy reach of the barracks, and she would be more comfortable there in married quarters. Regimental affairs were a little too hectic at the moment for barracks life.

In line with the concept developed by General Guderian, Claus's regiment was attached to an armoured division. As Guderian's panzer forces advanced, they were to take with them their own infantry, artillery, pioneers and repair workshops. There was to be no lagging behind the tanks, and infantry was to be taken forward in half-track armoured personnel carriers.

By that Friday morning, when the Army crossed into Poland, the expected numbers of carriers had not been supplied in sufficient numbers. Many mechanized infantry regiments, Claus's among them, had to follow up behind the tanks in lorries.

The first shot fired in the campaign, at 4.45am, was a bomb launched at a Polish bridge by a Stuka dive bomber, the Junkers Ju87. The Stuka too had its origins in the vastness of Russia; it was a development of the K47, a two-seater ground attack aircraft of forward-looking design which Junkers had built and tested at Lipetsk. Stukas were to form the spearhead of blitzkrieg, that technique of air attack in support of advancing land forces which had been worked out, tested and mastered over the plains of Russia. The years of military collaboration were paying off.

In her Moscow room, Erika was paying no attention to the radio news that morning. Production statistics were being quoted at length, as usual, This, that and the other industry had made enormous strides under the guidance of the Communist Party and thanks to the wisdom of Comrade Stalin. Agriculture, too, was flourishing. The victory of socialism was assured.

The key figures of industrial output having been communicated in detail, the announcer had one more incidental item to add. German forces had invaded Poland at dawn.

Had Erika heard right? The Soviet authorities evidently did not take this seriously.

The majority of the Polish people, too, received the entry of German troops into Poland in completely the wrong spirit. Poland's mood was one of self-assurance. Hadn't frenzied crowds shouted 'On to Berlin!' when Poland's forces paraded through Warsaw streets on that year's national holiday, May 3? No one believed in the possibility of defeat, and the Warsaw government refused all discussion about revision of borders.

An excess of self-belief on the part of Poland's military had led to purely offensive planning. Poland's armies were drawn up solely for forward thrusts into Germany, with no reserves held deep, or other provision made for warding off invading forces. This Polish miscalculation could not have worked out better for Germany's invasion troops.

Claus's experience was typical. Tough resistance for the first three days, then once the breakthrough had been achieved nothing but a rapid chase of what was left of Polish forces. Panzer thrusts swept away all resistance. Horses, wagons, weapons, ammunition and equipment of all kinds was left strewn about the countryside by the broken Polish formations. Many a Polish soldier was able to escape only thanks to the cover of thick forests. Already, retreating Poles were backed up against the River Narev.

For Claus, it was breathtaking. How long had it taken in the last war to dislodge an enemy from defensive positions? How long to cross a river? And at what cost in men? Now their panzers destroyed the enemy in no time, and where bridges were down pioneers had fresh ones across to the farther bank faster than Claus would have believed possible.

172

Once over the Narev, and they were on their way to the Bug. Between the two rivers, the forces' way was eased by Luftwaffe bombers which hammered the opposition in advance. When Claus's regiment followed up, it found only a foe already decimated, surrounded by the familiar debris of destruction.

Until now, the army from East Prussia had been heading roughly due south. Now it swung southeast, making for Brest-Litovsk along both banks of the Bug.

In accordance with the guarantees which they had given to the Polish Government, first Britain, then France, declared war on Germany. This news, too, was reserved by Moscow radio for the latter end of its news bulletins. Statistics demonstrating the enormous progress made by Soviet industry and agriculture had, as always, absolute priority.

It took her a day to work it out, then Erika had the solution to the whole vexed problem in her head. Of course! Comrade Stalin had led Hitler nicely up the garden path! He had guaranteed Soviet neutrality in order to encourage Hitler into beginning his war. Now Germany would have to fight against Britain and France as well. The imperialist powers would exhaust themselves, and the Soviet Union would be the clear and only winner. The way would be open for the entire world to be liberated for Communism.

Never at any time had Erika felt such a swelling of admiration, even of affection, for Comrade Stalin.

Her euphoria was dampened when Preiss appeared at the apartment, his face red, his manner vulgar and suggestive. The effects of drink on this pathetic specimen only emphasized the contrast with Claus's soldierly dignity. Preiss had not been a drinker in Germany, yet now he seemed to have fallen for the bottle in a heavy way.

Erika spent some minutes attempting to discuss the war with this intrusive guest, to expound Comrade Stalin's masterly overall strategy.

Preiss reached out for her, fingers clawing for her breasts. Erika's right hand swept into his cheek with such force that it jarred her palm. Preiss was knocked off balance, the black-rimmed glasses flew from his

173

face. Dark eyes flared with anger and hurt as Erika thrust the spectacles into his pocket and bundled the pitiful 'comrade' out of the door.

That, she hoped, would be last she would ever see, or hear, of Comrade Preiss.

German forces reached the Polish capital after only eight days of fighting. Claus did not see Warsaw, even from a distance. The panzer division of which his regiment was a part raced past the city well to the east, unhindered by serious resistance because the country's defenders had in the main already been bypassed.

Claus's regiment was already moving eastwards of Brest-Litovsk when urgent orders arrived. The Red Army was invading Poland to claim Russia's share of the booty, and all German forces were to withdraw behind the rivers Vistula, San and Narev. These waterways formed the demarcation line, and Claus's formation was pulled back to Brest-Litovsk.

Polish soldiers who found themselves unable to flee into Romania or Hungary now began streaming westwards, preferring to become prisoners of the Germans rather than fall into Russian hands.

For Claus far more than for any of his regimental comrades, the arrival of Soviet troops at the demarcation line was an exciting, even a thrilling moment. Claus had known Russia in his childhood and spent ten years working in intense cooperation with Soviet officers. This meeting now between the two armies was, he felt, the culmination of his life up to this point.

The Russian commanders were delighted to meet an officer who spoke their language almost like one of themselves. It was 'Tovarich Erlenbach' all over again. In the evening, the vodka flowed, but first the newsreel cameramen and the press photographers arrived to record comradely meetings between Soviet and German soldiers, with not a bottle in sight.

Solidarity

Everyone agreed that the Poles had fought bravely and well. Poland's defeat had been due to her own over-confident planning, the clear technical superiority of her opponent and the overwhelming nature of blitzkrieg.

Soviet leaders had every reason for satisfaction. After almost twenty years of persistent effort, the Kremlin had finally harvested a part of what it had always coveted. The end of Poland and the creation of a common frontier with the Reich was a reality. It was, nevertheless, only the beginning. For Russia, the Baltic states and Bessarabia were still to come, whereas Germany had not yet made any claims to further territory.

Conquest of Poland had cost Germany 10,572 dead, with a further 3,304 missing. Russian dead numbered 734. Despite the greater German effort and sacrifice, Germany's share of Polish territory was smaller than that of the Soviets: 188,500 square kilometres against 201,000. Stalin was about to make even larger gains, and announced that 'a strong Germany is an absolute prerequisite for peace in Europe'.

Molotov told Britain and France that it was 'criminal to wage a war under the pretext of fighting to defend democracy when it is really nothing other than a war for the destruction of National Socialism'. According to Molotov, 'the ideology of Hitler's Germany cannot be destroyed by war'.

Pravda added its voice with the assertion that 'the British and French imperialists want to turn this war into a world war. They want to drown the whole of humanity in a sea of suffering and sacrifice'.

This was exactly how the vast majority of the Soviet people came to view events. Pravda, Isvestia and the radio told them repeatedly that this was an imperialist war, and the British and French were responsible for it.

Now Moscow confirmed in writing the Kremlin's willingness to ensure that Germany should want for nothing in the way of raw materials essential to her war effort against the Western powers.

Immediately on declaring war, Britain had imposed a sea blockade on Germany. Making use of the world's largest warship fleet, their Lordships of the Admiralty had every reason to anticipate being able within six months to render Germany incapable of carrying on her war. Thanks to his new trade agreement with Russia, with its promise of practically unlimited supplies, Hitler could allow himself a hearty laugh over these British efforts. A sea blockade of the Reich had become meaningless. What Germany was unable to import across the seas rolled to her peacefully along the railway lines running directly across what had until recently been Poland.

A German-Russian frontier had been created along precisely the line promised to Germany in 1920, 'south of Lithuania, approximately on a level with Bialystok'. Across this frontier the long goods trains now rolled unhindered, carrying from the east directly into the expanded Reich foodstuffs and, more significantly, the raw materials needed for the manufacture of munitions.

Just as the men in the Kremlin had enabled Germany to overcome the military shackles of Versailles, so now they made a farce of Britain's carefully worked-out blockade. Hitler had the support which he needed for his war in Western Europe.

Unlike Germany's soldiers and airmen, her sailors had made little use of the generous offers of help made by the Russians between the wars. Now they began to make up for what they had missed. As the only port in the Arctic Ocean to remain ice-free all year round, Murmansk was to play a significant part in Hitler's war effort. The area round Murmansk was placed at the disposal of the German Navy, which at once established there its Basis Nord.

North of Murmansk, at Polarnoje, the Germans were even allowed to build their own U-boat base, from which submarines could slip out into the North Atlantic for action against British shipping. In Russia's far north, Hitler's U-boats – like all other hunted German vessels – enjoyed their own haven of sanctuary, safe from Royal Navy patrols.

Even the Bremen had fled to Murmansk on the outbreak of war, being unable to make her way home from New York past a waiting cordon of no fewer than fifty-one Royal Navy warships.

As part repayment for these services, the Germans presented their heavy cruiser Lützow to the Soviet Navy.

Where help for Hitler's war effort was concerned, nothing was too much trouble for the Russians. Now the Soviet Navy offered Germany submarines for attacking British shipping. German experts declined this offer with thanks, rejecting the Soviet vessels as inadequate for the task.

Among the Russian people, November's Red Army invasion of Finland caused confusion. After the start of hostilities it was announced that a Soviet-sponsored 'people's government' had been established in Finland. Good, thought Erika. That means one fewer country within the imperialists' grasp and one more nation about to be carried to ultimate happiness through the blessing of socialism.

Then the bread queues started forming outside Moscow shops. Wait a minute. If bread was short, didn't that indicate that something somewhere was not going to plan? Why should food supplies to the capital be disrupted? Were Russia's forces in Finland perhaps becoming bogged down? What about that 'people's government'?

Finland's legal government, it appeared, was still in office. It sent an appeal for help to the League of Nations in Geneva. The league did absolutely nothing to help the Finns, merely 'condemning' the USSR for aggression. On December 14, the Soviet Union was expelled from the league. This was the last act of an organization which had been founded with so many hopes for peace, and whose pretensions to preventing further wars had been made laughable by a simple conspiracy between two governments and their military men.

Yet Moscow's long dreamed-of annexation of Finland refused to run to plan. With only three divisions, not more than sixty out-of-date tanks and barely 100 aircraft, the resolute and courageous Finns inflicted severe losses on the thirty or so divisions of invading Russians. Finland's most spectacular weapon turned out to be the bottle of petrol hurled with the cry 'There's one for Molotov!' Soon, everyone was calling this device the 'Molotov cocktail'.

177

Communists worldwide fell over themselves to promote Germany's war effort. British comrades assembled a 'people's congress' against the UK's 'imperialist war', urging workers to end the 'unjust' hostilities in Marxist-Leninist fashion – that is, by revolution.

Belgian Communists fought bitterly against 'the determined efforts of the British Government to draw Belgium into the war'. Their French brethren threatened to stage a revolution if Paris continued to reject Hitler's offers of peace. France's soldiers were urged to 'unite to throw out the government'. Echoing Lenin's seditious press, newspapers printed specially for French troops called on them to 'make an end of the butchery', to 'fraternize' with the Germans and 'make an end of matters as quickly as possible'.

Communist sabotage of France's war effort included the destruction of two hundred gun barrels – the anti-tank equipment of four French infantry divisions – and the explosion of French aircraft in flight. These aerial losses remained a mystery until three Communists at the Farman works were caught red-handed loosening the nuts of fuel jets.

The leaders of Poland's government-in-exile, visiting the USA, were denounced as 'agents of British imperialism, who are trying to drag the United States into the war'. This seed did not always fall on stony ground. From among the Poles living in America General Vladislav Sikorsky, Premier of the Polish government-in-exile, had hoped for at least 45,000 volunteers for the Free Polish Army being raised in Scotland. Only 722 came forward.

American Communists opposed to the supply of weapons by the US to Britain and France organized strikes which brought one third of the US munitions industry to a standstill.

Hitler was not short of friends.

A renewed trade agreement concluded with the Soviets in February 1940 guaranteed Germany further deliveries of vital materials to the value of 800 million Reichsmarks within a period of only eighteen months – by a long way the largest volume of such an agreement. As with earlier arrangements, the goods to be supplied were chiefly oil, grain, cotton, wood and the raw materials for munitions. The oil to be delivered was to include 100,000 tons of high-octane aviation spirit, essential for the Luftwaffe's campaign against Britain.

This time Stalin's enthusiasm for the war led him to devise yet another method of bypassing Britain's blockade of Germany. He promised to buy in third countries those raw materials which Russia was unable to supply from her own resources, and to pass these on to the Reich.

Claus's regiment was withdrawn from occupied Poland in spring 1940 and returned to barracks in East Prussia. Eight days' leave followed. It was to be eight days of delirious happiness.

It was seven months since Claus had seen Marion. Somehow, she looked even younger to him than when he had left her. They rode, they went for long walks hand in hand, they sat side by side and did nothing, simply bathing in the warmth of each other's company.

'Once the war's finished, I'll resign my commission'.

'Oh, Claus!'

'I know it's what you'd like. It'll be time to retire, anyway, and one day I really shall have to turn my attention to Falkenstein'.

It turned out to have been embarkation leave. Claus had never envisaged going to sea before fighting a campaign, but within a week his regiment found itself on board a small troopship heading for Norway.

It was no pleasure cruise. Gale force winds set the vessel lurching as soon as she had cast off, with nothing to be seen thanks to an unfortunate combination of thick fog and heavy rain. Very few of the regiment had been to sea before, and most were unlikely to wish to repeat the experience.

If only they had landed on the southernmost tip of Norway, and reduced the time they had to spend in this kind of torture. But no. They were among those whose destination was further north. Their ship just kept on going, past Stavanger, past Haugesund, past the west coast islands, past the entrances to magnificent fjords which no one on board could see,

179

The fog was every bit as thick when the ship slowed down and changed course. It was 5.15am, and they were entering By Fjord for a landing at Bergen. Coastal batteries opened up, and there was nothing for it but to crouch below decks and pray that the poor visibility was as much a hindrance to the Norwegian gunners as it was for their own sailors.

Claus's ship was not hit. She ran into Bergen harbour unhindered and the city was in their hands without fighting. All the same, coastal artillery had hit two of their escort vessels.

The Army's first task was to capture the coastal batteries. After that, it was a question of waiting for a British Expeditionary Force to arrive. The British would come, and it would be tough. Claus's regiment had been detached from its panzer division and sent to Norway with a minimum of equipment, no longer motorized and without its heavy weapons.

Farther north still, paratroops who had landed at Narvik found themselves under heavy fire from British ships. Fierce sea battles ended with the loss of all ten German destroyers sent to protect the Wehrmacht occupation. British forces landed nearby, and the paratroops, also without heavy weapons, were isolated.

Every single supply ship despatched from Germany to Narvik was intercepted and sunk by the British, whose destroyers and submarines were waiting off the coast to the south of the port.

One supply vessel did reach Narvik. The Jan Wellem defeated the British blockade by the simple trick of coming in from the north, behind the back of the waiting Royal Navy forces. She had sailed from Murmansk, bringing material from Russia round the North Cape and coming as far as Narvik before the British knew what was happening. The Jan Wellem was the only supply ship to reach Narvik, and it was all due to Hitler's helpful Soviet allies. Basis Nord was paying massive dividends.

Erika was more confused now than at the time of the Hitler-Stalin pact and the destruction of Poland. It wasn't so much the press and the radio, as the ordinary people. Buying a loaf, she overheard a man behind her comment in admiring tones: 'That Hitler, he's giving it to

180

the Anglo-French imperialists'. 'Yes', responded his neighbour, 'Hitler's the chap to sort them out, all right'.

Was it possible? Admiration for Hitler by the man in the Moscow street. There was no mistaking the mood. Hitler was the hero of the hour in the Soviet Union. It was a threatened British invasion of Norway, said Erika's newspaper, which had provoked Germany's defensive measures.

Further 'defensive measures' of the same sort were undertaken with Germany's invasions of the Netherlands, Belgium, Luxembourg and France. This time, Soviet reporting went to town. The successes of German troops earned large headlines. For the first time, Erika saw people queuing at the newspaper stands for the evening paper, the Vetshovka. This was certainly something new. Normally, people contented themselves with either an evening paper or one of the morning titles. No one bought two newspapers in one day.

Now they did. People were not content to wait twenty-four hours for the next bulletin. They wanted the latest news just as soon as it was available.

When Paris fell, there was universal jubilation. 'Fantastic' and 'marvellous' were the words one everyone's lips. 'That's shown the French'. It was incredible. Despite Versailles, Erika's sympathies were all with the British and the French. The logical thing for everyone, surely, was to hope that the Western powers would win and the detested Nazi régime be swept away. Then they could begin building up in Germany the kind of advanced society which was being fashioned here, in the Soviet Union. Erika would then return to Germany – but would Claus have survived the war?

The same question was occupying Claus at that very moment. With no supplies having come through the British blockade, he had been forced to carry out a snap inventory of the regiment's ammunition, to see how many rounds were available for each man. They would use what there was, and then...

Would he have found a soldier's death, or would it be a British prison camp for the rest of the war? And how long would that last?

181

Well, they would have done their best. They would fight until they could fight no longer. No one could do more than that. It was the honourable way to go down.

The battles never materialized. With France on the edge of collapse, British forces were withdrawn from Norway in early June.

Claus's regiment settled down to the task of transforming itself from a fighting unit into an occupying force. The regiment's surroundings, mountains, fjords and dark green woods, offered the greatest imaginable contrast to the plains over which they had raced in Poland.

Control of Scandinavia meant that Hitler's mineral ore supplies, essential to further prosecution of the war, had been secured. The Navy now had harbours in convenient situations for putting out directly into the North Atlantic. The Luftwaffe gained bases extending its range for both reconnaissance and action, enabling British shipping to be located and sunk more easily. Bombers operating from Norwegian airfields now had within their range the harbours, shipyards, factories and cities of Scotland and even of Northern Ireland – an impossibility for aircraft taking off from Germany or the Low Countries.

Using the blitzkrieg tactics learned at Kama, German armies achieved in five weeks what Germany's old Imperial Army had not managed to do in four and a quarter years: the total defeat of France.

On such days, while the world was staring in horrified fascination at these unbelievable events, Red Army occupation of Lithuania, Latvia and Estonia failed to create a sensation. Confronted with the spectacular German victory, there were few outside the poor Baltic states themselves who felt much concern about their fate.

The Kremlin had ample reason to be thankful for so much covering fire from its ally. With the Baltic invasions complete, Molotov sent for Schulenburg to express, as the Ambassador reported to Berlin, 'the warmest congratulations of the Soviet Government on the splendid success of the German Wehrmacht'.

As the only people still resisting Hitler and Mussolini, the British began to prepare themselves for the expected invasion of their country

182

by the victorious Wehrmacht. In mid-June, the London government called for Local Defence Volunteers (the later Home Guard), who would reinforce regular troops in resisting an invasion. Soon, no fewer than 1.5 million men had volunteered – nearly as many as were in the wartime Army itself.

As expected, Moscow's accomplices were not among these volunteers. A British Communist who had fought in the Spanish Civil War against Franco's forces was asked to draw on his experience and give the Home Guard tips for anti-tank fighting. He refused with the explanation: 'We don't support the war yet'.

A 'final appeal to common sense' is what Hitler called his peace overture directed to Britain in July. With its customary decisiveness, the British Government rejected this approach. Hitler waited for another three weeks, in the vain hope that the British would after all eventually 'see reason'.

Instead, the British demonstrated their resolution with air raids on Hamburg, several other towns and cities, power stations at Cologne and Dortmund, railway installations at Hamm and Soest, and the Dortmund-Ems Canal.

Thank heaven, Claus reflected, that East Prussia is out of reach of the Royal Air Force. Particularly now. That morning a letter from Marion had arrived by the field post. She was pregnant.

If it should be a boy, that was at least a guarantee of an heir to take over Falkenstein should Claus not survive the war. Until now, Claus had never considered personal survival. All the same, a child did seem to make living through to the peace desirable.

Meanwhile the Russians had suggested establishing yet a second base for the German Navy at Kandalaksha. Yet now that Norwegian ports directly on the Atlantic coast were in German hands, this particular form of Soviet help had become superfluous. Basis Nord was closed down at the end of July,

With France out of the war and Germany faced now only by Britain and her dominions, Molotov sent for Schulenburg and told him that it was time to discuss the matter of Bessarabia. And, said Molotov, 'the

183

Soviet claim also includes Bukovina'. Should the Romanians resist 'a peaceful settlement', Russia would use force.

What would that do to Germany's supplies of oil? Romania was her only other source outside Russia.

Molotov knew the answer, and not just to this question. 'This war', he told the Lithuanian Foreign Minister, 'will make us rulers of Europe'.

A model Communist

'**C**omrade Wolf, you are under arrest'.

The eyes, so dark a brown as to be almost black, were hard. The mouth was tight and thin, the black hair roughly cut and obviously greasy. The man was shorter than Erika, his serge suit so tight that every muscle was accentuated, as if deliberately for intimidation.

Behind him, two green-uniformed NKVD soldiers were looking at her without expression.

'It must be a mistake'.

'No mistake. You are Comrade Erika Wolf?'

'Yes'.

'No mistake'. The man pushed Erika back into the apartment and followed her inside. The uniformed and armed pair stepped behind him into the doorway. 'You are under arrest by order of the Chief Directorate for State Security'.

It was impossible. Erika had done nothing wrong, was the most loyal of Party comrades. 'But what's the charge?'

'No questions. Pack some necessary things at once and come with us'.

'I haven't done anything wrong'.

'No talking. You will talk when you are questioned later. Now pack some things or we take you with us as you are'.

Pack some things. The first thing Erika saw when she turned away was her copy of Lenin's work Imperialism, the Highest Stage of Capitalism. She had only just started it, and was anxious to complete her reading. Erika picked it up without thinking.

'No books, no papers. You bring some necessary clothes and toilet things, that is all'.

185

Erika dropped the book at once. On the table beside it lay the previous day's Isvestia with its article praising the achievements of the German Wehrmacht in defeating the forces of imperialism and reaction in Western Europe.

Apart from her bed, a table and two chairs, Erika's room held only a narrow wardrobe and a small chest of drawers. In the bottom of the wardrobe was the haversack in which she had carried the few possessions she had brought when fleeing Germany. She took this out now, stuffed into it a dress, a jumper and underclothes, and added hairbrush, comb and toothbrush.

Then she dressed herself. The three NKVD men showed no sign of being prepared to look away, so Erika did not remove her nightdress but put on some day clothes over it.

'Davai!' Hurry up.

Before Erika had properly grasped the situation they had seized her arms and were bundling her into the rear of a black car. The two uniformed men sat either side of her, the plain clothes man with the bulging muscles in front beside the driver.

The streets were empty. It was the middle of the night. Erika had heard that they always came for people at about three a.m., but that of course applied only to counterrevolutionaries and other criminals. It couldn't apply to her. This was some mistake and they would soon clear it up.

Something else Erika had heard: It was always possible to know when someone was going to be arrested. If the gas wouldn't turn on, that was a sure sign. They always turned off the gas for the apartment block in question to prevent the criminal escaping justice by committing suicide.

Erika had been asleep when the banging came at her door. No gas appliance had been turned on, and she had had no idea of the time, just stumbled to the door with sleep-filled head and hazy eyes.

Mistake, mistake, ridiculous mistake. The words went round and round in Erika's head. She could think of nothing else. This was all some absurd mistake.

186

They were driving and driving. In the Soviet paradise, street lighting was sparse. The car's headlamps made ghostly lights and shadows dance up and down, chase one another, give a glimpse of buildings and at once make them vanish, sending one's surroundings flying past in a stark nightmare of black and white.

Only now did it strike Erika that they were in a part of Moscow that she had not seen. She had expected to be taken to the Lubyanka, the massive NKVD headquarters on Dzerzhinsky Square, where this silly mistake could be cleared up quickly. But no, this was certainly not the way to the Lubyanka.

A solid wall appeared ahead, stretching for the length of a street. At either end a round tower, not high but of considerable girth. They drove inside through huge gates. Stepping into the broad corridor of the main block in this establishment was to go instantly from night into day. The interior was brilliantly lit and spotlessly clean, giving an overall impression of great brightness. Small square yellow tiles with grooved surfaces made a bright street to the distant far end. On the walls to either side, green tiles stretched up to above the height of a man. Set into these walls, along their entire length, were doors, one after the other. Erika did not believe them to be the doors of offices.

Induction into this establishment began with waiting. Standing helpless and bewildered, while rubber stamps were wielded, paperwork and signatures exchanged.

The NKVD men left. All at once, Erika was weary. As soon as they put her into one of those cells, she would lie down and sleep. Then at least she would be fit for the morning. She had been arrested, so she was to be charged with some offence. That meant a court hearing. She must be at her best for that, so that she could show them that this was all some crass mistake. Whatever they were charging her with, she was innocent, and it would all be cleared up.

They would apologize, and she would soon be back with her pupils.

A cell was not the next step. First, they took her into a reception room.

'Strip',

Erika was not sure what she had heard.

'Strip!'

It was unbelievable. It was outrageous.

There was no choice.

'Davai!'

The command to hurry was the most frequently used word in the guards' vocabulary.

Erika removed her outer clothing. The guards were amused to see a nightdress underneath.

'That too!'

This was humiliation. This, surely, was not what the Party intended. Even were she a guilty prisoner, this could not be right. For a woman of childbearing years, there were days when she would be embarrassed to let her own mother see her naked.

It was a body search. Grotesque, unnecessary, inhuman. A violation. What on earth could these animals expect to find?

Animals? Erika was appalled that she had allowed herself to think of comrades in such terms. Later, she came to feel that it was the animal world she had insulted.

When they had finished, Erika threw her clothes back on, numb with shock and abasement, Emerging from the reception room, she barely noticed the two groups of NKVD men delivering other prisoners at the spot where she had been handed over. Impatient now to be alone in a cell, Erika hurried with the guards who led her along the row of doors. A cell was refuge, a cell was privacy. In a cell she could recover and wipe out – at least, she would try to wipe out – her shame and outrage. She needed to restore that composure which would be essential when she appeared in court.

The guards stopped at a door, unlocked it and swung it outwards. Erika could not wait to be inside, to be solitary, a heavy door between herself and these creatures. A cell was sanctuary.

She all but broke into a run as she stepped past the guards. The door was swinging to behind her in the same moment that she realized her mistake. A thump, and the rattle of key in lock.

This was no cell. A closet would be a nearer description. It was possible to stand in it. One could lean against the wall. One could squat, and prop one's back against the wall. It was not possible to lie. A vertical coffin. The description shot through her head like a bad joke. Dog kennels is what they were called by those who knew them. Just as a kennel tended to fit round the body of a dog without allowing room for activity, so these human receptacles fitted round the prisoner, and no more.

This was Butyrka Prison, with 25,000 inmates a town in itself. The dog kennels were reserved for new arrivals.

While the Tsars ruled, Butyrka had been notorious for its oppressive régime. During the real, pre-Communist revolution of 1917, workers had echoed the storming of the Bastille by freeing prisoners from their cells at Butyrka Now, under the Bolsheviks, the institution had become even more brutal than before.

The effect of being locked in what seemed little more than a box, coming on top of the bodily visitation, was disorientating and crushing. Erika was still fighting to control her outrage and anger, struggling for her brain to regain some control, when the prison seemed to waken.

Guards' feet were striding overhead, doors were being unlocked and closed again. A practically unbroken drone of orders gave a softer background to the clatter.

There were feet coming down cast iron stairs. Many feet, growing louder as they approached, then tramping along past Erika's door, some with solid steps, many shuffling. It took perhaps a quarter of an hour before all the footsteps ceased, and Erika could sense that many people were now gathered out there on the other side of the door which shut her in. Enough people perhaps to fill the main hall along its entire length. That was how it had sounded, like a battalion of soldiers taking up positions until there were men outside every one of all those doors.

At least the activity had the advantage of rousing Erika from her shocked numbness. It gave her something on which to concentrate her thoughts, taking them from the outrage and anger at her own situation and the cramp that she was suffering. What were all those people doing out there?

It was a guessing game, and Erika found no answer. There was a roll call. Voices came dully through the heavy door, but Erika could identify from the pattern of sounds that names were being checked.

About an hour of this, then the feet began to move again. Away they went, past her door a second time, hundreds of feet growing fainter, until there was silence.

Erika's legs, particularly her ankles, were numb. She forced herself not to think of her discomfort but to concentrate on what she would say at her trial. The difficulty was that she had no idea what particular mistaken charge it was intended to bring against her. Yet whatever it was, she would be able to convince her judges of her complete innocence.

Erika was disciplined, loyal, obedient and enthusiastic. She had scrupulously done everything the Party had required of her. She had attended, and been a vigorous participant in, repeated seminars on Marxism-Leninism, the history of the Soviet Communist Party and many other subjects. She had read everything that she could find from the pen of both Lenin and Comrade Stalin, and gone willingly to every meeting which had required her attendance. She had taken leading parts in demonstrations on Red Square, had frozen half to death parading a placard calling for death sentences on counterrevolutionaries. Once she had carried a picture of a giant fist with the words 'Long live the NKVD, the armoured fist of the revolution!'

It had been a matter of honour with Erika to serve and to obey. She was a model Communist, the perfect party member.

Whatever monstrous and unjustified suspicion had been raised against her, Erika could easily prove her innocence. And no one who was guiltless could be convicted. This was not Tsarist Russia, nor was it Nazi Germany. Thank goodness she was out of there.

190

They came for her much later that day. Two guards led her along a series of corridors to a room in which a fat man in civilian clothes sat behind a plain table, a uniformed officer to either side. Fat men usually had jolly, or at least kindly faces. This one had the cruellest eyes Erika had seen.

'Comrade Erika Ivanovna Wolf' – in the Russian style she was known as daughter of Ivan, the Russian form of Johann, her father's name – 'you told your pupils that you were sorry that Charles Chaplin's film The Great Dictator would not be shown in the Soviet Union'.

Had that been a question?

'Yes'.

'What were your reasons and motives for saying this, Comrade?'

Erika was caught off-balance. Was this what they wanted to talk about? She had thought that she was going to be charged with some offence.

'I admired Chaplin's work. So did my pupils. I particularly...'

'Your pupils admired Chaplin, you say. What are the names of those who admired him?'

'I... They all did. I'm sure everyone was of the same opinion'.

'In every one of your classes?'

'In those where we discussed films at all, yes'.

'Which classes were those?'

'Well, I ... we talked about films in all of my classes over the years'.

'I see. Tell me, Comrade, what was it about Chaplin that you and your pupils admired?'

'In particular his exposé of capitalism in Modern Times, not just exploitation of the workers in America, but the government suppression of progressive and democratic movements, too. If you have seen that film, Comrade Commissar, you will remember that Chaplin is arrested and thrown into prison merely for carrying a red flag'.

'So you admired Modern Times. Why did you regret not seeing The Great Dictator?'

That was easy. 'Comrade Commissar, you know that I was an activist in the German Communist Party who was ordered by the Central Committee to leave Germany because of Hitler's actions against us. I had read that The Great Dictator was Chaplin's satire on Hitler and I wanted to see what he would do with the subject, whether it would be as good as Modern Times and his other films'.

Erika now saw that the cruel eyes were reinforced by a mouth which was every bit as pitiless. Had this man ever laughed?

'Comrade Wolf, you know that The Great Dictator was not shown because of a decision of the Soviet Government?'

'I didn't know, but...' It was silly, and she realized it. Everything that happened in this country, or did not happen, was the result of a decision by the government.

'It was a decision of the Soviet Government and you tried to teach your students to oppose that decision'.

'I didn't. I simply...'

'What was your father's profession?'

'He was a schoolteacher, like myself'.

'You have had one lover, Claus-Dieter von Erlenbach. What is his social class?'

Nothing was sacred. 'He is an army officer'. They must have known that.

'I did not ask about his profession. Erlenbach is a capitalist'.

'He is an officer'.

'He owns an estate employing workers. He is a reactionary, an aristocrat, a class enemy and a police informer'.

A class enemy? Claus was the most loving and tolerant of men.

'In 1929 Erlenbach assaulted a meritorious member of the Red Front on a street in Berlin, rendered him unconscious and betrayed him to the reactionary police. This comrade later died in custody'.

Claus would have acted in the same way if it had been a Nazi with a gun in his hand, but this, it seemed, was irrelevant.

Afterwards, it was not, as Erika feared, back to the dog kennel.

It was worse still.

She was taken to a cell made to accommodate twenty-five. It already held 108. The twenty-five beds hinged to three of the walls had been folded down to form supports for a raised wooden floor.

The only place for Erika, clambering up with her haversack, was at the front by the door. At the far end, a barred window had been covered on the inside with opaque glass, so that no sun or sky could be seen. Life in this cell was lived in permanent half-darkness. Some of the women seemed to be constantly on the move, crawling from one group of fellow prisoners to another. There was no walking upright, but it was at least possible to move, so long as everyone was sitting.

When they slept, or tried to sleep, movement was out of the question. Packing the floor from wall to wall, each woman had only a bare foot of width available. There were neither mattresses nor blankets, and Erika found that the continuous burning of the single electrical bulb prevented any sleep.

It was the same fat unsmiling official behind the table next day, when Erika was taken from the cell and led again to the interrogation room.

'Comrade Erika Ivanovna Wolf, you have confessed to anti-Soviet activity by encouraging opposition to decisions of the Soviet Government among pupils entrusted to your care'.

Confessed?

'You are of bourgeois origin and the accomplice of a reactionary capitalist aristocrat and class enemy. It is clear that you are dangerous to the safety of the Soviet Union. The sentence is ten years' imprisonment'.

193

Bourgeois origin? Erika's parents were working class, had worked hard all their lives. Before she could form the words to respond, two guards had seized her arms and were hustling her out of the room.

Ten years? It could not be true. That was no trial. Where was the court? There had been only an interrogation, and even that was nonsense.

Erika had done nothing wrong. Wanting to see Charlie Chaplin; was that anti-Soviet? And calling her bourgeois. The whole thing was grotesque. Such injustice could not happen in the Soviet Union.

It was a mistake. Whatever the other people in here had done, she at any rate was innocent.

The other women tried to make it plain to her. They were all innocent.

Erika could not take it in. Cramped as she was, she fell into the sleep of total exhaustion.

It was weeks later, and before dawn, when the cell door was pulled open and Erika's name called, along with a half-dozen others. Already there were sounds of feet outside, the same activity, it seemed, as she had heard on her first morning from inside the dog kennel.

'Out!'

First, there was the humiliation of another body search. Then she was ordered with her haversack into the great main hall.

Already prisoners were lining up on both sides. Some had small suitcases beside them, most had bundles. Others, arriving down iron staircases, were joining the lines from both directions.

Erika was ordered to fall in at the end of the line on her side of the hall.

Twenty minutes later, the long hall was filled from end to end with prisoners standing on both sides in rows four deep. Guards walked along the length of the lines, checking lists of names.

So this was what Erika had heard from behind her door.

Massive doors at the far end opened, and the quadruple lines of prisoners began to move out into the early morning under the muzzles of several dozen guns.

The journey which now began was a continuation of the nightmare. It lasted for several days. The prisoners were loaded into the cattle trucks of a long train. So many prisoners were in each wagon that it was not possible to lie, only to crouch. It was barely possible to breathe. Each day the train was halted, and the prisoners given water and bread. This was the opportunity to throw out the bodies of those who had died since the previous day's halt.

When the train reached its destination and the prisoners were ordered to alight, most fell into a faint as soon as they had leaped to the ground. They were no longer used to breathing so much air.

Erika herself had to fight against light headedness. Managing somehow to retain both consciousness and balance, she found herself overwhelmed by an impression of endless space. After the suffocation of the dog kennel and the cattle truck, it was an unbelievable release.

Erika was standing – just – in the middle of an empty plain stretching flat in every direction. Not a tree, not a bush, was to be seen. The frequently changeable skies of Moscow had been exchanged for the magnificently blue heaven of Kazakhstan. Yet sky was unreality, only an unreachable canopy. Reality was here below, with Erika no more than a tiny entity in a long column of prisoners passing through barbed wire into a gigantic camp.

This was Karaganda, which with its 170,000 prisoners dwarfed even Butyrka. Karaganda was not one camp, but a series of camps.

The barracks buildings – separate for men and women – were huge. For those arriving, there was nothing to indicate the multiple activities in the various sections of the complex. Besides copper mining and a complete copper industry, Karaganda included silver and iron ore mines and, above all, coal mines.

Butyrka had resembled a small town. Karaganda was a big one. This was more than a resemblance. Karaganda actually was a big town by virtue of being largely self-sufficient. Karaganda had its own farms.

These produced the food needed to keep the prisoners alive. Sufficiently alive, that is, for them to maintain maximum performance at work.

And no more.

If an innocent prisoner can ever be considered to be lucky, Erika was lucky. For no reason that she could ascertain, she escaped Karaganda's mines and factories and was placed in charge of a tog. This was the name given to an area cleared in the grass of the steppe, where grain was cleaned and stored. Thefts were a regular occurrence, and Erika's duty was to guard the supply.

Did the NKVD consider Erika to be of such probity that she was unlikely herself ever to steal or to collude in theft? Or was it a trap? Were they simply giving her the opportunity this time to commit an actual crime, so that they could add to her sentence?

Erika was on duty fourteen hours a day, seven days each week, but she could not prevent all theft. That would have required a guard who never slept or turned away for any reason. It did not take Erika long to discover that prisoners stole grain, pounded it into flour with stones, added water and cooked it into a sort of porage in tin cans.

Erika had her own tin can. That and a wooden spoon were all that she possessed in the way of utensils. She never used her can for cooking stolen grain. Hunger was her permanent condition, but Erika resisted all temptation.

Sometimes she asked herself whether she was being sensible. Would it make any difference? As soon as the NKVD could establish that grain had been stolen, they would blame her anyway.

It had taken Erika seven years of living in the Soviet Union to do it, but at last she had learned the most important fact of all. One did not have to be guilty to be punished.

Nothing demonstrated this more clearly than the nickname given to several of the camps within the Karaganda gulag. They were referred to as wives' camps because they housed the wives of men who had been liquidated. In the Soviet Union it was a crime to be married to the wrong man.

Winter, everyone warned Erika, was the time most to be feared. Women who worked in Karaganda's market garden, growing potatoes and vegetables of all kinds, were unanimous that three seasons of the year could be survived despite the fourteen-hour, seven-day week.

In winter, their task was to shovel snow into great heaps and spread it in deep piles over all the fields and vegetable beds. This undertaking was called snow preservation; its purpose was to counteract dryness by creating a kind of water reserve for the event that there would be no rain in spring. It was work which froze the body, numbed the mind and reduced the number of prisoners.

Erika was not at Karaganda long enough to experience winter.

When the guards came to take her to the nachalnik, head of the NKVD in her camp, Erika assumed that the grain thefts, of which she was completely innocent, were to be visited on her. Now she regretted not having eaten some of the stocks.

The nachalnik's orders were different. Erika was to be taken back to Moscow.

There was no overfilled cattle wagon this time, but an ordinary train with wooden seats. Had the mistake been discovered and admitted? Was she to be released?

Her escort was unsmiling and uncommunicative. This was no surprise. Erika had learned by now to expect no information or answers to questions from officials at any level.

The car into which Erika was bundled at the Moscow station went straight to the Lubyanka. It was said of the great yellow building with its neo-classical façade that it had the finest view in Moscow. Even from its cellars one could see Siberia.

But Erika had come from there. Being brought back to Moscow must mean good news. The mistake had been discovered. That could mean a pardon. And an apology.

Erika was locked in a cell with a half-dozen frightened women and no explanation. This did not look like a pardon. Not for the first time, Erika was forced to curse herself for her naïvety.

197

Next morning Erika was subjected to a body search. Being used to this ordeal did not make it any easier.

There were around thirty of them who were taken to a train from the Lubyanka that morning, several of them women. Erika recognized six or seven of the group. They were German Communists, among them the well-known faces of prominent party intellectuals who had been living at the Hotel Lux.

The party was placed in a single carriage under NKVD guard. Once they were under way, Erika discovered that every one of her fellow travellers was either German or Austrian, had sought refuge from the Nazis and been arrested on one pretext or another.

There was speculation among three or four of the party about whether they had been denounced to the NKVD by Russians or by their own German comrades. One of the women in the group looked across at Erika.

'I know who denounced you'.

Erika stared.

'It was that swine Preiss'.

For a half-minute, Erika could say nothing.

Preiss, of course. She had rejected him; denunciation had been his revenge. Preiss had heard Erika criticize the ban on anti-Nazi works and the Chaplin film. Nothing, after all, was easier than representing disagreement with an official decree as anti-Soviet agitation.

'Anyway', the same woman went on, 'the swine's had his own come-uppance'.

Preiss, it seemed, had since been arrested himself. As in all similar cases, nothing further had been heard of him.

'And serve him right', the woman concluded.

There was now lively speculation about where the journey would take them. One of the group asked the guards.

'You'll find out soon enough', was all the response he received.

198

When the train stopped and they were ordered to alight, there was general relief. They did not find themselves in any desolate part of the country, but at the edge of a city.

Erika put on her back the haversack which had travelled with her ever since she had left her homeland, and dropped from the carriage.

Waiting to receive them were men in the black uniforms of Hitler's SS.

The shock could not have been greater had she looked up to find herself facing a firing squad.

'Davai!'

An NKVD hand pushed Erika in the back. Sheep collected by dogs, thought Erika, as the prisoners were prodded towards the SS men.

'Davai!'

The train had brought unwanted German Communists to the demarcation line at Brest-Litovsk in some sort of tit for tat exchange. What might the Nazis have given Moscow in return?

Two days later, Erika arrived at the women's concentration camp of Ravensbrück.

All change

What on earth was going through Hitler's mind? First he ordered the Army to be reduced by disbanding forty divisions and sending their soldiers home. That was on the day after German troops entered Paris.

Then he ordered war production to be reduced significantly. The main weight of arms manufacture was now to be based on the requirements of the Navy and the Luftwaffe. Aircraft and U-boats were to have priority.

These measures were clearly aimed at Britain. Evidently Hitler foresaw no further large-scale military undertakings on land. He would force Britain into capitulation by blockading her at sea and destroying her war production from the air.

Now Hitler reversed his orders. Not only were no divisions to be disbanded; the Army would have to be expanded for 1941.

What had happened?

First there had been the Soviet escalation of demands on Romania.

Then the British Ambassador, Sir Stafford Cripps, had taken to Moscow a promise that Britain would guarantee Russia a free hand in the Balkans if she entered into military alliance with her against Germany and Italy.

A free hand in the Balkans? That would include Romania, with those oilfields indispensable to Germany's war effort.

Molotov passed on the details of this offer to Berlin. It made Hitler realize that Stalin could after all decide to change sides, now that the prize being offered was becoming increasingly more alluring.

Stalin, reasoned Hitler, had until now been in favour of alliance with Germany because this promised him more than a pact with any other power. Should the Kremlin pragmatists realize that they could now close a better deal elsewhere, they would without hesitation abandon their pact with Germany.

A revision of Germany's munitions programme was soon ordered. The more he thought about it, explained Hitler to his top commanders, the more he was convinced that the British were remaining so stubborn only because they were hoping for Soviet help. British determination to keep fighting could be explained only by something such as an assurance from Moscow. But if Russia were once beaten, then London's last hopes would be dashed.

Now Molotov arrived in Berlin for two days of talks. Thanks to the Royal Air Force, negotiations took place under ominous circumstances. Twice, Molotov, his staff, his hosts and interpreters had to break off discussions for retirement to the Foreign Office air raid shelter.

Molotov asked for a free hand to force bases for Soviet troops from Turkey. Hitler tried to divert Kremlin interest towards Asia, inviting Russia to join the Berlin-Rome-Tokyo Axis. The Soviet 'sphere of interest' in any new pact could be defined, he suggested, in southern Asia, towards the Indian Ocean. Molotov was not interested. Instead, he asked for more in Europe: Bulgaria, Hungary, Yugoslavia and Greece, in addition to Turkey. Then there was also, he said, the question of Sweden.

Within two weeks, Stalin not only confirmed these demands; he added fresh ones. The Soviet Union now expected support for expansion southwards between the Black Sea and the Caspian, as far as the Persian Gulf. Russia also wanted sovereignty rights in Baltic waters up to and including the Skagarrak between northern Denmark and Norway – in other words, as far west as the entrance to the North Sea.

Had Hitler been naïve to expect Stalin to be satisfied with the gains he had already made?

In 1937, the Red Army totalled 1,433,000 men. It was now well on its way to numbering four million. Within the past year, 125 new Red Army divisions had been created.

The Soviet build-up was in full swing, German arms production was sinking, and America was struggling to fulfil the rôle which President Roosevelt had defined for her, as 'the great arsenal of democracy'.

Stalin's adherents in the USA saw their function as differing from Roosevelt's vision. The White House was ringed permanently by protesters for 'peace' opposing US backing for Britain's fight against Hitler. Among them were to be found sailors with signs stating simply 'No convoys'.

One week before Christmas 1940, four copies of Hitler's War Directive No. 21 went from his headquarters to Wehrmacht commanders-in-chief. It began: 'The German armed forces must be prepared, even before the conclusion of the war against Britain, to crush Soviet Russia in a rapid campaign'.

Yet why would Hitler turn against his indispensable partner and supplier? To wage war against the Soviet Union, when he was already fighting against others as well, would be tantamount to Hitler's cutting through his own main artery. There had never been so much trade between Germany and Russia as during the first twenty-one months of hostilities. So far during the war, Stalin had supplied Hitler with large quantities of cotton, 1,500,000 tons of wheat, rye and oats, a similar amount of crude oil and thousands of tons of valuable ores and metals such as chromium, manganese and platinum. Several special trains had been made available from the trans-Siberian railway to transport 4,000 tons of rubber to Germany.

Deliveries from the Soviet Union were extraordinarily prompt. Hitler could be well pleased with his partner. New agreements were signed with Moscow during January, as a result of which the volume of Soviet supplies was stepped up.

Now a contract was concluded for the Germans to build a factory in the Soviet Union. The first payment of 10,000,000 marks in gold was to be made on July 1.

The handling of such international transactions – but not this one, of course – had become the day-to-day business of Major Rolf Albrecht, Retired, late of the German Army. The New York banking house which employed him was not the sort of bank which saw cash passed across a counter. Its behind-the-scenes function was to facilitate deals between governments and large-scale businesses.

Albrecht had proved his value to the bank in affairs involving Switzerland and the Scandinavian countries. He was settled and content, and he, Julia and the children were now American citizens.

Jewish emigrants from Germany had been permitted to take only 200 marks out of the country, but the Albrechts had been fortunate. Julia's parents had both died before Hitler came to power, leaving their daughter a sizeable fortune at a bank in the Swiss town of Kreuzlingen. Opening this account had not only protected her father's assets from the inflation which had twice hit Germany during the 1920s; it had kept Julia's inheritance out of reach of the Nazi government.

The Albrechts now had a house on Long Island, and were members of a country club. In mid-life, Rolf had discovered a new sport to replace the shooting which he had once pursued in the Schorfheide.

He played golf every weekend, congratulating himself that he had found the ideal recreation. It was a pursuit which could give him exercise in the fresh air until quite late in life, right until he was actually infirm. The stiffness from his war wound prevented his executing the sort of corkscrew swing practiced by able-bodied players, but he had developed a compromise technique, a reduced half-swing in which he did not attempt either to twist himself or to raise his club too far. He finished with a full blooded follow-through, all the same, and despite being unable to hit the ball as far as others who used a full swing, in time became a competent and consistent golfer. He was a popular playing partner, and he and Julia were well liked members of the club.

Weekends at the country club were, both to Rolf and to Julia, one of the principal delights of being in America. Their children were doing well at school and were meanwhile as American as if they had been born in the country. It would have been possible to describe the Albrechts as happy, but for their concern over events in Europe. Julia was as much devoted to her German homeland as was her husband. The eruption of war had cast both of them into emotional turmoil and an intellectual quandary.

They wished Hitler to be overthrown, but could not bring themselves to hope for a German defeat. Not, that is, the sort of defeat which appeared to be necessary to dislodge the régime. To expect peace to be made without Germany's being completely crushed was, each recognized instinctively, to ask for a miracle. Nazis would fight to the end, and that end would have to mean total devastation for Germany.

If only Hitler could be assassinated! Would his successor then be sensible enough to seek peace?

The Albrechts followed the war news with the most intense interest. The collapse of France had horrified them, making it seem that nothing could stop the Hitler juggernaut. For several weeks they feared that the British might come to terms with Hitler. The dictator would then be in the saddle for life, causing who knew how much further mayhem.

Churchill's speeches, recorded and broadcast in the US, had reassured and heartened them both. Churchill was now their hero. Julia had acquired a portrait of the Prime Minister, and hung it up in their home. All their hopes were now carried by the British. If the British could only stick things out, it might be possible eventually to grind Hitler down, so that his hated régime could be collapsed without resorting to complete destruction of the Fatherland. If this war had to be fought to a finish, each of them knew, the terms imposed on Germany this time would far outstrip even the Versailles vindictiveness.

Anathema to them both were the activities of the American Peace Mobilization. This clumsily named movement devoted all its energies to attacking the British 'imperialists'. It was all 'Support Stalin's peace policy', 'Stop the warmongering aid to Britain' and 'Keep America out of war'. Any criticism of the Hitler-Stalin alliance was dismissed as 'capitalist lies'.

One after another, reports of Communist activity came in from around the country. The Army had to be brought in to resume working after union leader Wyndham Mortimer halted production at two California aircraft plants. Edward Cheyfitz masterminded strikes in Cleveland which lost the aircraft industry aluminium castings worth 60,000,000 dollars. John Anderson, once Communist candidate for governor of Michigan, brought out 5,000 more aluminium workers in Detroit. Harold Christoffel organized seventy-six days of strikes which set America's destroyer programme back three months.

Though American weapons were still being manufactured in works which Communists had not succeeded in bringing to a halt, strenuous efforts were made to prevent ships sailing with them to Britain.

Quite inexplicable to Rolf and Julia was the wilful blindness of people fully clever enough to have known better. Soviet crimes were defended by many of those very people to whom the great mass of the public looked with admiration and on whose judgement and wisdom they might be expected to rely.

Chaplin's satire The Great Dictator was a wonderful antidote to such näivety. Though it had been completed two years earlier, the film was not released until 1940. The Albrechts, children as well, went to one of the first performances. The children did most of the laughing; at the end, their parents stood and applauded.

It was at the country club that Julia first heard of the Aid to Britain Committee. This organization was holding a rally in New York at the weekend, and Julia thought that she and Rolf should attend.

'I'm sorry', Rolf told her. Despite his inward hopes for British success in ending Hitler's régime, Rolf could not bring himself openly to participate in activities against his homeland. Actual support for Britain's war effort would be incompatible with the most elementary notion of honour. In any case, meetings of that sort were political, and officers did not mix in politics.

It was what Julia had expected. She, though, was bound by no such officers' code, and went to the rally alone.

The crowd outside the venue for the rally was hostile and vocal. The usual mob of Communist protesters was shouting its denunciation of British resistance to Hitler, and the familiar placards were being waved. The demonstrators were planning a march from New York to Washington.

Julia hesitated. Herself only a little over five feet tall, she surely could not fight her way through such a crowd. On the other hand, she was damned if she was going to be prevented from attending a legitimate meeting.

A tall man wearing a grey hat took her arm. 'You want to go in, lady? Come with me'.

The man strode through the mob as though it did not exist. Julia was inside.

Nothing Julia had experienced since Churchill's 'We shall never surrender' speech had cheered her so much as the two-hour course of this rally. It was clear that there was no shortage of sound common sense among the American people. Julia clapped and clapped, cheered and cheered.

When the meeting ended, the same tall man took charge of her again. 'Don't worry', he told her. 'We'll get through them'.

Julia looked at her guardian. This man had the same bearing and confidence as Rolf. Was he an FBI man? They kept an eye, she knew, on Communists and Nazi sympathizers.

The man's hand lightly under Julia's arm, the two emerged onto the street, tensed and determined to run the gauntlet.

The shouting had ended. No placards were to be seen. The demonstrators had vanished.

Participants in the rally looked round, looked at one another. 'They've gone to Washington already', said someone.

They hadn't.

While the pro-British rally was taking place, news had reached America. Hitler had invaded his Russian ally.

Suddenly, Communists worldwide were no longer opposed to Britain's single-handed fight against the Nazi dictator.

In the first six months of that year, some 2,500,000 man hours had been lost to US defence industries through Communist strike action. In April, eight Americans died during violence in the course of these attempts at sabotage.

Now Stalin's admirers in the US could not urge striking workers back into the factories and shipyards fast enough to turn out for Russia those same arms which they had been desperate to keep from Britain.

News of the assault on Russia threw Claus off balance. Russia was the one enemy which Germany, in his view, should not make. Germany's natural enemies, the ones who begrudged her any kind of world status, were in western Europe. The safest stance for Germany on the international stage was, he believed, in partnership with Russia. Claus had devoted most of his life in the service to this end, which wise men – he was thinking above all of Hans von Seeckt – had determined was Germany's best course. Claus wondered that the Führer, in whom normally he had every confidence, had chosen to quarrel with his most reliable and most useful ally.

Still, he must presume that the Führer knew what he was doing. There would have been a sound reason for the invasion of Russia. Claus concluded that it must have been a pre-emptive strike. Soviet forces had presumably been planning an attack on Germany, and the Führer had now neatly scuppered their plans.

The invasion did indeed look as though it had been a pre-emptive master-stroke in the nick of time. A number of Soviet divisional and corps headquarters close to the front were overwhelmed so swiftly that masses of plans, records, orders, maps and other papers were captured intact.

Intelligence officers with 4th Army reported finding a duplicated document of more than twenty pages ordering preparations for an attack on German forces to be completed by late summer or autumn of 1941. A map found with the Soviet XX Motorized Corps showed the route planned for its advance: across the River Bug, then through German-occupied Poland along a path south of Warsaw and over the Vistula.

This appeared to confirm the assessment of the Soviet régime which Hitler had confided to his Wehrmacht adjutant, General Rudolf Schmundt. Stalin and his colleagues had been in power for a generation, said Hitler – ample time to have ensured the loyalty of, above all, the young. With the dissolution of the Austro-Hungarian Empire, Russia's traditional enemy had disappeared. There had been no threat to Russia – certainly not the pitiful 100,000-man German Army – yet the Soviets had devoted the 1920s and 1930s to building up gigantic forces with more than a million men in their peacetime army. This had all happened before Germany's military build-up had begun in 1935, so there could be no question of its having been a necessary defensive response. Why, then, all the Soviet forces with their steady and continued expansion? Hitler could reach only one conclusion: Stalin intended sooner or later to overrun Europe.

It was certainly true that the build-up of Soviet forces was on a monumental scale. Alexandra Kollontai was now the Soviet Ambassador in Stockholm, where she had been heard to comment that never in Russian history had her country deployed so many troop contingents along her western borders as now. This remark was reported to Berlin.

Basis Nord, after serving the German fleet so stoutly in its war against Britain, now became the port to which British sailors delivered supplies for Russia's war.

At Bergen, Claus wondered that he himself had not been transferred to a unit earmarked for the Eastern Front. Surely it was in Russia that he could be most useful.

The bulletins came in fast. Panzer at the gates of Moscow. Leningrad isolated and under siege. Massive advances in the south.

Claus began to fret. Russia was the place for him. His transfer ought to come.

It wasn't that he wanted to leave his regiment, which was functioning well as a unit and where he now had good friends. To Claus it seemed that everything in his life so far had combined to fit him for service in Russia on behalf of the Reich.

No orders arrived, and by December it was clear that there was going to be no peaceful occupation of the Soviet Union offering opportunities for Russian-speaking liaison officers. Claus resigned himself to staying where he was – as long as his regiment stayed there, of course. At any time they could be moved. Meanwhile, Norway was far being from the worst posting.

It was, relatively speaking, a comfortable position which Claus held in the occupying forces. Bergen was a beautiful location. The old town, with its row of wooden shops along the waterfront, was a charming complement to the modern city with its theatres and parks. Side by side were mountains and the sea. Not far outside the town was Troldhaugen, the home of Eduard Grieg. Claus had visited the house and sat at the composer's piano.

Many of his comrades were billeted with Norwegian families, but Claus was lucky in sharing a house with his commanding officer. It was a villa which when the Germans landed was standing empty and for sale, its owner and sole occupant having recently died. In a conveniently central position close to the harbour, the building had been requisitioned at once by the Germans for use as regimental headquarters. Claus and his CO had their batmen and orderlies there, and a guard was mounted day and night.

Norwegian resistance fighters were astonishingly tough and courageous, but so far Claus had not been involved in any serious trouble with them. From time to time he joined in a sweep through the countryside or a patrol in the town, but as regimental adjutant was chiefly occupied with paperwork. Records and reports, reports and records.

Claus liked the Norwegian people enormously, and could not blame them that his admiration was not reciprocated. He remembered how he himself had felt, when just part of his own country had been occupied by foreign troops.

The war took on a greater dimension with Japan's simultaneous attacks on Hong Kong, Malaya, Thailand and the US naval base at Pearl Harbor. Japan had opened hostilities against the British Empire and the USA; now Hitler, true to his pact with Tokyo, declared war on America as well.

Japan's actions were involving the Reich in a struggle against America which surely Germany could not win. Claus was far from being an expert on industrial or economic matters, but he did know enough to recognize that the manufacturing and manpower strength of America made her pretty nigh unbeatable.

Still, Claus had more immediate concerns than the broader sweeps of grand strategy. Here he was with a chance to go home, and it looked as though he might not be able to make the trip. At least, not yet.

That morning cloud was ten-tenths, the air was full of mixed rain and snow and the meteorologists advised against flying.

For the senior officers due at the Wolfsschanze, there was no question of not taking off. Even in perfect conditions the flight from Norway would be a protracted one. Hitler's headquarters were deep in an East Prussian forest near the Soviet border, and the good old Tante Ju could not fly that far without refuelling. There would have to be a stop at a Luftwaffe airfield in northern Germany. That would cost time. What was more, today headwinds would slow them down to the extent of adding anything between an hour and two hours to their flight time. The sooner they started, the better.

Claus had not been ordered to the Wolfsschanze, but home leave – twelve whole days of it – had come up at last. Since arriving at Bergen, Claus had been home once only. His CO had sent him off on eight days' leave shortly after Marion had given birth to their son, whom they named Alexander after Marion's father. The boy was nearly a year old now, and Claus's quarters were decorated with photographs of him, brought in Marion's letters by the field post.

A staff colonel visiting the troops at Bergen was among those on his way back to Hitler, and he invited Claus to join the flight.

'You'll get away from the Wolfsschanze more or less straight away', the colonel told him. 'There's transport in and out all the while. If you can't get a car or a truck, someone will at least be able to take you to the station at Rastenburg'.

That was only seventy-five miles or so from Marion and Alexander. This was December 1942, and the boy's second birthday was coming up. Claus had bought a stuffed toy seal for a present. Also in Claus's bag was a traditionally knitted woollen jacket for Marion.

They took off from Stavanger with the rain and sleet hammering on the aircraft skin with a sound like shipyard riveters. Almost at once the Junkers entered dense cloud.

Instrument trouble set in within an hour. Next, the machine became sluggish in responding to the controls. Wings iced up, that was obvious.

The answer to icing was to lose height. When the machine was low enough, the ice would begin to disappear and control could be regained.

Today the ice was forming at anything higher than 500 feet. To come down to that level over mountains was out of the question. Finding the correct height was critical, and a compromise. Too high, and the wings would ice up completely, dragging the aircraft down. Too low, and...

They needed to be over the sea.

Neither altimeter nor air speed indicator was giving a reliable reading, and nothing could be seen except cloud. Of the navigation instruments, only the compass was unaffected by the weather.

Sea was to the south.

Banking into the turn was a struggle against the frozen ailerons, and there was nothing for it but to juggle the engines. Behaving with their usual sewing-machine-like smoothness, the three BMW motors were already being pushed well above normal cruising speed in an effort to maintain minimum height. The port engine was induced to give a little more, and the change of course began.

A crash like sudden gunfire, a violent surge forwards, then with absurd slowness the aircraft cartwheeled sideways. It hit the ground roof downwards and began to slide downhill. A lesser crash. The machine gave a brief shudder and movement ceased.

A sledgehammer hit Claus on the forehead.

Insult to injury

'Erika'. He had said the name and was at once bemused. Why had his first word not been Marion?

The girl bending over him was blonde and blue-eyed. When she saw him open his eyes she smiled, and her smile reminded him of Erika. That at least was the excuse he made to himself for his slip. But did the girl not also resemble Marion?

'Hello'. The girl was looking into his eyes, searching for signs of what had happened inside Claus's skull.

Claus tried to raise his head and shoulders, but a sudden sharp pain in the left temple made him pause half way.

The girl laid a hand on each of his shoulders and eased him backwards. 'Don't try to move', she told him. 'We don't know what damage is done to you yet'.

Where the hell am I, Claus wondered. He was lying on his back on a grassy slope, looking into a sky covered with grey cloud. A turn of the head in either direction revealed nothing but heavy cloud. He was cold.

'How do you feel?'

'I'm all right'.

'Of course you would say that, but a doctor will be here soon to look at you. We must know what is wrong before we attempt to move you down the mountain'.

Mountain? What was he doing on a mountain?

Dizziness hit him now, and he lost consciousness again.

When he woke, the girl was still there, sitting two feet away.

There was a young man, too, with a gentle, amiable face and a pleasant voice. 'That looks a nasty one on your head. Just lie still while I have a look at the rest of you'.

So this was the doctor. How old might he be? Twenty-seven, twenty-eight?

The examination was slow and thorough. Besides the illusion that the front of his skull had swollen by a good inch, Claus could feel that both of his feet and ankles were very badly sprained. These had ballooned up.

While lights were being shone into his eyes, his pulse and blood pressure measured and his limbs manipulated to test their limits of movement, Claus was beginning to remember. The drive down the coast to Stavanger. Atrocious weather which mattered not a damn to him when all he could think of was that he was on his way home to see Marion and Alexander. The Junkers with engines running and the instruction to keep seat belts fastened. That was as far as he could recall.

The young doctor straightened up. 'Well, nothing broken. Amazing, that. Just concussion, but a bad one. You were unconscious for a long time, you know. They'll probably want to keep you in hospital for a few days, just to make sure, but I don't think there's any permanent damage'.

'What happened?'

'Your wing tip hit the side of a mountain. You are very fortunate'.

'How far did we get?'

'Near to Kristianstad'.

'Right on the southern tip'.

'No, that's Kristiansand. In Norway. This is Kristian*stad*. You're in Sweden. And you've been lucky'.

'What about the others?'

'We're still checking. How many were you?'

Claus needed to think. 'Eleven passengers. I'm not sure about the crew. Three of them, I think'.

They carried him down the mountain then. Two burly fellows who had appeared from nowhere put a blanket over Claus, strapped him to a stretcher and set off downhill. Memories of 1916 came back. The stretcher bearers then had zigzagged across uneven ground as rapidly as they could move; these men had to cope with the immense difficulty of going steeply downhill. The girl went with them.

It was to a house, not a hospital, that they took him. A wooden chalet, but a large one, some way down towards the valley, with a stony road leading from the front door. The room where they put him to bed had a window looking upwards to the mountain tops. The girl bathed the wound on his head, and disappeared. When she returned, she was carrying a tray with tea, ham and rye bread. Real butter, too.

Claus had not realized how empty he was. He sat up to eat, then lay back and closed his eyes.

How much the girl reminded him of Erika when she smiled!

He was in a neutral country, and neutral countries interned combatants. He'd be here until the war was over. He'd not see Marion or Alexander for years.

It was becoming dark, with little to be seen through the window, when he heard people entering the house. There were footsteps on the stairs, quiet voices and doors being opened and closed. The young doctor, looking very tired now, came in and sat down by the bed.

'How are you feeling, Major?'

'Fine, thank you. I'm very grateful'. Claus looked at the rustic furnishings of the room. 'Where are we?'

'Oh, this is the base for the mountain rescue teams in the area – a sort of halfway house to the hospital, if you like. But we shan't send you on there until tomorrow'.

The earnest way in which the doctor leaned forward in his chair had a familiar feel.

Déjà vû? Had Claus experienced this scene in a dream?

215

Then Claus remembered. Himmler had adopted that same confidential manner at his bedside in Berlin.

'Were you deserting, Major?'

Claus could not believe that he had heard correctly. 'I beg your pardon'.

'Were you deserting? Were you flying to Sweden to desert, and crashed because of the bad weather before you could reach an airfield?'

The question was outrageous. 'Deserting? Certainly not'.

'Were the others planning to desert?'

Claus groped for words, affronted beyond anything he could have imagined.

'I... I don't know. Nobody said anything. No, I'm sure nobody would'. The suggestion was offensive in the extreme.

'Your Army comrades maybe not, but the aircraft crew'.

How could Claus know? He didn't believe it, anyway.

'I'm asking because we found only four survivors from the crash. The other three are all badly hurt, and will almost certainly be returned to Germany. I want you to know that you do not have to go back. If you go to an ordinary internment camp for combatants, you are likely to be sent home with them, but there is a special camp here for deserters and refugees from Germany, and they might not tell you about that. I'm telling you this so that you can have the option, in case you don't want to go back'.

Claus felt anger rise in him. 'Of course I want to go back to Germany. I have my duty to do'. He was almost shouting.

The doctor lit a lamp and produced a syringe. 'Something to kill that pain, and then you should have a good night's rest. Think about it before you sleep, and perhaps you'll feel differently in the morning. You can let me know then'.

'I can let you know now. I shall never desert my country'. This was the supreme question of honour, particularly when his country was at war.

'All right, Major. I just wondered because your aircraft should not have been flying over Sweden at all. We couldn't ask the crew, because I am sorry to say that they are all dead, along with seven of the passengers.'.

A Swedish Army ambulance arrived along the rocky track next morning. Claus found himself in emotional difficulty. On the one hand he needed to thank the doctor for his attentions just as sincerely as he thanked the girl. On the other, he remained outraged at the impugning of his honour implicit in the doctor's questions. In the end, Claus reminded himself that he was a diplomat's son, and parted from each with equal courtesy.

The military orderlies in the ambulance were friendly, the first part of the drive, over unmetalled road, unsurprisingly bumpy. It was not to a military hospital that they took the four survivors, but to the main infirmary at Kristianstad. Here, Claus was examined by a doctor who was sixty if he was a day. The man spoke excellent German and seemed pleased with the results of his examination. 'We'll have to keep you for a couple of days just to make sure', he told Claus, 'but I think it's unlikely there's anything permanent'.

The other three survivors from the Junkers were being treated in the same hospital. One of them had lost a leg, and all were under guard.

The guard, it turned out, was minimal. Two soldiers sat in the corridor, accepting coffee when it was offered, from time to time reading Svenska Dagblatt and more frequently flirting with a passing nurse.

These pleasantries suffered temporary interruption with the arrival of an intelligence captain and a sergeant. Each of the German patients was accommodated in a single room, and the captain interviewed them separately. The sergeant took notes.

'Your embassy has been notified', the captain told Claus, 'and the International Red Cross'.

Of course they had everybody's details. They had put Claus into a hospital gown, holding on to his uniform, his pay book and all his papers. Including Marion's letters and his precious photographs.

At least the Swedish Army told him what the hospital staff had not: the site of the crash. Only some thirty miles or so from Kristianstad, apparently. The colonel with whom Claus had driven from Bergen was among the dead.

The captain recited the rules about internment. Claus braced himself, but the man did not mention desertion. Severely wounded combatants would be repatriated. That meant the man whose leg had to be taken off. As for the others, it was a matter for the discretion of the government whether they too went home before hostilities ended.

The words were non-committal, but the captain's manner suggested fundamental Swedish friendliness towards the Reich. 'I expect that somebody from your embassy will be coming down to see you'.

Nobody did. Five days after the crash, Claus and two other survivors were taken to Stockholm en route to internment. Only the amputee, recovering from his operation, was not yet fit to be moved.

The senior survivor was a general who had been pulled from the wreckage with multiple fractures but without his briefcase and the top secret papers intended for Hitler at the Wolfsschanze.

These documents were in Swedish hands, they would be photographed and copies could be passed on to any or all of Germany's enemies. Even though the government in Stockholm was to a great extent under German influence, who knew how far Swedish sympathies might not really be with the British and the Americans?

All the papers from the aircraft would, promised the Swedes, be returned in due course. This was no reassurance at all, now that their contents had been rendered valueless.

For the move into internment, uniforms had all been cleaned, pressed and where necessary repaired. Pay books were returned too, along with all personal papers, the contents of the officers' pockets and personal baggage. Claus had Marion's letters and the photographs again.

Claus was angry with himself that he had spent his days in the hospital bed thinking of Erika. He had made a conscious effort to replace her image in his mind with that of Marion, but always Erika's face came back. Erika laughing, Erika full of earnest conviction while arguing her case for female emancipation, Erika marking her pupils' exercise books in knitted-brow concentration. Erika contented and relaxed, with eyes closed and the suggestion of a smile animating her mouth.

Claus had blamed the girl who had tended him on the mountainside for recalling Erika to his mind so strongly, but was there not perhaps more to it than that? Had this girl not merely been a trigger, releasing something that was irremovably there, so deeply embedded in his psyche that it was a part of him that would never die, could never die, except when he died himself?

However Claus tried to look at it, he was ashamed that his thoughts had not been absorbed completely by Marion and their son.

The rail journey under formal Army guard from Kristianstad to Stockholm was an almost casual, but mainly silent affair. The German survivors were accommodated in a single first class compartment, with two Swedish officers on fold-down seats in the corridor. It struck Claus as a more comfortable version of Lenin's special train.

Despite the relaxed nature of their confinement, none of Claus's companions seemed inclined to conversation, and the prevailing mood remained one of thoughtfulness.

Were not all looking forward with as much eagerness as Claus to returning to Germany with a minimum of delay? Repatriation, they had been told, was probable because of their injuries, but no one seemed to be looking forward to a summons to the Wolfsschanze, with ensuing recriminations.

Accommodation at Stockholm was another surprise. Claus had no idea what the others had imagined, but his own expectation had been of being placed in an out-and-out prison camp, perhaps a military barracks converted for internment purposes.

219

Instead, they were taken to a large house on the outskirts of the capital and each given a single room. The two Swedish officers remained, and they carried pistols, but there were no rifle-carrying guards, no unscaleable perimeter fences, no machine gun towers and no searchlights.

'You will be here just for a day or two, while travelling arrangements are made for your repatriation', the senior of the Swedish officers told them.

'They want to interrogate us', warned the general.

Each man made up his mind that he would say nothing.

Food was excellent, a resident nurse was in attendance and there were playing cards, table tennis and an excellent billiards room. The men could listen to German radio broadcasts.

Two officials came next day from the German Embassy, confirming that repatriation arrangements were in hand. The bodies of those killed in the aircraft were being taken home to the Reich and the men's personal belongings returned to their families.

The embassy men seemed cock-a-hoop at the first class treatment given to the German officers. No internee had been accommodated in such surroundings before; no, not on the Allied side, either, they were sure. The diplomats attributed the favourable handling of the situation to the fact that the senior survivor was a general in Germany's High Command, and saw in this a sign that Sweden sided naturally with the Reich.

There was no interrogation. Apart from being summoned to the nurse's room for examination, change of dressings and other treatment, the men were left to amuse themselves.

Claus's visit to the nurse was mere routine. His head injury caused him no discomfort, and he was walking well again. The nurse closed the door and told him: 'You have a visitor'.

The Red Cross?

'He says he's an old school friend'.

An old school friend here? So there were more than just the three of them being held in this comfortable internment.

The nurse smiled and went into an adjoining room.

Would the old friend turn out to be another Army man? Navy? Or perhaps even Luftwaffe? Claus tried to remember what he had heard of the service careers of his old schoolmates.

Through the door which the nurse had used came a robust bald man in civilian clothes, who to Claus looked older than himself.

'Claus!'

The face meant nothing.

'Do you remember, Claus?' The man was speaking Russian. It was the last thing Claus had expected to hear. 'Fyodorov. At school together. St Petersburg. Same class six years'.

Fyodorov? The name meant nothing, either.

'Alexei Mikhailovich Fyodorov'.

When he tried, Claus could remember about half of his classmates from St Petersburg. Fyodorov was not among them.

Was this another trick like the one they had tried with Kandelaki? Surely this bald fellow was quite a few years older than Claus.

No. Wait a minute. Claus did remember him. That is, he remembered a classmate named Fyodorov, and he was an Alexei. About the Mikhailovich Claus was not sure.

Was this really the same chap, or was it just someone using Fyodorov's name? The man was Russian, though. That was beyond dispute.

In five minutes, the visitor had convinced Claus that he was the genuine article, Fyodorov reminded Claus of idiosyncrasies in classmates and their teachers. The more Claus looked into the man's face, the more he came to realize that this was indeed the same fellow. But goodness! How the years had changed him! It's a good thing, Claus told himself, that when we look at one another as boys we cannot see what we are going to become. He's bald and I'm beginning to turn grey.

Oh yes, it was Fyodorov, all right. But what was he doing here, among interned enemy soldiers in the middle of what was obviously becoming a war to the death?

'Claus, I have something very important for you to do'.

Fyodorov was a Soviet diplomat. Claus, he said, was far from unknown in Moscow Foreign Office circles. It appeared that the Russians had compiled a sizeable file on Claus through his years of work with Department R. In Moscow, they had followed his career in detail.

'We know', Fyodorov told him, 'what a good friend you are of the Soviet Union'.

'Not any more'.

'Claus, we are on neutral ground. Here you and I are not enemies. I beg you to consider what we two have in common'.

'So long as we are at war, we can have nothing in common'.

'No, Claus, you are wrong. What we have in common is that we both want what is best for our country. I know that is so. Now I beg you, Claus, to be pragmatic. What would be best for your country, and for my country as well?'

'For Germany to win, and to get rid of that abominable government of yours'.

Claus had hit home. Fyodorov was shaken.

'No, Claus. Our two governments are the right ones for our peoples. What our two countries need is peace. I think that what would be best for us both would be to end this war as soon as possible. Don't you agree?'

Claus looked at the Russian without answering. It was beginning to annoy him that this unrecognizable former classmate was insisting on calling him by his Christian name. It wasn't as if they had been friends. They had sat together for a while in the same room along with a score

222

of others, that was all – and that had not been since 1912, for goodness' sake. Good lord, that was thirty years ago!

'Claus, you speak of Germany winning. Do you really believe that Germany can win?'

'Of course I do, and we shall'.

'Claus, you could not knock Britain out of the war. The Luftwaffe was beaten and you could not invade. Can you invade now? Do you believe that you can beat the British now?'

Claus did not answer.

'The British have beaten you in Africa. The Afrika Korps is in full flight. I tell you, Claus, Montgomery has chased the Afrika Korps back so far, so fast, it must be a world record, the fastest advance in history. And you are still going to win?'

'That is one round. It is not the whole fight'.

'And in Russia you have come to a full stop. Soon you will be chased out. Your 6th Army is surrounded at Stalingrad. It is only a matter of days now before it is annihilated. The 6th Army will be lost completely, like all your forces in Africa. There will be no more going forward in Russia for you, Claus. There is only going back. And soon the Americans will be in Europe'.

Fyodorov leaned forward. He was uncomfortably close. 'We are old friends'. That is not how Claus would have put it. 'We can speak honestly to one another. You know what happened to Germany last time, at Versailles. What do you think will happen this time when you are beaten? Do you want to go on fighting so that Germany's enemies can destroy her completely?'

Claus could not speak.

Fydorov leaned back. 'Claus, I am here on behalf of Comrade Stalin and the Foreign Affairs Commissariat of the Soviet Union. I am authorized to tell you that Germany can have peace on her eastern border within a week. The Soviet Government and the Soviet peoples want peace. Germany needs peace in the east, so that she can concentrate her forces against her real enemies, the western imperialists. The Soviet Government is prepared to give Germany that peace. It is in both our countries' interests'.

'Peace within a week?' The absurdity of the notion had brought Claus's tongue to life.

'Yes, Claus, that is the message which we want you to take back to Germany. That is why you were brought here. That is why I am here'.

'What do you mean, that is why I was brought here? I am a combatant in a neutral country, interned prior to repatriation'.

Fyodorov smiled. It was not, Claus had to admit, an ugly or sinister smile. The man could be quite charming, and was not out of place in the diplomatic service.

'Claus, this is not a normal place of internment. You must have realized that. This house is owned by a rich Swedish plutocrat who sees it as his mission to act as an intermediary between governments in an effort to make and preserve peace. The man has many homes, and he has placed this one at the disposal of the Swedish government, to be a safe house for diplomatic negotiations. The Swedish Government too wishes us to have peace'.

'You mean we came here just so that I could meet you?'

'Yes. The others would have gone to an internment camp if you hadn't been with them. The Swedes thought it was better to keep you together. If they had taken you off on your own somewhere, it might have looked suspicious'.

'But how did you know..?'

Again that smile, knowing this time.

'As soon as your details reached Stockholm, they came to us. Madame Kollontai – she's our Ambassador here – probably knew that you'd been in that crash before anybody in Germany knew it. Somebody recognized who you were, and we asked for a meeting at once'. Fyodorov laughed. 'We just have to say the magic word peace and the Swedes fall over themselves to help'.

224

'But I'm not a diplomat. Somebody probably confused me with my father. I'm the adjutant of a motorized infantry regiment, that's all'.

'Panzer grenadier regiment now, isn't it? They changed the designation. No, we know your father retired years ago, and Claus, I am sorry to hear that he is dead. My father died, too. You, Claus, are the man we need'.

'How? I have absolutely no status'.

'No, but you can talk to the right people. You know the right people'.

'I know no one'.

Fyodorov ignored this. 'The offer is simple. The Soviet Union will make peace at once and asks only one condition: Germany must recognize the boundary line agreed between us in 1939. Withdraw your forces behind that line, that's all, and you can concentrate all your efforts on keeping the British and Americans out of Europe'.

It was scarcely credible. 'There's a general here, for goodness' sake', Claus protested. 'And what's more, he's in the High Command. He's the man for you to see'.

'We don't know him. We don't know how he would treat our offer, whether he would distort it in passing it on to Hitler, or whether he would even pass it on at all. We know you. We know you are a man of honour. We know you will pass on our offer honestly. Claus, think what this will mean for our two countries. Germany has been at war for more than three years. Continuing can only mean exhaustion in the end'.

Fyodorov rose. 'One thing, Claus. When you return with Germany's answer, do not stay at the Grand in Stockholm. That's where all the diplomats go, and I don't need to tell you that we are bypassing the usual channels. Wherever you check in, I'll know about it pretty quickly. Just stay in your hotel, and I'll contact you'.

The Russian seized Claus's hand rather than just extending his own. Was he afraid, Claus wondered, that I would not take his?

225

Fyodorov was gone, the nurse returned and Claus went back to his room dazed.

Kollontai again! Claus no longer resented the woman and her damned insane ideas. After all, she had saved him from marrying Erika, and that had left him free to wed Marion. He ought really to feel grateful to the Soviet Ambassador.

All the same, the headache was back.

Return with Germany's answer? There was no chance of that.

Wolfsschanze

Fyodorov's visit left Claus with more to think about than he had
been given since returning to regimental duties.

The first question was what on earth made the Russians think that
he had any kind of connection to Germany's leaders. They exaggerated
his importance even where his work in Department R was concerned.
His had been a junior position; he had carried out decisions, not made
them.

With whom did they now expect him to make contact? He had
never met Ribbentrop, and seen Hitler only from a distance. Did the
Russians think that he could make an appointment with some secretary,
then march in to see the Führer and say: The Russians would like to
make peace?

Even to try to see Ribbentrop was unlikely to lead anywhere. Claus
was a soldier on leave from the forces occupying Norway, nothing
more. Were his father alive, he would surely warn him to have nothing
further to do with the matter, to forget the approach, to forget
Fyodorov. He should go home as soon as he was able, enjoy his leave
and return to his regiment with fresh strength and enthusiasm for his
duties.

There was another puzzle. The school at St Petersburg had taken
only pupils from the ruling or moneyed classes. Therefore Fyodorov
had belonged to a family which was well situated under the Tsars. How
had he survived to reach a senior diplomatic position within the
Communist régime?

This worried Claus until he remembered that Tuchachevsky too had
been from an aristocratic family and was an officer in one of the Tsar's
guards regiment. Alexandra Kollontai herself was the daughter of a
general who was one of the Tsar's adjutants. Neither the marshal nor
the ambassador had found any difficulty in becoming loyal
Communists, so perhaps Fyodorov was not such a phenomenon after
all.

Repatriation came two days after Fyodorov's visit. All briefcases and their contents were returned, but what use were the supposedly top secret papers now?

The general was gratified that the small group had been accommodated in a sort of house arrest rather than in a camp. He attributed this to his own importance as a member of the German High Command and seemed to imply that the others were lucky to have been with him.

A German civil aircraft – also a Ju52, this time with Lufthansa markings – took the four from Stockholm to Tempelhof Airport in Berlin.

Interrogation was routine for servicemen returning from internment or a stay in an enemy PoW camp. What questions had been asked by their captors? What was it that they seemed particularly anxious to know? How devious were their interrogation methods? What threats were made, what promises? What attempts were made to enlist collaboration? What were conditions like, in the camp and in the country generally? Where did people's true sympathies appear to lie?

All of these questions, and more, would normally have been put to the crash survivors at a Wehrmacht intelligence establishment as soon as the men returned to the Reich. Because two of them were proceeding straight to Hitler's East Prussian headquarters, they were not subjected to this procedure. They would have questions enough to answer at the Wolfsschanze.

Claus, who had a ticket of leave in his pocket, was ordered to report to the War Ministry, as the Reichswehr Ministry had once again become. He was to complete a written statement there.

Entering the great building was like old times, or would have been, had Claus not been anxious to be on his way home to Marion and the boy. No convenient flight to East Prussia for him now. He would have to find a train.

The Bendlerstrasse was full of new faces. Claus had been gone from the ministry less than four years, yet saw no one there whom he knew. Enquiries about old friends confirmed the extent of the personnel changes. It was of little importance. Claus could think of no one at the ministry to whom he might communicate Fyodorov's offer. Who had the right connections to the top, these days? The war had changed so much, catapulted into positions of great power people who were little more than uneducated upstarts, while despatching into obscurity those very men of experience, erudition and judgement who were more than ever needed now that the Reich was struggling for its sheer existence.

Claus lodged a report detailing the circumstances leading to his being on board the crashed plane, and describing his treatment by the Swedes. This was all that was required for the record. He omitted all mention of the meeting with Fyodorov.

It had been Claus's intention to travel home as soon as his report was completed. Now he realized that this was something which he simply could not do.

There was an offer of peace. It might be serious, it might not be. Hitler might take it up, he might not. Either way, Claus could not neglect the opportunity. However great his personal concerns, it would be rank dishonour to neglect a task on which so much might depend.

Had his father not said that diplomacy was even more important in war than in peace? However dubious this particular mission might be, it was a chance which should be pursued. No, Claus would have to find the right person for dealing with the Fyodorov offer before he could think of going home on leave.

There was one man who had contacts in all the right quarters, and whom Claus had met several times. Baron Konstantin von Neurath, Ribbentrop's predecessor as Foreign Minister, had visited Falkenstein for the funeral of Claus's father and afterwards spent almost a half hour talking with Claus about his years in Bern. Neurath had known that Claus was at the Reichswehr Ministry, but asked no questions about his work there.

A fellow Württemberger, Neurath had been a good friend of Claus's father. He was old school, courteous, discreet and an opponent of the war. Nominally, he was still Reich Protector of Bohemia and Moravia, that is, of the occupied Czech state, but had been sent on extended leave more than a year ago for not being tough enough on the

229

Czechs. Affairs in Prague were now being run by the head of the Reich Security Main Office.

A telephone call from Haus Schwaben confirmed that Neurath was at his home in Württemberg and would be happy to receive a visit. It was an opportunity for Claus to go to Falkenstein for a few days before travelling to East Prussia. He had not seen his mother since his wedding, and that had been more than three years ago.

Baron von Neurath was a strongly built man of bullet-headed appearance, with a neatly clipped moustache. He received Claus with the courtesy that was his hallmark. Neurath was the epitome of tact, a quality which had earned him two years as Ambassador in London. Before Hitler came to power, Neurath had served two Chancellors as Foreign Minister. Hitler kept him in that office until 1938, when the baron opposed policies which must lead to war. Though Ribbentrop had taken over at the Foreign Office, Neurath was retained as minister without portfolio and as a member of the Reich Defence Council.

After the usual personal pleasantries – how was Claus's mother, how long would he be able to have with his family before returning to his regiment? – Neurath seated his guest in a leather armchair in a comfortable but uncluttered study. Each man had a glass of Courvoisier in his hand.

There was no time for approaching the question obliquely. Claus related all that had happened at Stockholm, describing the surprise nature of his brief 'internment' and repeating Fyodorov's words as accurately as he could recall them.

Neurath listened without comment or obvious reaction. When Claus had finished, he remained thoughtful for a few moments, then looked Claus directly in the eye. He spoke with deliberation.

'You must understand, Claus, that I am not a Russian expert. You are probably in a far better position to assess Russian conduct than I'. So he had known about Claus's work in Department R. 'Apart from a couple of years in Turkey, all my embassy experience was in western countries. As Foreign Minister I didn't have any serious business to settle with Russia, so my knowledge of them is based on the minor dealings I had with their ambassador, plus what I have heard from

Schulenburg and others. Bearing in mind these limitations to my knowledge, I can say the following:

'The meeting with Fyodorov that you describe seems to me to be exactly the way that the Russians would effect an approach. They love the indirect route. For some reason, they seem to have an aversion to tackling matters head-on, probably in case they meet with disaster. They like to begin things in an oblique, seemingly innocuous way, letting approaches seem almost like chance. Does that seem to you an accurate assessment of the Russian mentality?'

'Indeed it does. We had repeated instances of that when I was at the ministry'.

'Right, then. They would not do anything so crass as sending a radio message to Berlin, or a courier under a flag of truce, in case Germany turned them down flat. We should then trumpet the episode to the entire world, and they would look pretty silly. In particular, they would be totally discredited in the eyes of the British and Americans, on whose help they would still need to rely if they were forced to go on fighting against us. No, the Russians would never risk looking foolish in public. They like to be certain that they are going to win before they are seen to be undertaking anything at all. That is why they prefer the devious way of tackling things, so that if an affair goes wrong they can say that it was all unofficial'.

Neurath broke off. 'I saw a thought come into your head then, Claus'.

'It made me think of Hess'.

'Exactly. Hess flew to Scotland to try to make peace before we invaded Russia. He failed, as anyone who knows the British character would expect him to fail, and we promptly disowned him. He had flown on his own initiative, without the knowledge of the Führer, and the balance of his mind was probably disturbed. That was the official story, and it is exactly what the Russians will say about Fyodorov if your conversation is ever made public.

'The fact that the Swedes cooperated in letting Fyodorov visit their safe house means two things. First, the Swedes are as serious as the

Swiss in wanting to see an end to this war. Second, Fyodorov must have been introduced to the Swedish authorities at the highest level. That means it is certain that Alexandra Kollontai is acting through him. She's a very senior person indeed. I don't know if you realize it, but Kollontai is the only surviving member of Lenin's original 1917 cabinet. Stalin has had all the others killed, even sending someone to Mexico to finish off Trotsky, but Madame has managed to survive. She is said to have some kind of hold on Stalin, has stored away proof of the methods he used to achieve supreme power. If she dies an unnatural death, it is all supposed to come out. That's the rumour, anyway. Whether it's true or false, the fact is that Madame Kollontai is precisely the person Moscow would use for top-level negotiations. The only alternative would be Astachov, who is well known in Berlin and is now Ambassador in Switzerland. That's another place where they could talk to us in private.

'So we can assume that the approach is official. The next question is, what do the men in the Kremlin really want? So far as I can see, there are two possibilities. One, they want to use Germany in some kind of game against their Western allies, that is, threatening to conclude a separate peace with us in order to wring more concessions from the British and Americans. That, in my view, is very likely. Stalin will unquestionably want more than Roosevelt and Churchill are prepared to give. His idea will be to take over as much of Europe as possible, from Finland all the way south through Poland and the rest of the Slavonic countries right down to the Mediterranean. That means all of the Balkans, including Greece, and Turkey as well. Russia wants both to control the Dardanelles, and to rule the Baltic. So long as the Red Army has to keep on fighting against us, the Western powers will never agree to this sort of thing, but it will be a different story if Stalin frightens them into thinking that he might pull out of the war and leave them to face us, the Italians and the Japanese on their own'.

The baron sipped his Courvoisier. 'The second possibility is of course that their offer of peace is serious. This would be easy enough to test. We simply come back with a counter suggestion to their one about a return to the 1939 boundaries, and wait to see how they respond – or even whether they respond.

'One thing is certain. We cannot let this offer, if it is a genuine offer, simply lie. It is our duty out of simple humanity to do what we can to end this slaughter. You must realize, though, that I am to a large extent sidelined. I may be still a minister, but have neither power nor influence. I have been so long out of touch that I cannot interpret Hitler's possible attitude at this stage. There's only one thing for it. I shall contact Ribbentrop and request an appointment. He doesn't care for me, and I can't guarantee that he'll receive us. Also, I doubt whether even Ribbentrop can influence Hitler. Any decision will come from Hitler alone, I fear'.

Claus moved in his chair. 'You said receive us'.

'But of course. I can't go to Ribbentrop and say someone told me such and such, and ask him to put the case to Hitler. No, you will have to come with me and tell him exactly what Fyodorov said to you. I take it you have it written down?'

'I daren't write it down, because I didn't want anything on me that could fall into the wrong hands. It did occur to me that the Swedes had in any case probably bugged the room where I met Fyodorov, but all the same I just committed everything to memory word for word as far as I could, as soon as Fyodorov was gone'.

'Good. You can recall it still – word for word, as far as you can?'

'Oh yes. It's not a conversation one is likely ever to forget'.

'Of course. A once in a lifetime thing. I had better tell you that from all that I know of Hitler, I am convinced that what he would like is peace with the West. I'm sure that he is likely to want to keep on against Russia. What we are up against is an obsession, and all obsessions are dangerous. They blind people to reality, so that they can no longer act pragmatically. In Hitler's case it's partly what he sees as his mission to destroy Bolshevism, but it's also this idea of his about living space for the German people. Hitler expects an increase of fifty per cent in the German population over the next hundred years, and is convinced that the Reich needs to be expanded eastwards to accommodate this. So he'd probably want to keep on fighting to take territory off Russia even if the Communist government were to disappear overnight'.

233

Before Claus left for Falkenstein, Neurath had telephoned to Ribbentrop's adjutant, then spoken to the Foreign Minister himself. Ribbentrop agreed to a visit in two days' time.

They went to Berlin together, the baron and the major. Ribbentrop received Neurath in his palatial office without delay, while Claus sat in an anteroom. Memories began to pour back. This was how it had all started, waiting in a ministerial anteroom more than a quarter of a century earlier.

Claus had been seated for little more than ten minutes when he was himself summoned into the Foreign Minister's presence. Neurath and Ribbentrop had talked alone, and there was no aide in the room.

Ribbentrop received Claus with courtesy but a grave expression. He looked Claus searchingly in the eye, invited him to sit and asked for the details of Fyodorov's approach.

Claus's memory did not let him down. The image of Fyodorov was almost real in his mind, and he was able to quote the man's words as though performing a simultaneous translation.

Ribbentrop listened, thanked Claus and hastened to what was for him evidently the important question. 'You knew this Fyodorov at school in St Petersburg, you say?'

'Yes'.

'He's Jewish, is he?'

Claus found the question not just irrelevant but offensive. Images of Julia's distress on leaving Germany shot in front of his eyes. How dare anyone speak of someone's being a Jew as though this were in itself a crime?

'No. Russian Orthodox. I don't think we had any Jews in my class at all'.

'That's all right, then. As long as you are sure'.

'I am absolutely sure'.

Ribbentrop was looking down at his desk. He seemed almost to be speaking to himself. 'Seven days. The Führer must be told at once'.

Claus saw the Foreign Minister's head come up, the light blue eyes turn to his own. 'You will have to come with me, Major'.

Ribbentrop's 'at once' was no longer to be taken as literally as in the past. Even for the Foreign Minister of the Reich, access to the Führer was these days not such a matter of course as it had once been.

Claus was instructed to continue his leave as planned. He would be contacted at Mohrungen immediately the appointment with Hitler had been made. He was not to leave East Prussia, and if necessary his leave would be extended.

Claus wondered that Neurath had not also been invited to accompany Ribbentrop to the Wolfsschanze, but the baron was not at all surprised.

'I was only the means of introducing you to Ribbentrop', he told Claus. 'I can contribute nothing to what you have to tell Hitler. I did not hear Fyodorov's offer'.

'But surely you can contribute advice, how to handle the offer. Your experience...'

'The Führer does not need advice. The Führer knows himself what to do'.

Claus found Neurath's tone intriguing.

'I'm not a Russian expert', Neurath told him, 'but I do know that Stalin will expect a counter offer. I'm not sure that Hitler understands that. In 1939 he agreed to Stalin's demands far too quickly'.

'Can it be bad, if we agree at once to a ceasefire in the East? Can that ever be too quick?'

'Peace at once would be admirable – but along lines that Stalin suggests? We have to think of what the Kremlin's next move would be once we had withdrawn our forces back to the 1939 boundaries. We should then be devoting our full efforts to facing the British and Americans. Do you think the Red Army would just sit by and watch?'

'No, of course I don't'.

235

'The boundary was drawn in 1939 along rivers in Poland. Hitler's response to this offer ought to be to suggest a boundary along rivers well inside Russia. This is what Stalin will expect. Then he can start the haggling'.

Neurath reflected for a moment. 'If a separate peace could be concluded at all, then it would certainly be with the Russians. The West seems to me unlikely ever to treat with Hitler. Really, we have no reason to be at war with the West at all, but Hitler brought off the incredible trick of making enemies even when he was making justified claims. Versailles was unjust, and the British knew it. If Hitler had carried on using diplomacy, he could have had a revision of the Polish question, an end to the Corridor and a return to the 1914 boundaries, oh, probably within ten years. By 1950, say. His mistake was to break his word over Czechoslovakia, saying that the Sudetenland was his last territorial demand and then going on to occupy the remainder of the Czech state. This showed the world that his word could not be trusted. It simply prepared the British and French mentally for declaring war the next time Hitler put a foot wrong. They were practically waiting for him to use force against Poland'.

It was an illusion, of course, born of impatience, but the train home to East Prussia seemed to Claus slower than any he had ever ridden in.

The reunion with Marion brought a joy which exceeded all Claus's expectations. Alexander was a delight, and Claus was astonished to find how much he had grown. Had he been away that long? Claus spent hours playing with the boy. Outside, the snow was deep, and there were only indoor games to be played. Claus and Marion did go for walks, but Claus was careful not to let Marion stay out too long. He could not bear to think of her becoming chilled.

Love was rapture, but love was also care. It was the games with Alexander which made Claus realize that what he wanted was peace. Peace as quickly as possible, and no wars again, ever. All over the world there were children like this, girls as well as boys, and they needed to grow up in a world in which war was something which mankind had outgrown, a concept belonging to the past, like witchcraft or a belief that the earth was flat.

Claus was a soldier. He had spent his life as a soldier. It had been a matter of honour to serve his country in her time of need. Yet most fervently he hoped that Alexander would never have any need to put on a uniform.

What had Seeckt said? Perhaps nations would in future allow themselves time to think things over calmly before going for the other fellow's throat.

A consummation devoutly to be wished. The line emerged from a schoolboy memory.

The telephone summons to the Wolfsschanze came from Ribbentrop's office, but it did not come for five days. A car from the Foreign Minister's pool would fetch Claus next morning, and he was to say nothing to anyone about his destination.

The drive took two hours and a quarter. The sky was black and threatening, the snow unrelieved. Only their crisp white dressing, frozen into crust, mitigated the sombre darkness of the trees on either hand.

Bolt upright on the car's leather seat, Claus reviewed for the hundredth time all that Fyodorov had said. No, there was no denying the irresistible impression. The offer, Claus was sure, was genuine.

The forest thickened, and there in front of them waited a cluster of SS vehicles.

Spread altogether over some one and half square miles, the Wolfsschanze was ringed by six miles of barbed wire and something like 55,000 mines concealed in a perimeter strip varying in width between fifty and 150 yards. The car's arrival had been announced to the checkpoints in advance, and the driver carried the passes essential to enter the massive complex.

Entry through that outer fence was only the first stage. Next came an inner fence where checks were tighter still. SS guards were everywhere. Round the innermost zone was yet a third fence. At each of these three rings of fence, a different pass was required. Security was naturally at its highest in the heart of the place. Here with Hitler were

237

his bodyguard battalion, the commanders in chief of the armed services and leading men from the Nazi Party.

More than 2,000 persons lived within the Wolfsschanze, which included some forty offices, barracks, utility buildings and the like, plus seven massive and forty not quite so massive ferro-concrete bunkers. The roofs of the stronger bunkers were anything up to nine yards thick. The roofs of several of them supported anti-aircraft guns and machine gun nests.

Every evening a special train left Berlin for the Wolfsschanze, which had a railway line running right through its heart. There were two airfields, one for light aircraft only. Permanent telephone and radio contact was maintained with Berlin and with every sector of the fronts where German forces were fighting. Within the central core, Ribbentrop maintained offices of his own, a kind of Foreign Ministry annex housing his liaison staff. It was here that the car stopped and Claus had once again to identify himself.

Ribbentrop was nervous. So much was apparent. He greeted Claus with what looked like relief, as though he had been afraid that his witness would not appear and he would be left to face the Führer alone.

The Foreign Minister was indeed called to the presence on his own, and not until late in the afternoon. Claus waited in another barrack block, running over and over in his memory the conversation with Fyodorov. Would Hitler simply want to hear what had been the Russian's exact words, or would he ask Claus for his opinion, an interpretation? Claus had given the episode a great deal of thought – indeed, it had been practically impossible to stop thinking about it – and had made up his mind that Fyodorov and the offer were completely genuine. If asked for his view, he would tell Hitler so.

Claus waited for a full hour before Ribbentrop returned. The Foreign Minister took him to a room where they could speak with no one else present.

'The Führer', he began, 'has asked me to thank you for your trouble. The Führer of course sees the bigger picture. He knows that if we make peace with Russia now, the West will see this as a sign of weakness. Quite rightly, therefore, the Führer will enter peace talks

238

only after a significant military victory. Our army will be pushing forward again in the spring, and after we have made some spectacular gains that will be the time to entertain the Russian offer. At present, this is not the right time, that is, not the right moment in the course of the war'.

So that was it. Claus was not to be called in to meet Hitler.

Where did that leave matters? Fyodorov was expecting a response.

Since their introduction in Berlin, Ribbentrop had evidently made enquiries about Claus. He congratulated him on the work that he had done in Department R, and praised his late father, of whom he had heard much but whom he had not had the privilege of knowing.

Ribbentrop was keen to deliver a success to Hitler. He knew that Hitler's first choice would have been peace in the West, but failing that, if Ribbentrop could secure peace with Russia it would restore his own importance in Hitler's entourage. As the war widened, the Foreign Minister's status had inevitably been eclipsed by that of others.

Here, with Stalin's offer, was Ribbentrop's chance. It was just a matter now of waiting for a significant German victory on the Eastern Front. Until then, he would keep open the lines of communication via Fyodorov and Madame Kollontai.

'How much more leave do you have, Major?'

'Nine days. It has been extended into convalescent leave because of my injuries'.

'Of course. Well, go on home and enjoy the rest of your leave and wait for your orders. The car will take you back now'.

Three hours later, Claus was back with Marion. Alexander had just been put to bed, and Claus went into the nursery to gaze at his son. The stuffed toy seal which he had brought from Norway was at the top of the sleeping child's cot, and the boy's hand was touching it.

Claus stayed looking at the boy for some ten minutes. Yes, they must end this war, but it must be in such a fashion that there could not be another. No more vindictiveness as at Versailles. They had to create a peace that would be just and free of lingering resentment. This was the duty that they owed to their children.

Claus's orders arrived on the fourth day after his visit to the Wolfsschanze. The Army was seconding him to the Foreign Office for duties as a special military attaché. He would be at the disposal of the Foreign Minister of the Reich.

Evidently Ribbentrop had not lost all of his influence. Claus was sorry to be leaving his regiment, sorry not to be returning to Norway. Yet if there was anything that he could do in the search for peace, he would of course do it with the utmost dedication.

Unlike his reaction on being posted to Switzerland, this time Claus did not resent the change of assignment. He was to report to Ribbentrop personally on January 25, 1943.

A conference of the 'Big Three' – Churchill, Stalin and Roosevelt – had been arranged for mid-January at the Moroccan city of Casablanca. When the agreed date arrived, only Churchill and Roosevelt turned up to plot the course of future overall strategy. Stalin used the Battle of Stalingrad, now nearing its conclusion, as the excuse for his absence.

The real reason for Stalin's failure to attend at Casablanca was that he was awaiting the outcome of his peace feelers to Hitler. There was not the slightest practical need for him to remain in Russia. The German 6th Army had been surrounded at Stalingrad by no fewer than ten Soviet armies. The outcome of the battle for the city was inevitable, with or without Stalin's presence on Soviet soil.

Claus was conducting a last check of his uniforms and equipment, ready for the journey to Berlin, when news came through from Casablanca. Churchill and Roosevelt had concluded their conference with an announcement that they were demanding unconditional surrender from Germany, Italy and Japan.

The one hope for peace, said Roosevelt, lay in depriving the Germans and Japanese of all military power.

So now they knew where they stood. In the West it would have to be a fight to the finish. All the more important now, then, that peace should be concluded with the Russians.

Shuttlecock

The language that was in Marion's eyes as Claus left her for Berlin was the same he had seen in his mother's face when boarding the train for Switzerland more than a quarter-century earlier.

Ribbentrop received Claus alone to instruct him in his duties. Erlenbach was his special courier who would report only to him. No one else was to be admitted to the transactions until there was something to report to Hitler himself. When that time came, it would be Ribbentrop who would do the reporting.

Claus had the impression that Ribbentrop was inwardly depressed – probably by the announcement from Casablanca – and was whipping himself into activity to conquer this. Claus told him that the Russians were pragmatists from first to last and unlikely to tie their hands by committing themselves to any unconditional surrender nonsense.

This was Claus's honest assessment, and it was also what the Foreign Minister needed to hear. He was anxious for Claus to see Fyodorov again right away. 'Find out if they are intending to associate themselves with this unconditional surrender business, or if their offer still stands. See how far they are prepared to go, how serious they are with this offer. You will have to be given diplomatic status, of course'.

It wasn't that easy.

Sympathetic though the Swedish Government might be, it was not going to accept as a fresh German diplomat in Stockholm a professional soldier who only weeks earlier had been a combatant subject to internment on their soil under the terms of the Geneva Convention.

What if the Army discharged Claus pro forma, as officers had been temporarily discharged for trips to Russia during the years of collaboration? They could invalid him out on the grounds of the injuries he had sustained in the Junkers crash.

Swedish doctors, though, had treated Claus and knew that his injuries had not been serious enough to leave permanent effects. They would not justify invalidity, particularly in time of war.

Claus himself came up with the answer. His years in Department R had given him plenty of practice in finding ways round problems of this kind.

They applied for a transit visa.

Claus was to visit German forces in Finland. En route he would make a stopover of one night at Stockholm. On the way back, he would do the same.

This was unobjectionable. The visa was there in five days.

Claus flew from Tempelhof to Stockholm in civilian clothes.

Arrival in Sweden was like emerging from a tunnel. The general atmosphere was one of light and cheerfulness. After the deprivations of the Reich, this was almost like going on holiday. A policeman looked hard into Claus's face at Stockholm airport, and the customs men let it be seen that their inspection of his luggage was going to be thorough. This, though, was normal and without significance.

Ribbentrop was anxious for the Stockholm Embassy to know nothing of Claus's visit. Who knew what reports might not go back from the Ambassador to other institutions in the Reich? To Himmler, for example, who might want to settle a personal score by suggesting that Ribbentrop was pursuing contact with the enemy which the Führer had not authorized.

Yet could they really keep Claus's travels secret? Fyodorov had means of learning Claus's whereabouts; was the Gestapo any less efficient?

All the same, as Fyodorov had suggested, Claus avoided the hotel customarily used by diplomats. He booked instead into the quieter Strand Hotel, nearly all of whose rooms overlooked Stockholm's waterways.

The stay in the hospital at Kristianstad and those few days in the Stockholm safe house had given Claus a brief return to the variety and plenty of peacetime food. He found himself looking forward to the solid portions available at the Strand, and felt guilty when he remembered conditions at home. Even at the Wolfsschanze, Claus had

242

learned, austerity was the rule. Hitler insisted on Wehrmacht rations, for himself and for everyone else.

Claus would not risk being seen in the hotel restaurant, or anywhere else, dining with Fyodorov. He went to the restaurant early, ate without lingering and returned to his room. He would let the Russian come to him here.

Fyodorov arrived in the early evening. He was excited, and shook Claus's hand with vigour.

'You've heard the news, Claus?'

Claus had heard nothing.

'Paulus has surrendered at Stalingrad'.

It was perhaps not unexpected, but nonetheless devastating.

Under no circumstances must Claus let it be seen that the outcome of this one battle in any way weakened Germany's position. He went onto the offensive.

'You have offered peace with a return to the boundaries agreed in 1939. These boundaries no longer satisfy the needs of the German Reich. The minimum demands which would serve as a basis for discussion would include all of the former Polish state as established at Versailles. I stress that this is a minimum German requirement. In addition, the Reich must take into account the needs of its loyal allies. The territory taken from Finland in the peace of 1940 must therefore be returned to the Finns'.

'Claus, you are asking the impossible!'

'In return, the German Reich will support the aspirations of the Soviet Union in other directions, in so far as they do not impinge on the legitimate needs of the German people'.

'If this is what they told you to say in Berlin, Claus, it is already out of date. You are in no position to make any demands. You have lost an entire army at Stalingrad, and we are now in the driving seat'.

Ribbentrop had not told Claus to say anything of the kind. The Foreign Minister had been no help at all. Either he had no ideas

243

himself, or he preferred to leave things to Claus so that if anything went wrong he could legitimately dissociate himself from what his subordinate had said.

Claus had been forced to extemporize, and remembered what Neurath had told him about making a counter demand. In the absence of a specific response from Hitler, Claus had to say something in order to find out, as Ribbentrop had said, how far the Russians would go.

Claus was aware that his actions could be interpreted as treasonable. Yet the risk to himself was irrelevant so long as there was the least chance of peace.

'You cannot dictate terms', Fyodorov insisted. 'The Soviet Union has made a most generous offer'.

Claus refused to concede that events at Stalingrad were in any way decisive for the ultimate outcome of hostilities. On the contrary, Moscow's peace overture clearly indicated that the Kremlin had been forced to acknowledge the weakness of the Soviet situation.

The two of them argued for nearly three hours. While Claus was in Finland, Fyodorov would be reporting to Madame – this was how he always referred to Ambassador Kollontai. Madame, he promised, would have a response ready when Claus stopped again at Stockholm on his return from Helsinki.

The contrast between Stockholm and Helsinki was perhaps even greater than that between Stockholm and wartime Berlin. It was back into the tunnel again. Claus found the Finnish capital blacked out, the daily life one of austerity and the national mood grim. For more than eighteen months now the courageous Finns had been fighting to regain what the Russians had taken off them. The continuation war, they called it. Claus's impression was that what really mattered to them was not the lost territory itself so much as preserving their independence as a nation.

Claus reported to Finnish military headquarters and to the commanding general of German troops in Finland. His visits were of dubious value. Officially he was a liaison officer from the German Foreign Office. The information he was given, and the complaints made to him, concerned matters about which Ribbentrop could probably do nothing.

One fact which he did learn interested Claus greatly. All the other nations fighting on Germany's side had fallen into line with Nazi policy and rid their armed forces of Jews. Only the Finnish government had resisted all German efforts at persuading it to adopt this policy. Finland's army had Jews fighting in its ranks.

Six days after checking out of the Strand Hotel at Stockholm, Claus booked in there again. Fyodorov did not keep him waiting long.

Madame, Fyodorov reported, wanted to know which specific Soviet aspirations would enjoy German support. The Soviet Union expected more than had been in the draft agreement of November 1940. Reich demands vis-à-vis Poland were not up for discussion.

Claus was out of his depth. He knew nothing of any 1940 agreement. All Claus could do was promise another meeting under the same circumstances.

Had Claus done what Ribbentrop had asked him to do? Had he established whether the Russians were really serious, how far they would go, and whether they were likely to abandon their offer and adopt the Western stance of unconditional surrender? Wasn't Kollontai merely playing for time? And what on earth was in the 1940 agreement?

Claus wrestled with these questions throughout his flight back to Berlin. A feeling of having failed completely alternated with the reflection that Madame Kollontai at least seemed not actually to have slammed the door shut. In any case, interpretation was up to Ribbentrop. Claus was merely the messenger.

Ribbentrop was appalled. The draft agreement of November 1940 had been drawn up in the utmost secrecy. It was a document under lock and key, of whose existence only a literal handful of people in Germany knew. If this Fyodorov had been admitted to the secret and was trotting the agreement out in negotiations, Ribbentrop had no choice but to tell Major von Erlenbach of its provisions.

The draft was of a projected pact between Germany, Italy, Japan and the Soviet Union. The pact had not been signed, and existed only in its draft form. Spheres of interest were defined in the first of two secret additional protocols. The first of these defined Soviet ambitions in Asia, the second protocol was directed against Turkey, giving Russia those rights in the Dardanelles which she had long coveted. It was these gains, then, which Moscow was now saying would not be enough.

The fact that Madame Kollontai had been informed of the planned agreement showed that she was working directly on the instructions of Stalin and Molotov. But did that make the peace offer genuine? The whole thing could still be a ploy to secure withdrawal of German forces from Soviet territory, giving the Red Army the chance to regroup and achieve overwhelming strength.

And then?

The game went on all year.

Four more times Claus flew to Helsinki with stopovers at Stockholm, and four more times Ribbentrop's subsequent audiences with Hitler produced nothing.

This, at last, was what the Foreign Minister told Claus. The truth was that Hitler had categorically forbidden further peace talks with the Russians, and Claus's travels remained a secret from the Führer. Ribbentrop was keeping Claus on a string in the hope that the course of the war would cause Hitler to change his mind. If Claus were successful, it would then be he, Ribbentrop, who would be in a position to deliver what the Führer wanted. Anything going wrong, on the other hand, would leave Claus as the scapegoat.

Japan, having pacts with both Germany and the USSR, offered Berlin her services in mediation. It was this which convinced both Ribbentrop and Hitler that the Russians were indeed in deadly earnest with their offer. So anxious was Stalin to secure peace that he had approached Tokyo with a request for assistance.

Hitler declined the Japanese offer with thanks.

Mussolini wrote to Hitler, urging him, in view of the intransigence of the West, at least to make peace with Russia. Turkey, neutral but friendly with Germany, recommended the same course.

Hitler rejected all these promptings, but still Ribbentrop kept Claus in the dark, sending him repeatedly backwards and forwards on a pointless mission.

Fyodorov was becoming impatient. Claus, he complained, was simply wasting his time. The Germans did not seem to know what they wanted.

Hitler did know what he wanted, but knew too that it was no use talking to Stalin about his objectives. These could be achieved only through decisive military victory. Any return to the status quo in the East was out of the question for Hitler. What Germany needed to continue the fight were Stalin's oilfields in the Caucasus.

That summer, Hitler launched a massive offensive which was broken by the Red Army's superiority in tanks. Wehrmacht losses near Kursk were disastrous, and in the middle of it all came news that British and American forces had taken the war to Sicily. Only two months after losing his entire African forces, Hitler was once again faced with land war in Europe – this time with the addition of US opposition.

Now, argued Fyodorov, now you must talk about peace. Claus was beginning to feel almost apologetic towards his old classmate. He too had become frustrated over the lack of progress. With defeat at Kursk following the loss of an entire army at Stalingrad, the Russians would have every reason to expect that Hitler might be prepared to cut his losses and continue the war against the Western powers only.

Was Hitler perhaps uncertain, Fyodorov wondered, about dealing with Madame? If the Germans preferred, they could talk in Switzerland, via Astachov, who was well known in Berlin.

And there was always the Swedish Government, Claus suggested. The Swedes were obviously keen to help. After all, they had brought the two of them together.

Fyodorov laughed. 'The Swedes would like to see peace, yes, but at this stage of the war their government doesn't want to do anything official. Since you and I met at that house we've passed the turning point. If the Swedes were to be a party to helping Germany concentrate all her resources against the West, they would put themselves into a very bad position vis-à-vis Britain and America. They're already looking to the post-war world'. Fyodorov poured himself a cognac and grinned. 'No, Claus, there's nothing doing with the Swedes officially. It's all up to you and me'.

By this time, Claus had grown to like Fyodorov. At school he had really taken no particular notice of him. Now he could see that the boy had blossomed into a good natured, erudite companion of considerable charm. Fyodorov drank French cognac in preference to vodka, and though his thirst was considerable he was not one of those who through drink became over-friendly, boastful, boisterous or aggressive. The two men had grown to understand one another very well. Each took his duty with the seriousness which it deserved, while never sacrificing elementary courtesies or neglecting mutual respect.

Stalin was due to meet Churchill and Roosevelt at Teheran in late November. Before this, he made one last effort to take the Soviet Union out of the war. Fyodorov gave Claus a copy of the agenda which had been drawn up for the Teheran conference, with the message for Hitler that Stalin would prefer to resume talks with Germany rather than continue with his Western allies.

True to form, Stalin ignored both his Anglo-Russian pact and the United Nations Declaration of January 1, 1942, in which Britain, China, the USSR and the USA had pledged to cooperate with each other 'and not to make a separate armistice or peace with the enemies'.

Ribbentrop waited. Claus waited. No reaction came from Hitler. The Führer gave the impression that what the Allies would decide at Teheran was, to him, a matter of supreme indifference.

What the Big Three agreed, among other things, was that simultaneous invasions of Northern and Southern France would be mounted by Western forces in May 1944, and that after Germany's defeat Poland was to be shifted westwards to incorporate all of

Germany east of the rivers Oder and Neisse. East Prussia would disappear completely.

These results, too, were handed to Claus for forwarding to Berlin. The West, Fyodorov pointed out, would not negotiate with Germany, irrespective of whether the country was led by Adolf Hitler or by a Cardinal of the Roman Catholic Church. Germany's only chance to cut her losses was to make a swift peace with Russia. The 1939 boundaries were better than the ones proposed at Teheran, and peace on the Eastern Front would give Germany a chance of fighting off the invasions scheduled for May.

There's no arguing with that, Claus told himself during the flight back to Berlin. Ribbentrop, he was sure, would agree. The only question was whether the Foreign Minister would be able to persuade Hitler this time that peace on the Eastern Front would be expedient.

The Lufthansa machine circled slowly over Tempelhof, allowing for about a minute a splendid view of the Reich capital. Then the Junkers began its approach, and the ground rose up quickly.

A rattling, a bumping, a rushing, and one could feel the brakes going on. Once down to walking pace, the Ju52 turned slowly, and they were rolling towards the airport buildings.

The BMW motors were stopped one after another, the passengers rose from their seats, the door was opened.

Claus went down the gangway, and was immediately surrounded by five men.

Gestapo, that was obvious.

One of the five took Claus's briefcase from his hand. He was led to a black Mercedes.

The Prinz Albrecht Strasse, that was where the interrogations took place, in Gestapo cellars. His previous visit had been by invitation; this time five men and a car made it an arrest.

Then probably the prison at Plötzensee, the usual spot for executions. A concentration camp was unlikely for him. What he had done could unquestionably be interpreted as compounding with the enemy. No doubt about it, that was high treason.

The Mercedes was moving fast. When it slowed, it did not turn into Gestapo headquarters, but slid into the courtyard of a palace.

They did not take him to the cellar he had expected. The man behind the desk of superb wood received Claus politely, spoke quietly, invited him to take a seat opposite and regarded him silently for some seconds through his pince-nez.

He's looking at me now, thought Claus, in a quite different light from that at our last meeting.

'Now, Erlenbach', asked Himmler finally, 'what's the latest with this Fyodorov?'

Claus looked into the eyes that were examining him. They were calmer than those of the Foreign Minister. This man, he said to himself rapidly, already knows everything. In any case, there's no point trying to lie. Cards on the table is the only way with him. 'Fyodorov has just given me a report on what the Allies decided at Teheran'.

'Did he give it you in writing?'

'No, Reichsführer'.

'But you've seen the decisions in writing?'

'Seen them, yes, in Russian. I didn't make a copy, though. I didn't want anything on me at Stockholm airport'.

Himmler was looking at Claus completely without expression. 'But you committed it to memory?'

'Certainly, Reichsführer'.

Claus looked Himmler directly in the eyes throughout his descriptions of the Allied plans for Germany's boundaries and the invasions of France scheduled for May.

Himmler could not hide the fact that he was shaken. He remained silent for a while, removed his pince-nez, polished the lenses one after the other and replaced the item.

This was a man beginning to worry.

'Erlenbach, the game that you are playing is one that in certain circumstances can cost one's head. If you wish to play safe, I advise you in future to report on all future contact with the Russians to me first, before you communicate with the Foreign Minister'.

The Reichsführer fixed Claus with a serious stare, but spoke in amiable tones. 'This is a piece of friendly advice, Erlenbach. Remember: to me first'.

Even as he left the palace of the SS head, Claus remained incapable of imagining the sort of intrigue which was taking him in its grip. Never had the outside air seemed so clean and fresh to him, nor Berlin – even Berlin in her grey wartime dress – so beautiful. Claus himself was straightforward, honest, upright, forthright and loyal, and would be until the day he died. Now he had become a disposable object in the middle of a game played by two men each using him in the hope of gaining favour with Hitler – or at least of surviving the war in the Allies' good books.

The Erlenbach file had been studied by the Reichsführer with his customary concern for detail. There was not the least thing to be said against the major; he was indeed the very personification of the selfless servant of the Reich.

Ribbentrop, Himmler knew, was not in Berlin. Erlenbach would have to sit around until the day after tomorrow before he could report to his master. Meanwhile he, Heinrich Himmler, would the first to bring the Führer details of the plans agreed in Teheran.

Another triumph for the SS intelligence service. Erlenbach could prove very useful. If future contacts with the Russians went wrong, it would be Ribbentrop who was the villain. And Erlenbach's role would reflect on the Army. High treason by a career officer, and Erlenbach had brought it all on himself by refusing to join the SS.

Before flying to Rastenburg, Himmler would spend a diverting hour with Hedwig. He was living with his secretary now, having finally parted from Margarethe, the wife who was eight years his senior.

At the end of March 1944 Claus flew again to Helsinki, stopping off as usual at the Strand in Stockholm. He had booked his stay in advance, so Fyodorov would know of his arrival.

As had become his routine, Claus dined early and retired to his room with a bottle of Remy Martin. This was, he knew, Fyodorov's favourite cognac. Claus placed two armchairs facing the window, poured himself a drink and settled down to watch the waterfront scene.

At Bergen, Claus had found himself watching the seabirds in off duty moments. He was fascinated by the diving of the cormorants, with their long, flexible necks, and by the ability of the herring gulls to ride on a wind with a minimum of wing movement.

He watched the gulls at Stockholm now, patrolling over a stretch of water by gliding on the breeze above it back and forth like sentries, merely tilting from one side to the other to change direction and only occasionally needing to make a single flap of wings to stay aloft.

It was as he was pouring himself a third cognac that Claus realized how much time had gone by. Fyodorov had not arrived.

He decided not to drink the spirit. Not yet, at any rate. He wanted a clear head for talking to Fyodorov, and would empty the glass only after his visitor had gone.

There was still plenty of light, and in Berlin it would already be dark. Claus had always found it astonishing that just a few hundred miles north or south could make such a difference to the length of days and nights.

Over the next two hours, waterborne traffic slackened and shadows between the ripples darkened. The Russian, it seemed, would not turn up.

As daylight faded, the lights of the city appeared to strengthen and to rejoice in their function.

Obviously Fyodorov was not coming.

Claus drank his cognac and began to prepare for bed. Tomorrow it was back into the gloom that was Helsinki at war.

Three days later, Claus was at the Strand again on his return journey. Once more he sat in his room with a bottle of Remy Martin, watching the water and the sea birds and marvelling at the changing tones of red in the sky as the sun disappeared. Still there was no sign of Fyodorov.

Stalin had pursued his clandestine contacts throughout a full year. Hitler had evidently decided to fight things out to the end, and it looked as though Stalin were giving him no more chances.

Germany had thrown away an opportunity.

It was almost, Claus felt, an occasion for mourning. He drank more cognac than usual.

Himmler received his report without comment, thanking Claus with his usual courtesy. Even so, Claus told himself, it was certain now that the Reichsführer was very worried indeed.

The same was true of Ribbentrop. Claus's news forced the Foreign Minister to acknowledge his powerlessness to deliver peace. Germany's future lay in the hands of the Wehrmacht alone.

Claus was sent home on leave, pending a new posting.

The approach of the Red Army towards East Prussia seemed to have aged Marion's parents by some fifteen years. Marion herself had lost weight and was pale. Alexander, on the other hand, was thriving. How wonderful, Claus reflected, to know nothing of what was happening in the world around one!

The last time Claus had been at Mohrungen, the ground had been covered with several inches of snow. Now the spring was so advanced that it was almost summer-like. He and Marion went for lengthy walks with Alexander, sat in the sun under trees which were just bursting into blossom and did their best to distract each other from the events of the war. The final day of Claus's leave was heartbreaking. Claus was in agony at the thought of leaving Marion and the boy to face a Red Army invasion which he knew must come.

May failed to bring the threatened assault on France. Had the Soviet information been deliberately misleading? Or had the stiffness of

German resistance in Italy forced the British and Americans to a postponement?

The landing came early in June. By this time, Claus had been released from his secondment to Ribbentrop's staff and transferred to the headquarters of an Army Group on the Eastern Front.

It was back to interpreting. Claus's function was to question prisoners. Building up from these interrogations a picture of Soviet preparations and dispositions was not difficult. It proved equally easy to establish the high level of opposition to the Soviet régime within Red Army ranks. It was clear that a large proportion of the Soviet forces would have been ripe for recruitment to General Vlassov's Free Russian Army, but Allied forces were too much in control of the war by this time. No sensible Russian soldier was going to change sides at this stage in the fighting.

Apart from this, German brutality in occupied areas of the Soviet Union had alienated many who might earlier have been prepared to join an anti-Communist crusade. From prisoners, Claus learned for the first time of the crass blunders committed by men such as Erich Koch, whom Hitler had installed with the title Reich Commissioner as civilian ruler of the Ukraine. Koch's heavy handedness had turned against Germany millions who in 1941 had welcomed Wehrmacht soldiers with flowers as liberators from Stalin's tyranny. Sheer stupidity had wasted a golden opportunity for Germany to acquire much needed friends. This was on a par with the contumely accorded to Stalin's status quo offer.

Yet for once Hitler was giving serious consideration to the idea of a separate peace on his eastern front. Western forces had consolidated their bridgeheads in Normandy and were beginning a push inland. The Japanese Ambassador in Berlin, Hiroshi Oshima, took to Hitler personally an urgent message from Emperor Hirohito. If Hitler wished it, the Emperor was prepared at any time to negotiate peace between Germany and the Soviet Union.

This was one offer which Hitler did not dismiss at once.

There was an important personal message for Claus, too. Marion was expecting their second child early in the new year.

Flight

It was one of the Czech women who lost her head, but it could have happened to anyone.

Just the old, old story. Imprisonment, particularly when it was unjust, could so easily tip the mind over the edge. From time to time somebody would make a dash for it, either somehow fantasizing that the bullets would miss and the fence give way, or simply not caring, perhaps even hoping for death.

Whatever motivated the Czech prisoner, no one would ever know. She was one of a working party crossing between barracks when she broke away and made a sudden run at the perimeter fence.

By now, Erika was an old hand at Ravensbrück. Her experiences at Karaganda had inured her to that mental agony which was driving the poor Czech woman crazy.

After the initial shock of abrupt incarceration at Butyrka, Erika had learned how to switch off her feelings and to live for the moment alone.

The grapevine at Ravensbrück was astonishingly efficient. Everyone knew how the war was going. Just a matter of a few more months, Erika promised herself, and the Red Army would be here to liberate them.

To her surprise, the first time this thought came, Erika immediately wished that the Americans or the British would be here first, instead. What, after all, were the Russians likely to do to her?

Perhaps, though, she would not live to see any Allied troops at all. Would the SS not liquidate the camp, and the prisoners with it, before the liberators arrived?

Had Claus survived? Would Claus survive? These were the questions which occupied Erika more than any concern about her own future.

And if he came through, would she ever find him again in the chaos which Germany would undoubtedly become?

Night after night they heard the British bombers flying to some target or other. If the target were not hundreds of miles away, they could hear the flak and the bombs too. They could see searchlights and from time to time the red glow of a burning city over the horizon.

By day the Americans came. If the prisoners were working outside, they would pause in what they were doing, to look up at the trails of condensed vapour streaming from the wingtips of the great four-engine machines.

This would make the guards angry; they would shout at the women to look down and get on with their work. The more loudly the guards shouted, the more nervous they were growing. The prisoners were certain of this, and it delighted them.

The noose was tightening round the Third Reich.

Erika had been ordered by a guard to carry a file from a barracks office to the main administration block. She was thinking of Claus as she walked.

When peace came and they were reunited, he would hold her softly in his arms, touch her cheek with his lips as lightly as a warm breath, lay the palm of his hand on her hair with gossamer tenderness, whisper words of adoration into her ear.

The Czech prisoner shrieked and dashed across in front of her. Erika flung herself after the woman to stop the madness.

The first bullet from the tower passed straight through Erika's skull, spreading brains and blood for a distance of two and a half feet. The Czech woman was killed by the next three rounds.

Claus was thinking of Erika that same morning. If in the end Germany was unable to withstand the pressure from east and west, would Erika enter Germany in triumph along with all the other Communist exiles, to be installed by the Red Army into some sort of position of power?

It was curious that Soviet forces, which had come to a halt outside Warsaw, had still not launched their final offensive towards the Reich.

256

It looked very much as though Stalin were waiting for a response to Hirohito's offer, that he was after all giving Hitler one final chance of peace. The Red Army stood still until the Western Allies reached the German border.

Even under such pressure, still Hitler declined to take up the chance of peace with Russia.

Stalin had waited long enough. On January 12, 1945, he unleashed 1,350,000 Red Army men against German forces which they outnumbered by six to one. The German front burst apart.

Claus's Army Group included an SS Panzer Corps. Attached to headquarters was an SS liaison officer with whom Claus had little to do until necessity threw them together in the same staff car.

Their Mercedes was not forty miles northwest of Mohrungen when the driver spotted Soviet tanks.

'Go north!'

Stones sprayed, the nearside rear wheel skidded off the edge of the road, earth flew. The two passengers in the rear seats had to hang on to the doors.

In seconds the heavy car was heading towards the Baltic. Here, approaching Elbing on the Nogat estuary, the land was flat, the view extensive.

Three miles on, they saw more Red Army tanks to the east, and these were closer.

It turned into a race back to their headquarters.

Another couple of miles, and there were more tanks. Visibility was poor, with ground mist thickening. These tanks might be German.

'Stop! In cover!'

The driver skidded the Mercedes to a halt behind a large brick-built warehouse, already isolated in its location and now abandoned by those who had used it. Claus seized his binoculars, raced with the SS officer up wooden stairs to the top floor.

There was no doubt about it. The first Red Army tanks had reached Elbing.

This effectively cut off East Prussia from the rest of the Reich.

Perhaps half a million Red Army men might now stand between Claus and his family.

Claus called the driver and posted him at another top floor window where the man could keep watch to the south and west.

The SS officer and Claus were agreed. The only way back to their headquarters, if it was reachable at all, would be from the south.

Their car was hidden from the Russians, but the warehouse was within range of the Soviet guns.

Both men knew that it was precisely the type of building which the enemy must assume at least to hold a German observation post, and possibly to house gun positions. It would be a matter of routine for the tanks to destroy it before continuing their advance westwards.

On the other hand, for the Mercedes to move at present would invite quick destruction, if not by the tanks then from the air. The Red Army, too, had studied blitzkrieg, and moved under the cover of Sturmoviks, those two-seater fighter-bombers used primarily for low level attacks on armoured vehicles.

The Russians were showing no interest in continuing westwards, and that was understandable. They were moving north to occupy Elbing and reach the coast. It was clear that they would not move on until they had consolidated their positions there.

In another hour there would be considerably less light. The two German officers agreed that they would wait for a little more than semi-darkness and then make a dash for it in the Mercedes.

Yes, the driver confirmed, she had enough fuel for, oh, probably a hundred and twenty miles yet.

While they watched for movement among the Russian units, the SS man talked. An Austrian named Steinegger, he had a bottle of a very poor cognac which he sent the driver to fetch from the car.

Claus accepted the first dram offered, but declined more. He wanted to keep a clear head.

Steinegger put the bottle to his own lips repeatedly. As he drank, his talk became more confiding and less discreet. He was becoming, thought Claus, like a Russian in vodka.

Steinegger had volunteered for the Waffen-SS as soon as war broke out. The Waffen-SS was the military arm of Himmler's organization, fighting alongside the Army as an élite wherever the situation was toughest. Concentration camp guards and the like were provided by the General SS.

What impressed Steinegger, he told Claus, had been a recruiting poster with Himmler's words 'I ask of an SS man that he does more than his duty'.

Since the Anschluss which had brought Austria into the Greater German Reich, Claus had known many Austrians who seemed determined to become more Prussian than the Prussians.

Steinegger had earned rapid battlefield promotion and as a junior officer taken a Russian bullet through the knee.

While recovering from his leg wound, Steinegger was visited in a military hospital by a senior SS officer who made it clear that he was not to enjoy the rest of the war as a passenger. Until he was completely fit to go back to the front, he would be assigned to other duties.

The outcome was that Steinegger was posted temporarily to a concentration camp as a driver.

'I was a pioneer', he boasted. 'It was the vans I drove that proved you needed petrol, not diesel. It would have taken all day and all night to finish them off with diesel, and that surprised everybody, because the smoke is always blacker with a diesel. But that doesn't mean anything. The stuff that works fast is in petrol fumes, not diesel'.

What on earth was the man talking about?

It was a mistake to ask.

The prisoners locked into the back of a van, the exhaust routed so that it went inside. The drive round the countryside, then back into the camp to unload the bodies.

It had been Russian prisoners they used for the experiments. Now they had found a better way. They didn't take people for rides any more. They finished them off in the camps.

Was the man unhinged?

What camps? What people?

The Jews. The ones who'd been deported, telling them they were going to be resettled in the East.

It was impossible. The Jews had been resettled in the East, hadn't they?

'No. that's what I'm telling you. They've got great camps in Poland and they're getting rid of the Jews by the thousand in giant gas chambers. Pesticides, that's what they're using now. What else would you use on a Jew?'

Not since he was a small boy had Claus lost control. He lost control now. His head caught fire, his arms flew up.

'You damned swine!'

With both hands Claus seized Steinegger by the collar of his tunic. The edges of the metal SS insignia dug into his palms.

'Liar!'

The collar was not the sort with lapels. It was not deep enough for Claus to keep a secure hold.

Steinegger pulled himself free without effort. 'What the hell's wrong with you?'

'We don't kill prisoners. We don't kill people because they are Jews'.

'You idiot! What do you think we have been doing all these years? Of course we are wiping out the Jews'.

If war should come, the outcome will not be world bolshevization, but the destruction of the Jewish race in Europe. They had all heard Hitler, but had not listened.

'Murderer!' Claus shot out his right fist, caught Steinegger on the point of the jaw. Berserk now, he swung his left. The Austrian tumbled backwards, landed flat on the wooden floor.

Claus leaped towards him. 'You murderers! You've ruined everything! You've ruined Germany!'

Steinegger drew his P38 and fired.

Claus fell face downwards into the dust of dead industry.

'Weakling! No wonder we're losing'.

Steinegger picked himself up, called the driver and hurried down the wooden stairs.

The Mercedes disappeared southwards without attracting any Russian attention.

Both in the official Soviet work Voinna (The War) and the Soviet forces newspaper Krasnaya Svesda, Red Army soldiers were instructed: 'Germans are not human beings... There is nothing more amusing for us than German corpses... Kill the German!'

The Red Army order of the day for January 12, 1945 decreed: 'Germany must be turned into a desert', and stressed: 'There will be no mercy – for anyone'.

The official order for mass murder was unequivocal, a government policy directed against the civilian population, against women, against children, against the aged, the sick and the infirm.

What became the great treks began with a few families. Then the numbers of those leaving their homes swelled all at once.

Nearly all were old or elderly, women and children, taking to the roads with carts and prams and carrying with them the most essential or precious of their earthly goods.

Soon all the roads westwards were jammed with seemingly endless columns of refugees. Three weeks into the new year all movement in the area round Danzig came to a full stop. It was impossible to move any farther westwards.

To the south the Russians were already a lot farther west, well onto German soil. They had reached the Oder at several points and were threatening Breslau. From the east, the mass of the Red Army was rolling ever closer.

As though by unspoken command, the mass of freezing and hungry refugees began to move northwards of Danzig towards the port of Gotenhafen.

For some four years, great cruise ships had lain tied up at the piers of Gotenhafen. More than a dozen other vessels, mostly freighters, were in the harbour. If they stayed where they were, they would soon be sitting targets for the rockets, bombs and cannon of the Sturmoviks.

The Navy had performed wonders in collecting civilian refugees from Baltic ports and shipping them to harbours well ahead of the Soviet advance. Now the cruise ships were to be readied for sea.

It took three days, while the waiting thousands shivered and huddled together on the frozen quays. Everything on board was organized with scrupulous orderliness.

The largest of the cruise ships, a 25,000-tonner, had her own printing press, and this was put into action now to produce tickets for the voyage, along with food and milk vouchers.

A number of women in the later stages of pregnancy were among the shivering throng on the piers, and a labour ward was improvised in the ship's hospital.

Normally the ship catered for nearly 1,500 passengers, with a crew of more than 400. It was clear that many more persons would need to be carried, and supplies for several thousand were taken on board.

When embarkation began at last, the crew began by handing out tickets, meal vouchers and lifejackets. Soon the lifejackets ran out and it became a case of tickets and vouchers only.

By the time the refugees were on board, 7,956 passengers had been registered and the first baby born in the hospital.

A passenger list was handed to the harbour office, and shortly after midday on the twelfth anniversary of Hitler's appointment as Chancellor, the vessel cast off.

She did not go far before her captain stopped her.

Several smaller vessels, included the Gotenhafen ferry, were hastening across the water to the great ship. They were full of old people, women and children. The women were holding up their children and shouting 'Take us with you!'

Captain Friedrich Petersen had rope ladders put over the side and sent down sailors to help the refugees board his ship. That was another 500 or so, and of these there was no record on land. A pregnant woman was among the newcomers. She was taken down at once to the hospital deck. One of the small boats handed over a number of wounded servicemen.

Petersen was well out into the open sea when a radio signal from Gotenhafen arrived. Return to port and pick up another 2,000 refugees.

It was impossible, and the harbour commandant should have known that. With 8,500 on board a vessel built to carry a maximum of 2,000, Petersen already had a dangerously overfilled ship.

What was more, she was struggling through a force seven wind, and with the temperature at minus ten degrees there were already ice floes in the water.

Beginning at seven pm, passengers were admitted in a series of sessions to the two restaurants, fore and aft. Dinner raised everyone's morale. They were moving quickly away from the Russians, and after the freezing wait on the harbour quays they were now warm and well fed.

In the labour ward, the pregnant woman who had come on board from a small vessel at the harbour entrance gave birth to a lusty girl.

'You're not on the passenger list', said the nurse. 'May I have your name?'

'Erlenbach. Well, von Erlenbach, actually'.

'Your first name?'

'Marion. Marion Elisabeth'.

'The father's name?'

'Major Claus-Dieter von Erlenbach'.

'Your child is beautiful, and she will have an unusual entry on her birth certificate. Place of birth: MS Wilhelm Gustloff'.

'Oh. I didn't know that was the ship's name'.

'Do you have a name already for the baby?'

'Well, I haven't had a chance to discuss this with my husband. I don't know that he has any particular preferences in girl's names, and I really hadn't thought about it myself'. Marion considered for a few moments. 'Erika. That's a nice name. I've always liked that. I don't know if my husband will, though. I know he likes my name, so perhaps we should put down Erika Marion. Yes, Erika Marion. I'm sure he'll like that'.

'Erika Marion von Erlenbach', repeated the nurse, writing it down. 'Yes, it sounds lovely. He's sure to like it'.

'Nurse, can my little boy..?'

'Of course'.

Erika was weary. When the nurse brought Alexander, she tucked him under her arm. The three of them, at least, were safe now. But what about Claus? Marion's last waking thoughts were of Claus. She fell asleep quickly, Alexander and the baby sleeping with her.

It was snowing, and visibility on the sea varied between one and three miles. Red Navy Seaman Second Class Vinogradov, who was on watch, could see a black shape and that was all. Apart from the fact that the German ship was a big one.

His skipper, Commandant Captain Alexander Ivanovich Marinesko, estimated the German at 20,000 tons, if not more. He decided to play a dangerous game. To match the liner's speed, he would have to use his diesel engines. That meant remaining on the surface so that the motors could breathe. The Germans had lookouts as well, so to avoid detection Marinesko dived just sufficiently to keep his conning tower above water. The hatch would have to stay open for air – a chancy proceeding in the rough winter sea. One small error in keeping the boat level, and she would be flooded through the open hatch and sink at once. Marinesko ordered full speed, and was soon four miles ahead of the great cruise ship. Now he stopped, closed the hatch, went down to periscope depth and waited.

In the Wilhelm Gustloff's hospital, an orderly was checking dressings. They were a mixed bunch who had come aboard from that small boat just as they were reaching the open sea. Infantrymen, tank men, artillery men, signals personnel, even a couple of Luftwaffe mechanics. Their wounds were a varied lot, too. All that the men appeared to have in common was that none was fit for further action. Not for a while yet, anyway.

One man seemed to be delirious. He claimed to have been shot by a fellow officer and was rambling about 'honour' and 'dishonour'.

His wound was not a fatal one. They would pull the man through all right, but meanwhile his mind was swinging backwards and forwards between two obsessions.

At one moment he would be cursing about dishonour and the betrayal of all for which a decent German fought. At the next he was clamouring to get back to the front as quickly as possible. Germany was losing the war, and now more than ever it was a matter of honour to stay at one's post.

The officer had been wounded in some sort of building, had fallen more than walked down the stairs and begun stumbling towards his headquarters. He had been picked up lying at the roadside by a column of ambulances taking wounded westwards. When the ambulances could travel no farther, their occupants were loaded onto a small boat which put out from Oxhöft to intercept this ship.

They would have to watch this man. He was the type who, as soon as they docked, would try to walk straight back to the front.

Marinesko had ten torpedoes on board, and fired four, with intervals of two seconds between them.

The first tore into pieces Marion, Alexander and the daughter of whom Claus knew nothing.

The second exploded into the hull farther astern, the third directly amidships.

The fourth torpedo jammed in its tube. It could explode right there.

Seaman Kurockin crawled into the tube after the torpedo, and by an incredible exercise of strength managed to withdraw it for disarming.

The entire crew of the S-13 cheered.

Broken in two by the third hit, the Wilhelm Gustloff sank by the bows.

Bulwarks groaned, then cracked. There was no maternity section any more, and water filled what was left of the hospital.

It was strange.

Claus had imagined that the last image he would see in his mind as he died would be Marion's beautiful face. Or Erika's.

It was neither of them. It was no one's face at all.

Claus saw with total clarity a wooden plaque bearing a carved illustration and an inscription.

A picture of the S-13 breaking a large ship in two, and the words 'Ten glorious years of Soviet-German comradeship'.

Charlottenburg

The British corporal grinned at Tommy.

'Would be nice if once I've got this running again, the owner turns up. Not killed after all. Would he be pleased to see this!'

Tommy looked at the white two-seater and remembered the smiling, open face of the man who had owned it.

'Yes. That would be nice'.

END

Readers of German can examine the evidence of Soviet participation in the conspiracy to 'plan, prepare, initiate and wage aggressive war' at the Foreign and Commonwealth Office annexe in London. Housed there is the collection of documents used to prosecute the major German leaders at Nuremberg.

Key pages recording Soviet urgings to destroy Poland are those numbered K095851-3, K095871-2, K095947-8, H111755-63, H276190-1 and E579400-17. There are many more, and the Foreign Office will supply photocopies.

An alternative is to secure the two volume history ...*die Polen verprügeln...*, ISBNs 3-921-730-33-3 and 3-921-730-34-1, in which these documents and more are reproduced. Illustrations also include both the Russian and German versions of the secret agreement dividing up Eastern Europe, and a map with the Polish demarcation line inked in, signed by Stalin and Ribbentrop. These documents are not in the Foreign Office collection, and were acquired directly from the horse's mouth.

The diplomat who travelled repeatedly to Sweden in response to Stalin's peace overtures was Dr Peter von Kleist. Immediately on landing from one trip, Kleist was arrested and taken before Ernst Kaltenbrunner, who had succeeded Heydrich as head of the SD and the Gestapo. Kaltenbrunner let Kleist carry on.

Among the Communists shipped back to Germany by Stalin was Margarete Buber-Neumann, who landed in Ravensbrück and survived.

So you see, I have done little more than change a few names.

To know only what was used in evidence at Nuremberg, without having heard what was not introduced, is like knowing only of Brady as the sole Moors murderer, while remaining ignorant of Hyndley's complicity. Still, many people do find ignorance bliss, and we all dislike having our perceptions disturbed.

Gordon Lang
Carnoustie,Scotland, 2008